VAMPIRE VENDETTA

ALEXIS MORGAN

MILLS & BOON

All the characters in this book have no existence outside the imagination of the author, and have no relation whatsoever to anyone bearing the same name or names. They are not even distantly inspired by any individual known or unknown to the author, and all the incidents are pure invention.

First published in Great Britain 2011
Harlequin Mills & Boon Limited,
Eton House, 18-24 Paradise Road, Richmond, Surrey TW9 1SR

ISBN: 978 0 263 87931 5

89-0211

Harlequin Mills & Boon policy is to use papers that are natural, renewable and recyclable products and made from wood grown in sustainable forests. The logging and manufacturing processes conform to the legal environmental regulations of the country of origin.

Printed and bound in Spain
by Litografia Rosés S.A., Barcelona

Alexis Morgan grew up in St. Louis, Missouri, graduating from the University of Missouri, St. Louis, with a BA in English, cum laude. She met her future husband sitting outside one of her classes in her freshman year. Eventually her husband's job took them to the Pacific Northwest where they've now lived for close to thirty years.

Author of more than nineteen full-length books, short stories and novellas, Alexis began her career writing contemporary romances and then moved on to Western historicals. However, beginning in 2006, she crossed over to the dark side. She really loves writing paranormal romances, finding the world-building and developing her own mythology for characters especially satisfying.

She loves to hear from fans and can be reached at www.alexismorgan.com.

To Mom—I really miss you.

“An… …ent that… …rst plac…

That … …ntire life, but his arrogance shattered her control. His vampire reflexes kicked in, enabling him to catch her wrist before her hand made contact with his face. Her temper flamed hot as she struggled to pull free of his grasp. Instead of letting her go, his other arm snapped around her and yanked her up against his chest.

“Seamus.”

She meant to yell his name, to protest his rough treatment of her. But the single word came out as a whisper, almost a prayer as his lips touched hers and their burning anger changed into a whole different type of heat.

Dear Reader,

I am so excited that the release of *Vampire Vendetta* is finally here. I've always had a thing for vampire stories. Vampires have been the standard-bearers for the paranormal genre. And I love how each author takes the mythology and makes it her own.

For *Vampire Vendetta*, I envisioned a world in which the vampires and humans live side by side. That led me to creating a hybrid species, the Chancellors. As half bloods, they have the strengths of both humans and vampires—and few of their weaknesses. The hero is a vampire out to restore his family's honour. The heroine is a Chancellor who has experienced prejudice due to her mixed blood.

I hope you enjoy reading Seamus and Megan's story of love and redemption as much as I did writing it.

Alexis Morgan

Chapter 1

Had these humans never seen a vampire before?

Seamus had gone too long since his last feeding and their rapid pulses were straining his control. As he sidestepped his way down the narrow aisle toward the nearest exit, he flashed his fangs at those closest to him, sneering when they shrank back in fear. The only exceptions were a couple of chancellors in the last row. At least they kept their own fangs safely out of sight. Their mixed blood might give them the strength of their vampire ancestors, but they weren't stupid enough to unnecessarily challenge a purebred like Seamus. What a shame.

Their blood would've given him a much needed energy boost.

The door whooshed closed as soon as he set foot on the rustic platform outside, and the turbo jerked forward to speed on its way, his existence quickly forgotten. He watched as the train departed, taking his old life with it. From this point forward, he was no longer the person he'd been.

Now wasn't the time to think about that, not when he had to reach his destination before daybreak. He set off at a brisk pace but had to slow down when the path narrowed to little better than a game trail. The uneven terrain made for rough going as sweat dripped down his face and the strap from his garment bag dug painfully into his shoulder. He'd only packed the bare necessities, the kinds of things that a vampire lacking strong ties to one of the more influential clans could afford: well-worn jeans, a handful of shirts, two lab coats and his shaving kit.

In his other hand, Seamus carefully clutched a custom-made case containing the tools of his trade, the ones that he hoped would prove to be his way into the O'Day estate. His newly purchased paperwork listed him as a licensed medic, a far cry from his real qualifications. However, a medical school graduate only a few weeks short of being certified as a surgeon would draw far too much attention, something Seamus couldn't afford right now.

He approached the perimeter fence of the estate cautiously. High-level energy crackled through the wires, pretty much confirming the rumor that Rafferty had forked out big money for first-rate security around his property. Turning east, Seamus followed the fence line, finally spotting a cluster of low-lying buildings in the distance.

"That must be the gate."

Maybe he should be embarrassed about talking to himself, but all he could feel was relief that he was on the right track. Besides, lately, if he didn't talk to himself, he had no one to talk to at all. Once word of his half sister's scandal had filtered through his peers and professors, he'd become totally isolated. It had been weeks since anyone had spoken to him at all except when absolutely necessary.

Among his kind, status was everything. Once that was gone, there was nothing left except for the driving need for revenge. With the death of his half sister, he was the last of his clan, its lost honor his to defend.

The sky to the east already had a faint pink cast. The first rays of the sun wouldn't harm him. However, if he didn't get inside the compound soon, he'd have to rig some kind of shelter to avoid being fried by the rising sun.

He looked at the dry, dusty ground in disgust. His early ancestors had reportedly dug holes and covered themselves with dirt in order to survive. If his life had reached that point, he'd be better off to burn and be done with it. But he still had a goal to accomplish, one that gave him a powerful reason to keep breathing. With that in mind, he picked up speed. He adjusted the strap of his bag one last time and hurried down the slope, eager to get on with his mission.

Outside the gate, Seamus rang the button to announce his arrival, wincing at the effect the shrill bell had on his sensitive hearing. When there was no immediate response, he pushed it several times in a row. A soon as he let up, he heard a stream of cursing coming from the rustic single-story building that sat about twenty meters inside the electrified fence. He huddled close to the scant cover of the gatepost and waited.

A few seconds later the front door slammed open. An irate male stepped out into the shade of the wraparound porch with an automatic in his hand and looking pissed off enough to use it. He glared across at Seamus before boldly stepping out into the morning light to open up a control panel on the far side of the gate. After he hit a few keys, the gate rolled open with a loud creak.

At the moment, Seamus was less concerned about his dignity than the effects of the increasingly bright sun. He squeezed through the opening and hustled toward the shelter of the porch. The roof offered some respite, but soon even that wouldn't be enough protection.

In contrast, his silent companion showed no discomfort at all as he waited for the gate to close before joining Seamus in the shade. That combined with a brief flash of fangs identified him as a chancellor rather than either purely vampire or human. Most of Seamus's kind tended to look down on the other two species, but right now the hybrid chancellor was all that stood between Seamus and sure death.

"Come on inside."

The chancellor stepped back to let Seamus lead the way into the office, probably not eager to turn his back to an unknown vampire. Smart of him. Inside, Seamus sighed with relief to be out of the sun. When his eyes adjusted to the dim light, he noted the office had no windows. No doubt a fair number of the estate's residents, including the owner, were severely allergic to the sun.

The man took a seat behind a cluttered desk

and waved Seamus toward one of the other chairs. "Dump your stuff on the counter. I'll have to search it before you can go beyond this point. But first, fill out these forms." He pushed the papers across the scarred desktop and tossed a pen down beside them.

"By the way, I'm Conlan Shea, head of security around here." He gave Seamus a pointed look when he didn't immediately respond.

Seamus picked up the pen and clicked it a couple of times before answering. He met Conlan's gaze head-on. "I'm Seamus. Seamus Fitzhugh."

He immediately looked back down at the paper in front of him and started writing furiously to avoid answering any more questions for the moment. Now that he'd successfully crossed the first hurdle, he needed time to gather his thoughts.

"So, Seamus, when's the last time you fed?"

Conlan was talking about blood, not food, and it was beyond rude to ask a vampire that question. Obviously, the chancellor had no time and no patience to pussyfoot around anyone's delicate sensibilities. They both knew older vampires could go long periods of time with only regular food and no blood. Younger ones, not so much. The last thing a chancellor would want to deal with was a vampire lost in bloodlust.

"Not since the day before yesterday, right before I got on the turbo to come here." Seamus's hand trembled, as much from temper as hunger, despite his best efforts to conceal it.

Conlan rolled his chair back to open the small fridge built into the cabinet. "Looks like I have a couple of A pos and one O neg. Name your poison."

"The A would be fine."

Conlan tossed him both of the As before turning his attention back to the computer. Keeping his eyes focused on the screen afforded Seamus some much appreciated privacy. Watching a vampire drink blood, either from a pack or directly from the source, probably didn't bother a chancellor like Conlan, but most vampires were pretty sensitive about it.

A few minutes later, Seamus tossed the second pack into the trash can. "Thank you. That helped."

"I live to serve," Conlan said with a sardonic smile. "So tell me, Seamus Fitzhugh, what brings you to our little piece of paradise?"

Seamus signed his name with a flourish, striving to act far more calm than he was. Knowing it wouldn't be easy getting inside Rafferty's estate, he should've expected to be greeted by a hard-eyed chancellor as the security officer. Because of their physical strength combined with a fierce sense of right and wrong, the word *chancellor* had become synonymous with justice and loyalty within the Coalition.

Seamus had spent the long hours on the turbo practicing his story, but right now he was choking on the words he'd rehearsed. Finally, he set the pen down and pushed the stack of papers back across the desk and settled for the bitter truth.

"I have nowhere else to go."

If the chancellor was shocked at the blunt statement, it didn't show. Conlan quickly scanned the papers, his eyebrows shooting up when he reached the part where Seamus had listed his marketable skills.

"You're really a medic?"

Seamus let his bitterness show. "I would've eventually become a doctor, but I lost my scholarship because of a scandal. I was asked to leave medical school midyear. Luckily, I had accumulated enough credits to force them to license me as a medic."

"What kind of scandal?"

Once again, Seamus answered truthfully. "It involved a woman. The situation got out of control and destroyed both of us."

Conlan blinked in surprise at Seamus's stark

honesty. Maybe he expected Seamus to act embarrassed or even ashamed, but it wasn't in him to cower. Instead, he let the chancellor look his fill. Finally, Conlan nodded, as if reaching a decision.

"Well, okay then. Here's how this will work—we'll check out your story, top to bottom, inside and out. You don't want to be caught in a lie. Rafferty O'Day doesn't offer second chances."

The chancellor met Seamus's gaze again and held it for a few seconds before releasing it. "So you have a choice. If you want to leave, you can wait here until nightfall. If you decide to stay, you'll live here in our guest quarters until I know more about you than your own mother does. Pass muster and you'll meet Rafferty and his wife, Joss, next. It's up to them whether you've found a new home. Clear?"

Seamus nodded. "Yes. I want to stay."

"Let me see your gear, and then we can get you settled in."

The chancellor rooted through Seamus's worldly goods with ruthless efficiency. It was hard not to take offense, but the man was just doing his job. At least he treated Seamus's med kit with respect.

After snapping the lock closed, he handed the case to Seamus. "I can't promise anything, but I know Rafferty has been hoping to find a licensed medic for the estate. If your credentials pan out, he'll be anxious to talk to you."

Then Conlan hefted Seamus's heavy duffel off the counter and headed for a different door than the one they'd entered through. "If you'll follow me, I'll get you set up. Right now, you're my only guest, so you can have your pick of rooms. There's a common bath at the end of the hallway we keep stocked with towels and the like. Help yourself."

There were about ten doors lining the hallway. A quick peek told Seamus they were all more or less the same, so he settled on the convenience of being near the bathroom. Conlan dumped Seamus's bag inside the door, but then stepped back out in the hall.

"It's been a long night, so get some sleep. I'm going to turn in myself." He paused outside the door. "By the way, the electric fence also separates this facility from the estate itself. One way or the other, you're stuck here until I let you out. If you get hungry during the day, that O neg is still in the fridge. You're welcome to join me for meals while you're here, too. Any questions?"

"Not that I can think of." Especially none he could ask of one of Rafferty's trusted employees, anyway.

"Okay. We'll talk some more tonight."

Seamus listened as Conlan's footsteps disappeared down the hallway to his own quarters. When he was sure the grim-faced chancellor was really gone, he sank down on the edge of the bed. He was fed, safe from the sun and ready for some sleep. The first part of his journey toward vengeance was over and without mishap.

Amazing.

Suddenly, a shower sounded awfully good. Just like the bedroom, the bathing facility was strictly utilitarian in design, but fresh and clean. He stripped off his sweat-stained travel clothes and tossed them in the refurbisher. After programming the water temperature to parboil, he ducked under the stinging spray to wash away the grime and grit from the train and subsequent hike to the gate. Fifteen minutes later, he crawled under the covers and closed his eyes.

Megan's stomach cramped; that was nothing new. She'd been feeling that way for days now, but it was getting progressively worse. In between the waves of crippling pain, she tried to convince herself that the twinge was nothing to be concerned about, but it was a losing argument. When the sharp pangs began to fade, she staggered forward again.

Only a few minutes had passed before the

next wave of agony started. The pain built to a sharp crescendo, the intensity worsening with each new attack. It took every scrap of will-power to keep moving when all she wanted to do was lie down in the dirt. If it were only her own welfare she had to worry about, she'd have given in, given up and surrendered to her body's demands for rest.

But she wasn't alone in this, so she trudged on, step by step as the sun slowly rose overhead. At least that made traveling a little easier along the rough path. Her knee ached from an earlier mishap, and she could ill afford to risk an injury that would leave her stranded out in the middle of nowhere.

She was concentrating so hard on walking that it startled her to realize that she'd finally reached the gate. Tears of relief burned down her cheeks as she rang the bell, asking—no, begging—for admittance. As she waited for someone to answer her summons, she did her best to scrub the dust off her face and straighten her hair. She had no baggage, having abandoned it some distance back when it became too much for her waning strength. Only the small pack she carried on her back mattered.

No one came. She rang the bell again, this time really leaning on it. There was no way to know who manned the gate for her cousin Joss's husband. But if Rafferty had hired a vampire, she might have to wait for nightfall to get in. The sour taste of fear burned the back of her throat as she prayed that someone would hear her.

She was about to give up and sink to the ground when she heard a voice. The yet unseen male sounded more than a little put out about the disturbance, but she didn't care. He could yell at her all he wanted if he'd just let her lie down first.

He finally appeared on the porch, shading his eyes with his hand. She could see his fangs from where she stood, but he had to be a fellow chancellor since he didn't hesitate to step out into the sunshine.

He held a gun in his hand, but kept it aimed at the ground while he punched some buttons. As soon as the gate opened wide enough, she stumbled inside, barely catching herself from falling headfirst through the narrow gap.

"What the hell?"

The chancellor immediately holstered his weapon and loped across to where she leaned against the gate trying to ride out another wave of pain. He did his best to support her as they shuffled toward the porch.

"Sorry, I don't mean to be a bother," Megan managed to gasp as she clung to his strong arm. The pain was back, already sharper than ever.

When she bent almost double, he muttered a curse and swept her up in his arms. She wasn't particularly petite, but the chancellor handled her weight with ease. He carried her carefully, but the motion was making her sicker. If he didn't put her down soon, she was sorely afraid she was going to humiliate herself even further.

Finally, he set her down on a bed. "I'll be right back. Stay there."

Like she needed to be told that. Did he think she was an imbecile? Well, if so, maybe he had a point. Now that she was horizontal, the pain eased up. She only hoped that her reluctant rescuer returned soon.

The door to Seamus's room slammed open with enough force to wake the dead. Most vampires his age slept throughout the day, but the irregular hours in medical school had forced him to adjust. He went from sound asleep to wide-awake by the time the door bounced off the wall and a rough hand grabbed him by the shoulder.

Seamus recognized Conlan by scent even as he knocked his hand away. "What's wrong?"

"You say you're a medic. Well, now's your chance to prove it." The chancellor was already heading back out into the hallway. "Get dressed and then meet me in the first room on the right. Bring that fancy gear of yours because I guarantee you're damn well going to need it."

The familiar surge of adrenaline roared through Seamus's veins as he yanked on a clean shirt and jeans. Picking up the med kit, he trotted after the chancellor. Obviously someone else had arrived, someone who was in need of medical care. Conlan didn't strike Seamus as the kind to panic. If he said to hurry, he meant it.

Out in the hallway, Seamus's fangs ran out at the sour scent of fresh blood mixed with something else, something foul. The smell grew stronger the closer he got to where Conlan stood waiting for him. The other man stepped aside to let Seamus pass. It didn't take long to assess the situation. He'd been expecting an injury, but instead found a desperately ill female chancellor.

He pegged Conlan with a hard glance. "Stay with her while I wash up—then, would you clean my instruments?"

He weighed Conlan's response, trying to judge just how much help the other man would be. Enough, he decided, even though Conlan clearly was not happy about his guest quarters suddenly being turned into a makeshift hospital.

Seamus set his case down and ran for the

bathroom to scrub himself clean. When he got back, he picked out the instruments he'd be most likely to need and handed them to Conlan. "Scrub up and use alcohol to wipe these down. Then wrap them all in a clean towel. I don't need to tell you to hurry."

Conlan glanced past him to the woman hanging off the edge of the bed and retching up blood into a wastebasket. "No, you don't."

When he was gone, Seamus approached his patient. She lay curled up on her side, her arms wrapped around her stomach. He took her pulse and listened to her heart. As soon as he touched her, she stirred and opened her eyes. He answered her unspoken questions.

"My name is Seamus Fitzhugh, and I'm a…a medic," he told her, stumbling a bit over the last word. "We're going to get you through this, you understand?"

She nodded and immediately tensed. He helped her lean out over the wastebasket again and supported her forehead as dry heaves racked her body.

When the spasm finally passed, he asked, "Can you tell me your name?"

She answered through gritted teeth. "Megan Perez."

"How long have you been sick?" he asked as

he mentally cataloged her symptoms. No fever, but clammy. Racing pulse. Vomiting. Severely dehydrated.

Conlan appeared in the doorway with a stack of clean towels and sheets. "Thought you might need these."

"Thanks. Set them there and bring me a pan of cool water and some smaller rags. After that, find me any emergency medical supplies you have."

As soon as he disappeared again, Seamus picked up one of the sheets and a couple of the towels. "Okay, Megan, I'm going to have to do a quick exam. Are you all right with that?" She had no choice, but he needed her to trust him.

She grabbed his arm, a wild look in her eyes. "Not me. Where's my baby? Is she all right?"

Conlan hadn't mentioned a baby. Seamus looked around the room and spotted a pack lying on the dresser across the room. It was the right shape and size, but way too quiet. Knowing his patient wouldn't relax until he checked her baby, he crossed the room with a sick knot twisting in his gut. Positioning himself to block the worried mother's view, he reluctantly peeled back the tightly wrapped blanket from around the pack, dreading what he was about to uncover.

A pair of eyes, more lavender than blue,

blinked up at him as the baby contentedly sucked on her fist. The relief at seeing the child alive was overwhelming.

“Hey, there, little one. I’m surprised you’re not screaming your lungs out.”

Conlan chose that moment to return. “Why would I be screaming?”

“Not you—the baby.”

The chancellor set down the pan and rags near Megan’s bed and then looked over Seamus’s shoulder. “Holy hell, she didn’t tell me it was a baby. No wonder the woman pitched a fit when I took the pack away from her.”

Seamus lifted the infant out of the carrier and cuddled her up on his shoulder. He held her out to show his patient. “The baby’s fine.”

The woman struggled to lift her head, but was unable to hold it up for more than a second. Her eyes, so like her daughter’s, caught Seamus’s as she tried to talk.

He crossed the room and knelt down beside the bed as she whispered, “Tell Joss, if I don’t make it…my daughter…hers now. Promise.”

Seamus told her what she wanted to hear. “I promise, but you can tell her yourself when you’re stronger.”

When the tension abruptly drained out of

Megan and her eyes rolled back, Seamus shoved the infant at Conlan. "Here, take her."

Any other time Seamus would've found the panic in the tough-looking chancellor's expression amusing, but not now. He grabbed Megan's wrist and felt for her pulse. It was thready and weak, but definitely still there.

Conlan glanced toward the mother. "Is she…"

"No, but she will be if I don't get some fluids in her. I still need those medical supplies."

"Where can I put this?" he asked, awkwardly holding the baby straight out from his chest.

"It's a youngling, not a *this.*" Seamus shot Conlan a disgusted look. "Make a bed for her out of a basket or a box of some kind. Hell, as small as she is even an empty drawer will do. Just pad it with towels or a blanket first."

The chancellor disappeared, allowing Seamus to turn his attention back to his primary patient. He resumed his assessment of her condition. She was practically skin and bones, far too thin for her height and build, as if she'd been too long without even basic nutrition. Nursing the child would have robbed her body's resources, but not enough to account for her condition. Right now, she'd definitely be vulnerable to any variety of illnesses.

Back at the medical center, an array of machinery and a battery of tests would've told him everything necessary to make an accurate diagnosis in a matter of minutes. But here, in the middle of nowhere, he was going to have to go with his gut instincts, and he wasn't liking what they were telling him.

He considered his options. A medic would treat her with IVs and maybe some antinausea medication. If he were smart, that's exactly what he'd do rather than risk blowing his cover story. But maybe he wasn't all that bright or maybe his vow to heal took precedence over his mission of revenge. Either way, it didn't matter. He opened his med kit and triggered the release for the shallow hidden compartment at the bottom.

His hand hovered over the vial he needed to save this woman's life. Controlled substances weren't as readily available to medics as they would be for physicians. If he used it, he might not be able to replace it, but then he'd already made his decision. Reaching for a syringe, he drew up the full dose and injected it in Megan's hip before he could second-guess himself. Then he sat back and waited to see if he'd gotten to her in time or if his efforts had been wasted.

After all, Megan Perez wasn't sick. She'd been poisoned.

Chapter 2

As the sun went down, Seamus collapsed on the chair Conlan had brought in sometime during the long daylight hours. The antidote he'd given Megan had done its job, although it had been touch and go there for a while. He'd hesitated before administering a full dose of the anti-iron medication. Meant for vampires, it was a dicey move to give it to a chancellor. Despite the genetic characteristics they shared in common with vampires, they were just as much human.

All of which meant that the injection had stood about an equal chance of killing her as it did counteracting the poison, especially in her weakened condition. As soon as the drug hit her bloodstream, it had triggered a series of violent seizures. But once those had passed, her color had gradually improved and the stomach spasms stopped, finally allowing her to rest.

Seamus shifted, trying to get comfortable on the hard chair. Right then, he wasn't sure which hurt more—his feet, his legs or his head. Not that it mattered; he was too busy being exhausted to care. Leaning his head back against the wall, he closed his eyes. The relief lasted all of fifteen seconds before Conlan walked into the room.

"How are they?" At least he kept his voice to a soft whisper.

Seamus straightened up and stretched. "Better. Sleeping for now."

"You okay?"

Why did the man care? It wasn't like they'd spent the day bonding. They'd been too busy emptying basins and changing Megan's bed linens over and over again for them to get chummy. Still, he couldn't deny that the chancellor had followed every order Seamus had barked at him right up until Megan had finally settled into peaceful sleep. Seamus studied the woman's exhausted face.

"She'll need to eat soon, preferably something bland and light." He would, too, but the patient came first.

Conlan nodded and tossed Seamus a warm blood pack. "Why don't you snack on that while I heat up some soup for both of you? I'll also go through some more of the emergency supplies and see if Rafferty thought to stock some diapers. We've already used up the few she'd stashed in the baby's carrier."

Seamus smiled at the worried note in the chancellor's voice. He was willing to bet the man could face down vampires on a rampage without blinking, but evidently a baby without diapers was more than he could handle.

"Soft toweling will do in a pinch." He leaned back again, preferring to feed after Conlan left.

"Odd that she didn't have any luggage," the chancellor said.

Seamus stored that bit of information with the few facts he'd been able to put together. None of it was adding up to anything good. "When you let her in the gate, did she say how she got here? She wasn't on the turbo. I was the only one who got off at this stop."

Conlan leaned against the door frame. "Walked, I guess. I would've heard a vehicle or an air drop."

"Think she might've jettisoned the luggage on her way? Frankly, as sick as she was, I'm amazed she made it this far."

"The thought crossed my mind, too. When the soup's ready, I'll take a run down the trail and look. If it's out there, I'll find it."

"I'm sure she'd appreciate having her own things."

"Back in a few." He eyed the blood pack in Seamus's hand. "Drain that. You look like hell."

When he was gone, Seamus opened his eyes to study his patient. The thought of her out there on that rough trail alone and in pain made him furious. What would've possessed her to risk such a crazy trip instead of seeking medical help? Judging by how thin she was, he knew damn well she hadn't gotten into such bad shape overnight. There was only one logical answer to that—she'd do anything to protect her baby, even if it meant her own death.

So the real question wasn't *what* had driven her to such a desperate move, but *who?* He'd already noted the lack of a wedding ring. By itself, that didn't mean much, although most human pairings went through some kind of marriage ceremony, as did betrothed vampire couples. He ignored the twinge of bitterness over the outcome of his sister's fractured betrothal. Now wasn't the time.

But Megan was a chancellor with a purebred vampire baby. If she'd mated with another of her own kind, there was only a twenty-five percent chance of that happening. No, it was more likely that the child's father was a vampire.

And maybe that's why Megan had run.

It was guesswork on his part, but it felt right. Other than making sure both mother and child were physically all right, none of this was his problem, but he hated the fear in Megan's pretty eyes. Since Conlan was head of security, Seamus considered whether or not to tell him his suspicions. Then the chancellor and his vampire boss could worry about what kind of trouble might be trailing after Megan Perez.

But revealing Megan's secrets meant endangering his own. A mere medic wouldn't have the training to diagnose and treat Megan's condition. O'Day and Conlan might not know that, but he couldn't risk them finding out.

A few minutes later Conlan returned with the soup. "If you don't need me for anything, I'll head out to look for her stuff. I shouldn't be gone more than an hour. Any farther than that, it will be too dark to see anything."

"We'll be fine."

"I've got to say, you did a heck of a job, kid." His voice was gruff, as if giving compliments wasn't his usual habit. Then Conlan hesitated in the doorway. "I hope she knows how lucky she was that you were here."

A soft voice joined the conversation. "Believe me, I know. The two of us owe you both more than we can repay."

The whispered comment brought both men to full attention. Seamus stood up, setting his unopened blood pack aside. He approached the bed. "How are you feeling?"

Her smile looked shaky, but the expression in her eyes was definitely warm. "I've been better, but I'm not complaining."

Seamus did a quick check of her pulse. "I regret that I couldn't risk giving you anything for the pain."

"I'm just grateful I made it here in time."

Her daughter stirred in her makeshift bed, immediately bringing a touch of worry to Megan's expression. "She's all right, isn't she?"

Seamus nodded as he settled the baby in her mother's arms. "You can check for yourself, but I did a thorough exam. Conlan found some formula among his supplies. Your youngling fussed a bit, probably because of the odd taste, but with some coaxing she took a full bottle."

The new mother's smile grew stronger as she gently unwrapped her tiny daughter. Seamus figured it would take a lot harder heart than his to not enjoy watching a mother fuss over her youngling. It was a shame that life itself would wear away that sweet innocence all too soon.

The baby protested, her cry sounding hungry to Seamus. "Try nursing her if you feel up to it. We can always supplement with another bottle if necessary. Right now physical proximity is the important thing for both of you."

Megan immediately tried to sit up, but couldn't quite make it on her own.

"Here, let me help."

Seamus immediately fluffed a couple of pillows to put behind her. Then he tried to hand the baby to Conlan to hold, so he could help shift the weary woman up into a sitting position. The chancellor immediately backed away, holding his hands up.

"No, that's okay."

"Come on, Conlan. The baby won't bite. She won't even have fangs for at least ten years." The needs of younglings of all three races were virtually interchangeable until puberty hit.

"It's not that. If I don't head out now, I'll lose

the light." He looked past Seamus to Megan. "We were pretty sure that you'd left luggage somewhere along the trail here. I was leaving to go look when you woke up."

The twinkle in her eyes said she wasn't buying that story, not completely, anyway. However, she didn't call him on it. "I had a small cart with several bags and boxes on it. It shouldn't be hard to spot if it's still there."

"I'll be back."

Seamus waited until Conlan disappeared to speak in a stage whisper, knowing his comment would easily carry to the chancellor. "To think a big, tough chancellor would be afraid of someone that small."

"Shut up, Seamus!" Conlan shouted from down the hall.

Seamus chuckled and helped both mother and baby into a better position for Megan to feed her child. "I'll give you some privacy, but I won't go far. Yell if you need anything."

"I will. But before you go, I have to ask you something." The good humor was gone, replaced by a deep-rooted fear.

"What?"

"How sick was I? Is Phoebe in any danger?"

"No, she's not." Time for some hard truths. "Because you weren't sick."

She didn't look as shocked as she should have, and her eyes slid away from his. "Of course I was. I haven't been careful about what I've been eating. Maybe it was food poisoning."

"You're half right—it was poisoning, but not the kind you get from bad food."

She looked past him toward the door. "Does he know?"

Where was she going with this? "Not yet."

"Can you not tell him? At least for now?" Her voice cracked.

"Conlan is the head of security around here. He's your best bet for keeping you and your daughter safe." Not to mention focusing on Megan's problems might delay Conlan's investigation of Seamus for a while.

"Please." The word cost her.

"All right—for now." He'd saved her life, but if he needed to out her problems to save his own butt, he would.

"Thank you." She settled back against her pillow, her focus riveted on her daughter.

He picked up his blood pack on the way out the door. The baby wasn't the only one overdue for a feeding. Out in the hallway, he leaned against the wall, glad for the breather. What a relief that mother and daughter were doing well. It had been a close call.

But she'd rallied after he'd gotten the IV started, although the journey had clearly cost her the last of her energy reserves. She'd be needing lots of fluids and protein to build up her strength.

After kneading the blood pack to mix it thoroughly, he popped it with his fangs and sucked it down. At least it was relatively fresh. According to Conlan, another delivery would arrive sometime during the night.

"Seamus?" Megan sounded hesitant. "I'm ready to lie down again."

He tossed the empty blood pack in the trash and prepared to face his patient, not that he'd ever be a real doctor again. "Let me get the baby settled back in her bed while you eat the soup Conlan fixed. Then you can get some sleep."

A short time later, he let himself out of the room after both mother and daughter had dozed off. The sun would be down in a few minutes, and he could finally escape the closed-in feeling of the dorm building. Fresh air would definitely be a welcome change, as would a chance to be alone for a while. It had been ages since he'd had this much intense interaction with anyone. He wasn't sure he liked it.

He had one, and only one, goal: avenge his sister. His role as a medic had been intended as a means to accomplish it. He hadn't expected to become entangled with any other resident of Rafferty's estate, especially a woman with lavender eyes and dark secrets of her own.

Conlan returned shortly after dark, dragging Megan's cart behind him. Seamus helped him lug the various bags and boxes inside to stack in the hall outside of her room. Neither man wanted to wake up the two females sleeping inside.

After they'd carried the last of the boxes in, Conlan led the way back to his office. When they were seated at his desk, the inquisition began.

"I've got to know—how contagious is Megan? Do we need to quarantine the compound until we find out if either of us or the baby come down with whatever knocked her flat? The supply shipment is due soon, and I don't want to put the rest of the estate at risk."

Seamus considered how much to tell him and settled for the truth. "You understand that without a fully equipped medical lab at my disposal, I can only make an educated guess about what the problem was?"

Conlan had been leaning back in his chair with his feet propped up on the desk. He immediately dropped them back down on the ground and leaned forward, a lawman scenting potential trouble. "After watching you all day, I'm willing to trust your gut. Spit it out, Seamus."

"I would guess that if we're not sick within twenty-four hours, we should be fine." A safe enough assessment given poison wasn't contagious. "I think whatever it was hit her hard because of her recent pregnancy. If she hadn't gotten here when she did, she'd have died out there on the trail. As it was, I barely managed to pull her back from the edge."

Seamus's fangs ran out to full length, a fact he couldn't hide from Conlan. "I can't believe no one helped her before it got that bad."

By now, the furious chancellor was sporting an impressive set of fangs of his own. Seamus wasn't the only one who hated knowing Megan had gone through hell. Chancellors came hardwired with a strong sense of right and wrong.

Conlan pulled a pad of paper from his top drawer. "What kind of symptoms should we be watching for? I need to give the boss a heads-up."

"Vomiting, clammy skin, weight loss and possibly gastric bleeding."

Conlan looked up from his notes. "Sounds like fun."

Seamus smiled at his black humor. "Chances are a healthy individual wouldn't get the extreme version Ms. Perez did. She was already weakened from her youngling's recent delivery."

Definitely time to change subjects. "Which reminds me, why would Megan say that Joss O'Day should end up with her daughter?"

Conlan relaxed, but only slightly. "They're cousins. Joss said they haven't had much contact over the past few years, but were pretty close when they were kids."

"That puts things in a different light. At least it would explain why Megan would risk so much to reach the compound, especially if she thought she was dying."

The chancellor leaned back again, his boots landing on the desktop with a loud thump. "You've got to wonder why she didn't turn to her parents for help or at least go to the local hospital."

"It's hard to think straight when you're that sick. Most likely she didn't know who to turn to, especially if she didn't know who could be trusted."

Seamus knew all about that—feeling so

damned alone because he no longer knew friend from foe. After all, that's why he'd ended here up on the outskirts of Rafferty O'Day's estate. The bastard had managed to rob Seamus of everything that had held meaning in his life: family, status, honor. And for that, the vampire would pay dearly.

Something of what he was thinking must have shown on his face because when he looked up Conlan was giving him the evil eye. Before Seamus could decide what would distract his all-too-discerning host, Conlan jerked as if someone had just yanked on his strings. If Seamus hadn't been so lost in his own thoughts, he would've heard the transport sooner.

"Sounds like we've got company."

Conlan grabbed packets of gloves and masks off his desk and headed out the door before Seamus even managed to stand up. By the time he joined him out on the porch, the gate from the estate side had rolled open. The chancellor shaded his eyes, trying to see past the glare of the headlights. Once he recognized the vehicle, he slammed the office door closed and stalked down the steps.

"This is all I need," he muttered as he waited for the vehicle to clear the gate before closing it again.

Seamus hung back to see who had the chancellor looking as if he'd swallowed something nasty. A tall woman climbed out of the passenger's side of the transport as an even taller male slid out of the driver's side. Seamus's chest tightened as his mind jumped to the obvious conclusion. However, the last thing he wanted to do was raise suspicions. If he was right about the couple's identity, he was about to finally meet Rafferty O'Day and his new chancellor bride, Josalyn Sloan O'Day.

He'd hoped to put that pleasure off for a few more days at least, but he had no choice but to act curious and wait for an introduction. He drew comfort from the fact that Conlan also didn't seem particularly happy to see his employer. What was his relationship to the vampire and his wife? Could the man be a possible ally?

There was no use in thinking that way. Without bothering to try to disguise his interest, he listened in on the conversation out in the courtyard.

"Since when do you two run a delivery service?" Conlan tossed them each a mask. "Here, put these on before you come any closer. We don't know whether or not Megan is contagious."

Without bothering to wait for a reply, Conlan picked up a box from the back of Rafferty's vehicle and started toward his office. Rather than be left alone with Rafferty and his wife, Seamus decided to lend a hand without waiting to be asked.

He nodded at the couple, careful to keep his expression neutral, but friendly. They picked up the remaining two cartons and carried them inside. He noticed one was a blood cooler. Good. At least he wouldn't go hungry.

Conlan's small office was even more crowded with the clutter of supplies and two additional people. Rather than hang around, Seamus set his box down with the others and started for his room.

"Get back here, kid." Conlan sounded more like he had when Seamus had first arrived, but Seamus had the impression that his bad mood wasn't directed at him.

"Seamus, this is Rafferty O'Day and his wife Josalyn, Joss for short. They own the roof over our heads and the floor under our feet."

There was no mistaking the bitterness in Conlan's voice. Before Seamus could decide what to think about that, the security officer continued on. "Rafferty, Joss, this is Seamus Fitzhugh. He's the one I told you about."

Rafferty ignored his employee's poor manners and stepped forward, his gloved hand held out. "We have you to thank for saving Megan's life. We both owe you for that."

Seamus forced himself to accept the handshake. "Ms. Perez is a fighter."

Joss smiled and followed Rafferty's example. Her grip was every bit as strong as her husband's. "Even so, it was a miracle that we had a medic appear at just the right moment. A person with your credentials would've been welcome, anyway, but your timing couldn't have been more perfect."

"Glad to be of service. Now, if you'll excuse me, I'll get out of your way."

He sensed their surprise at his abrupt departure, but he had to put some space between himself and the O'Days. Even though their gratitude seemed genuine, he wanted nothing to do with it—or them. Of course, it was easy to be gracious when they were the ones in a position of power. Not that he'd let his resentment show.

What had Petra ever seen in that man, anyway? No amount of money was worth shackling herself to a bastard like O'Day, especially considering the price she'd paid for doing so. The vampire obviously thought he ruled the world. Well, once Seamus established himself on the estate, they'd see who really was calling the shots.

Conlan stared after Seamus, wondering if he'd only imagined that sudden predatory gleam in the vampire's eyes. It was gone before he could be sure. He didn't want to raise any unnecessary suspicions about Seamus at the moment. After all, the kid was running on empty, same as he was. Under the circumstances, they were both entitled to be a bit testy.

But neither would Conlan ignore the possibility that Seamus wasn't exactly what he seemed. Tomorrow would be time enough to start digging into his past. If there was a problem, he'd find it. A question from Joss jerked him back to the conversation at hand.

"When can I see Megan?"

"Last I looked she was sleeping, but you can peek in on her and the baby, if you'd like."

After Joss left, he turned to Rafferty. "Why don't you ask your questions? I'm hungry and short on sleep. The longer this takes, the less likely I am to have many answers."

The vampire didn't blink at Conlan's blunt offer, but he didn't act all warm and fuzzy, either. Rafferty had hired Conlan because Joss had asked him to. Conlan had accepted the offer because he'd had no other options. It didn't make for the friendliest working relationship.

Rafferty pulled up a chair. "What do you know about the medic?"

"So far, just what he told me. He lost his scholarship because of a scandal involving a woman. He had enough credits to get licensed as a medic. He says he had nowhere else to go."

Steepling his fingers, Conlan stared at them briefly before continuing. "He's hiding something, but I don't know what. All hell broke loose right after he arrived, so I haven't even done a preliminary check. Judging by how he handled himself today, though, his credentials are legit. I was damn glad to have him here when Megan Perez collapsed coming through the gate."

Rafferty sat up straighter. "How bad was it?"

"Bad enough. I can't believe she walked all the way here."

"What was she thinking? If she'd sent a message to Joss, we would have picked her up." The anger in Rafferty's voice was clearly due to frustration.

"My guess would be that she didn't want to stay in any one spot long enough to wait for an answer or a pickup. Our young medic isn't the only one with secrets."

"You didn't say what the baby is."

Joss rejoined them. "She's female and a full-blooded vampire. Megan didn't mention the father, and I didn't press."

Rafferty frowned. "Well, that narrows it down to either a chancellor or a vampire, not that it matters. If Megan wants a home here, she's got one."

Then he shot Conlan a look. "So does Seamus Fitzhugh. Tell him we'll come back for him and Megan as soon as she's fit to travel."

Conlan held his coffee in a white-knuckled grip. If Rafferty wasn't going to follow his own rules, then why bother having them at all? "I'm not worried about your cousin, Joss, but I haven't had time to check into Seamus's story at all."

"I know, but I think this exception is necessary. We need a medic, especially until we know if Megan will make a full recovery. Do your normal search. If he proves to be a problem, I'll handle it." Rafferty rose to his feet and walked out.

Joss hung back for a few seconds. "Thanks again, Conlan, for contacting us immediately. I appreciate it."

"Just doing my job."

Despite his curt response, Joss smiled at him. "I know, but I sleep better knowing that you're here. Rafferty does, too, even though he won't admit it."

"Don't worry about me and Rafferty. We understand each other just fine."

She laughed. "Oh, I know you do. It's like watching two peas in a pod that don't really like each other."

He followed her to the door. "Liking each other has nothing to do with us trusting each other, especially when both of us have a tendency to bite first and ask questions later. However, because of you, we try to be civil."

"If you call what passes between the two of you civil conversation, I'd hate to see you when you're rude." Joss softened the comment with a quick kiss on his cheek.

He opened the gate and watched them drive off. Time for some sleep and then he'd start digging into Seamus Fitzhugh's past. He'd feel a heck of a lot better if he had a nice fat background report in hand before letting the young medic out of his sight.

After all, Joss might be Rafferty's wife, but she was the last real friend Conlan had.

Chapter 3

Megan eyed the huge breakfast Seamus had set in front of her. When was the last time she'd really felt like eating at all? It didn't help that she felt a bit self-conscious wearing nothing but a nightgown in front of someone she barely knew. How silly was that? During the worst of her illness, Seamus Fitzhugh had seen far more of her than what the rather demure gown revealed.

But he was a vampire, reason enough to be on her guard around him even if he had saved her life.

At the moment he was too busy walking her daughter back and forth in the small room to pay much attention to Megan herself. She didn't want to get caught staring, but she couldn't seem to pull her eyes away. There was no mistaking the strength in Seamus Fitzhugh.

Sure, part of that was standard equipment for vampires, but there was something about him that reminded her of tempered steel. As if he'd been sorely tested, but survived the experience all the stronger for it. It was there in the set of his shoulders and the faint lines that bracketed his mouth.

Whatever had happened had left shadows in his intensely blue eyes, which also reflected a powerful intelligence that at times saw far too much. He hadn't asked her many questions, but she could feel them coming.

"Little one, your momma needs to eat every bite on her plate," he crooned, the order intended for Megan although he was looking at the baby. "Or we'll have to spoon-feed her."

"I'm eating, I'm eating," Megan groused. Did the man think she was an idiot? As a nursing mother, she was still eating for two. She took another bite of the eggs.

He still stopped to check out the contents of her plate. Her steady progress evidently pleased him because he resumed his pacing.

"Hey, pretty girl, I still don't know your name."

Megan could take a hint. "Her name is Phoebe Perez."

"A beautiful name for a beautiful girl." Then he wrinkled his nose and grimaced. "And you're still beautiful, little Phoebe, even if I do have to change your diaper. Again."

"I can do that." Megan started to set the tray aside.

The medic headed right for the makeshift changing table. "Concentrate on eating your breakfast. You have years of diaper changing ahead of you. I'll take care of this one."

While he very efficiently handled that little chore, she considered the best way to broach a touchy subject. Finally, she just spit it out.

"Have you updated our medical records?"

He gave her a hard look. "No, I haven't had access to a computer yet. Why do you ask?"

"Because I haven't registered Phoebe's birth and want to keep it that way for the time being."

If Seamus was surprised, he didn't show it. Instead, he finished bundling Phoebe back up in her blanket before answering. He turned back to face Megan, speaking softly.

"Conlan still thinks you were sick with an infection."

Her heart jumped in her chest. "And is that

what you think now?" she asked, although it was a sure bet he didn't from the expression on his face.

"Rather than your being poisoned?" he asked, tossing the problem back in her lap. "No, and it wasn't an accident, either. You really need to tell Conlan and Rafferty."

She could no longer look him straight in the eye. "No, and no matter what you think, it was some kind of infection."

"Believe that if you want to. But antidotes for iron poisoning don't work on infections, and that's what I gave you."

Fear threatened to choke off her breath. "So why aren't you telling him the truth yourself?"

His eyes were glacier cold. "Let's just say you're not the only one with secrets and let it go at that."

He turned his attention back to the daughter, his voice softening again. "So, let's see, little girl. Coalition law states attending physicians must keep careful records, especially for infants and children, complete with the mother's name, the father's name and the species of the child in question."

He stopped in front of Megan. "Unfortunately, there was no attending physician anywhere in sight when you and little Phoebe arrived at the compound, so none of that could be done. However, if I were to suddenly stumble across a doctor, legally I might have to report the services I've rendered, as well as an accurate diagnosis."

With an enigmatic look on his face, he lifted Phoebe high against his chest and swayed gently, cupping the back of her head with his hand. "Personally, I don't see that happening anytime soon, especially since Conlan mentioned that Rafferty had been searching for a medic to service the estate. I would take that to mean there are no physicians living there now."

Relief washed over her. "Thank you, Seamus."

He merely nodded, clearly uncomfortable with her gratitude. "Now, finish eating."

Eventually her pursuers would find her trail, but she was too tired to think about that. For the moment, she and Phoebe were safe; that's all that mattered. After being on the run for weeks, the knowledge that she could relax enough to really sleep was a blessing. Once she recuperated enough of her normal energy, she'd be better able to make plans.

If Seamus really did have his own secrets, that explained why he didn't seem all that curious about her reasons for wanting to keep her daughter's birth a secret. Odd that Conlan O'Shea, the chancellor in charge of security, had yet to ask her a single question about how she came to be at the gate. Maybe it was because she was Joss's cousin. Once he'd verified that much, he'd left it up to Joss and Rafferty to decide what to do about her.

Joss had promised another visit soon. Megan appreciated all the vampire medic and the security chief had done for her, but seeing her cousin had meant a lot, too. She just hoped her presence on the estate didn't bring a heap of trouble down on everyone's head.

Seamus murmured something about a sleepy girl and gently settled Phoebe in her bed.

"Thank you," she whispered. "For everything."

"It's not like I have anything else to do." He straightened up but didn't look in Megan's direction. "Get some rest."

Megan stared at the closed door. She hoped she hadn't offended him, especially since he knew the truth about her illness, if not the reasons behind it. She didn't really know how far she could trust Seamus. Rather than worry about it, she took his advice and let herself drift off to sleep.

His departure had been abrupt, bordering on rude. Maybe he should feel bad about it, but Seamus couldn't muster up enough energy to care. Yes, the baby girl was a heartbreaker, and Megan herself was an attractive woman, or would be when she was back to full strength. But he needed to put some distance between them and soon, because he was fighting a powerful urge to protect her and the baby from whoever had sent Megan running. The strength of that impulse was a shocker. It had been a long time since he'd cared about anything but his own troubles. Now wasn't the best time to start.

He couldn't risk getting any further involved in Megan's predicament. That didn't keep him from wanting to beat the asshole senseless who'd left that fear in her eyes and poison flowing in her bloodstream. Worse yet, he'd gone along with Megan's request to protect Phoebe's unregistered birth. If that came to light, he could lose his medic license.

Granted, he didn't much expect to live any longer than it took to bring down Rafferty O'Day, but he still needed to maintain his cover story. Would it look suspicious to the chancellor to find out that Seamus was willing to risk his future for a woman who was little better than a stranger?

It was too late to worry about it. The damage

was already done. If necessary, he'd deal with the fallout.

He wandered toward Conlan's office in need of something to eat—blood or food, it didn't matter. Either would help him stabilize his volatile mood. The door to the security chief's office was closed. Despite the thickness of the wood, Seamus's vampire senses made it possible to hear Conlan talking to someone. From the tone, the conversation was definitely not a happy one. He hesitated, unsure of his welcome.

Conlan solved the problem for him, calling out, "Seamus, if you're going to eavesdrop, you might as well come in and sit down. At least you'll be comfortable."

As soon as Seamus sat down, Conlan rolled his chair back toward the fridge and pulled out a pair of blood bags and tossed them across the desk. Even as he was playing host, he didn't miss a beat in railing at the voice on the other end of the line.

Finally, the chancellor disconnected the call and slammed the phone down on the desk.

"God, save me from idiots!"

While Seamus fed, Conlan shuffled through a stack of papers. From appearances, all he accomplished was moving the pile from the right side of his desk to the left and back again.

When he cursed and started back through it a third time, Seamus had to stifle a laugh.

Conlan heard it anyway. "You think this is funny? I hope not, because I can tell you right now that I'm in no mood to be laughed at."

Seamus managed to maintain a straight face. "Sorry. I think perhaps I choked a bit on this excellent blood, and you may have mistaken that for a laugh."

"Yeah, right. I must have."

Conlan gave up on the paperwork altogether and leaned back in his chair, as usual propping his feet on the desktop. "So, how are your patients?"

"Fine. When I left the room, they were both falling asleep, which is normal for a baby and the best thing for the mother."

Not to mention him. And at least while they were sleeping, they weren't looking at him with those huge lavender eyes that drew him like a moth to a flame.

Conlan nodded. "Makes sense. How soon can they be moved?"

"It depends on how they'd be traveling and how far."

"About half an hour's ride. Joss and Rafferty are anxious to get Megan and her daughter settled into a house on the estate right away."

"I'd say late tomorrow should be all right. If either Megan or her daughter are going to develop any complications, we should know by then."

"Sounds good. Be packed up and ready at dusk tomorrow. Someone will be here to drive all of you into the estate." He rolled his shoulders to loosen up tight muscles. "I wouldn't be surprised if Rafferty comes for you himself."

Seamus's surprise verged on the edge of shock. "I thought there was a waiting period before I'd find out if I was accepted."

Resentment glittered in the chancellor's eyes. "Yeah, well, the rules are supposed to apply to everyone who walks through that gate. However, since Rafferty elected himself God around here, when he says break a rule, we stomp it into little pieces. He wants you close by for Megan and her baby, so you get a free pass on the waiting period."

"And you're not happy about that?"

"Don't take it personally. I don't trust anybody. Besides, that free pass only extends to the waiting period. I'll still have my shovel in hand digging into your background even as you drive out of the gate."

"Shouldn't take you long. Medical school doesn't leave much room for a social life."

Then he injected what he hoped was just the right note of mild concern in his voice. "But there's one thing I should probably tell you. Coalition law requires all newborns be registered. Megan Perez never registered Phoebe, and I agreed to keep it that way."

The chancellor's sole reaction was a slight narrowing of his eyes. Seamus bet he'd been an intimidating interrogator at some point in his life. That steely-eyed stare and blank expression would've broken a harder man than Seamus.

"So, why risk your license for a woman you've only barely met?"

Good question, one that Seamus had no real answer for, none that made any sense under his own precarious circumstances. If Conlan O'Shea was a stickler for the law, as most chancellors were by nature, Seamus might have just screwed up his only chance to get inside the estate. He gave the only explanation that made any sense at all—the truth.

"Someone had her running sick and scared. I wasn't going to be the one to lead the bastard straight to her."

Conlan nodded. "Good decision. I'll let Rafferty know in case it blows up in our face at some point. We try to maintain a low profile, but we also protect our own people."

Seamus was unsure if he was now included in that group, but he wasn't going to press for that information. It was enough that Rafferty was willing to let him onto the estate proper.

One step closer to bringing the vampire down.

"Well, I'm going to go for a walk. If you need me for anything, give a holler."

Conlan turned back to his computer. "Will do."

As soon as Seamus was out of sight, Conlan opened the file he'd started on the young vampire. The information was pretty thin, although the lack of it wasn't a concern in and of itself. It was early in his investigation, and as the kid had said, medical school was a tough discipline that left students little time for getting into trouble.

Yet, according to Seamus's own confession, he'd managed to get entangled in a situation that had resulted in him losing his scholarship and being forced to leave school, all over a woman. At first Conlan had a hard time believing that, but this latest confession gave some credence to his story. If Seamus was willing to risk his professional career for Megan Perez so soon after meeting her, what would he have been willing to do for someone he knew far better? Especially if that someone and Seamus had a more intimate relationship.

Conlan updated his notes with both his impressions and the facts about the registration irregularity. As a former investigator for the North American Coalition, he knew how to build a case, block by block until the whole took shape and stood on its own. Seamus might be exactly what he seemed—a well-intentioned, competent medic who'd screwed up big-time.

But Conlan's gut twitched when he read over the scant details. Something was missing. And although Conlan realized he liked the vampire, he wouldn't rest until all of the blanks were filled in.

By the next evening Megan was getting tired of the same four walls and of lying in bed. It was a relief when Conlan stopped in to tell her to get packed up because Joss was coming to take Phoebe and her to their new home. It hadn't taken long to get their meager belongings organized. The only downside of moving out was they were taking Seamus Fitzhugh with them.

The jerk! Despite his compassionate attention when she'd been so sick and afterward with Phoebe, he'd quickly grown cold and distant.

Had she offended him somehow by asking him not to register Phoebe? He could've insisted on following the law, and she would have understood. At best it was only a delay tactic. Eventually Banan and his family would figure out where she'd gone to ground.

She stuffed the last of her things in the box and sealed it. Before she could look around for something else to keep her hands busy, there was a soft knock at the door.

"Yes?" she called in a soft voice.

"It's Seamus, Ms. Perez. May I come in?"

Ms. Perez? What happened to calling her Megan?

"Yes, of course." She opened the door and stood back to let him in. She was surprised to see him wearing a lab coat and his stethoscope around his neck. His hand held his med kit in a white-knuckled grip.

His eyes instantly went to where Phoebe lay sucking on her fist in her sleep. For a brief second, his expression softened. But when he turned in Megan's direction, the chilly distance was back in full force.

"Is there something you needed? I'm trying to finish packing before Joss gets here."

He looked decidedly uncomfortable, which

meant she wasn't going to like what he had to say. Rather than ask, she waited him out.

Suddenly, his eyes focused somewhere over her shoulder, as if he couldn't stand to look her straight in the eye. "Medical protocol dictates that I do one last examination before we risk your traveling any distance, Ms. Perez. You know, to ensure there aren't any complications that would put you at risk."

Despite his naturally pale vampire complexion there was a definite hint of pink in his cheeks. For that matter, she suspected she blushed, too.

"Are you sure this is absolutely necessary?"

His eyes flashed dark with anger. "I assure you, Ms. Perez, I'm not in the habit of putting patients through unnecessary examinations. It is standard procedure before anyone is released from a medical facility. I'd be considered derelict in my duty if I failed to offer my services."

Her stomach churned, and she felt cornered. But he was right. If she'd been in a hospital, she wouldn't have questioned the need for the exam.

"I apologize, Mr. Fitzhugh. I didn't mean to insult you."

He nodded. "Shall we get started, then?"

The awkwardness didn't go away as he

listened to her heart and lungs. The rest of the exam was quick and thorough, the touch of his gloved hands gentle.

"Any more nausea or cramping?"

"No. The infection is gone."

He gave her a hard look. "So we're back to that again. I repeat—there was no infection, Ms. Perez. You were poisoned. Ignoring the truth is not only foolish, but dangerous."

Why did he insist on confirming her worst nightmare? "I knew I'd been losing weight, but that was because I hadn't been eating right. I picked up an infection. That's all it was."

"Fine, lie to yourself if you want to, but someone had been feeding you an iron supplement meant for vampires. In large enough doses, it's toxic for both humans and chancellors."

She doubled up in pain, but this time the cause was emotional, not physical. "He said I needed it for her."

"Well, whoever *he* is, he lied. Phoebe's needs are the same as any other youngling until she hits puberty. I'm sure Conlan or Rafferty O'Day will help you bring charges against him for attempted murder."

She didn't have to think twice. "*No!* That's the last thing I want to do."

Seamus was looking at her as if she'd grown a second head. "The bastard tries to kill you, and you still want to protect him?"

"No, I want to protect my daughter."

"Very well, but you know he'll try again. Don't wait until it's too late to seek help."

As he peeled off the gloves, he met her gaze. "You should be fine for the duration of the trip. Continue to rest as much as possible. Light exercise is fine, but nothing more strenuous than walking. Concentrate on eating lots of fresh vegetables and protein."

"I will."

"If you change your mind or if you need me for anything…uh, medical, that is, please don't hesitate to ask."

Then he was gone without another word, leaving her alone to get dressed again. Somehow she thought the thirty-minute drive to Joss's home with Seamus in the same vehicle was going to be the longest half hour of her life.

Because of their mixed blood, Megan and Joss could travel in daylight, but that wasn't true for Seamus or Rafferty. The hours dragged by until finally there was a knock at her door. Joss poked her head in and smiled.

"Hey, are my two favorite cousins ready to hit the road?"

The friendly welcome in Joss's voice was all it took to have Megan's eyes burning. She blinked back the tears as she embraced her cousin. "It's so good to see you."

Joss held her at arm's length for a few seconds. "Megan, I'm so glad you came to us. Rafferty and I won't press for details, but we're here for you. You'll spend tonight at our house, and tomorrow you and I will look at the cottage we thought you'd like. There are other choices if it's not what you have in mind."

Megan managed to smile through her tears. "I'm sure it will be perfect, Joss."

"I'll get Rafferty and Conlan to load the transport. After we grab your medic, we'll head home."

Megan bit back the protest that Seamus wasn't *her* anything. She was in no position to fault someone for wanting to maintain some distance, and she certainly didn't want to make things awkward for him with Joss and Rafferty. Once she and Phoebe were settled in their new home, it was doubtful that she and Seamus would have to see each other except when Phoebe needed a checkup.

The men made quick work of stowing her

luggage as well as Seamus's. Finally, the four adults and Phoebe were settled in the transport. Megan rolled her window down to say goodbye to Conlan.

"Thank you for everything. I don't know what Phoebe and I would have done without your help."

The chancellor looked uncomfortable with her gratitude. "Take care of that pretty daughter of yours."

"I will. Once I'm settled in, I'd love to have you over for dinner to show my thanks."

He jerked back as if she'd just insulted him. "That's not necessary."

She watched in confusion as he stalked away. "Did I say something wrong?"

Joss shook her head. "Don't take it personally, Megan. Conlan—"

Rafferty finished the sentence for his wife. "Is a jerk most of the time."

Joss punched her husband on the arm. "Rafferty, cut the man some slack. Conlan's had his problems, but then who hasn't?" Joss smiled down at Phoebe in her arms. "Except this little lady. She has all of us wrapped around all her adorable little fingers. Isn't that true, Seamus?"

The medic, riding up front with Rafferty, had

been silent since getting in the car. If her cousin or her husband thought his withdrawn attitude odd, neither gave any indication of it. That he finally answered surprised her.

"Phoebe is and will always be a heart-breaker."

Then he turned his head to stare out the window into the night. An odd thought crossed Megan's mind as she watched him from the backseat. Despite there being four other people in the enclosed space of the car, she'd never seen anyone look quite so alone.

Chapter 4

Seamus paced the length of the room and back. If the sun didn't set soon, he'd go into a total meltdown. Feeling caged, he started another useless trip across the carpet and counted off the minutes until he could escape the confines of Rafferty O'Day's home.

He'd already consumed three packs of blood, but they'd barely taken the edge off his hunger, much less his anger. Right now, his craving for blood demanded more than sucking it out of plastic. No, far better to plunge his fangs into the soft flesh of someone's neck and take a long, deep pull of life pulsing straight from the source—rich, vibrant and still warm. Somehow he doubted Rafferty would extend his hospitality that far.

It had been decades since the blood hunger of his kind had shaken Seamus's control. But right now his enemy was just down the hall, patiently waiting for Seamus to make an appearance. To make nice. To petition to be part of Rafferty's new world vision. Instead Seamus wanted to stake the bastard, and that only after he found a way to destroy everything that meant anything to the older vampire.

That was the problem with schemes based on sketchy intelligence—they fell apart at the first sign of an unexpected complication. Clearly his original plan had been shortsighted, not extending much past finding a way into the estate to study Rafferty O'Day from a distance. Instead, thanks to Megan Perez's untimely arrival, Seamus was the hero of the hour, an honored guest in Rafferty's own home.

Wearing out the carpet was getting him nowhere. He stopped in front of the dresser and forced his reflection to appear in the mirror. Good thing he did, because he looked as over the edge as he felt with his hair standing up in ragged spikes and his clothes disheveled. He finger-combed his hair and tucked in his shirt as he concentrated on slowing his pulse. His host might be willing to give Seamus a free pass because of his service to Joss's cousin, but that didn't imply blind trust on his part. If Seamus appeared rattled or was acting guilty, the older vampire was bound to wonder why.

After one last glance at the mirror, Seamus let his image fade and braced himself to face his host. Outside of his room, he paused to listen. A soft murmur of voices drifted down the hallway. He recognized both females and Rafferty himself. Great. He'd have preferred a private audience.

When the voices went silent, he realized the others had heard his approach and were waiting for him to join them. Further delay would only make things more difficult. He carefully schooled his expression, going for reluctance to interrupt his hosts' visit with Megan.

Joss looked up and smiled as soon as he came into sight. "Come on in, Seamus. We were just making plans to give Megan a quick tour of the estate. We'd like you to join us."

Just what he needed—more time shut up in a transport with his enemies. "If you're sure I won't be in the way."

Rafferty answered that one. "Not at all. While we're out, we can stop by the infirmary, so you can take a look around."

All of which would prevent Seamus from having free run of their home while they were out playing host to Megan. That last part went unsaid, but that didn't make it any less true.

"Then I'm sorry to have kept you waiting."

Megan had been awfully quiet, her eyes focused on her lap. Finally she looked up. "We were actually waiting for Phoebe to wake up from her nap."

Right on cue, the youngling in question announced her need for attention with a loud wail. Megan was immediately up and moving, barely giving Seamus time to step out of her way. He fought the urge to follow her, preferring to be with her and Phoebe than being left alone with the O'Days. He was also fighting a strong urge to take care of Phoebe's needs himself and to find out how Megan was feeling.

Joss moved up beside him, her hand coming to rest on his arm. He flinched, causing her to quickly withdraw her touch.

"Sorry." Keeping her voice low, she told him, "I just wanted to thank you again, Seamus. We would've lost her if you hadn't been there."

The last thing he wanted was gratitude, especially hers. "No thanks are necessary. Besides, I couldn't have done it if you hadn't had the foresight to make sure Conlan had all the right supplies on hand."

Rafferty entered the conversation. "Which brings me back to the infirmary. First thing, go through the inventory and make a list of anything that's missing because we only bought the basics. There's bound to be more we need, especially now that we have a licensed medic on-site."

"I can do that."

The vampire looked as if he had more to say, but Megan was back. Joss held out her hand to take the baby's bag.

As Megan relinquished it, she said, "We'd better get moving. I'd like to get settled in the cottage tonight."

Joss looked both surprised and hurt. "Surely there's no rush, Megan. You just got here."

"I know, but I don't want to be an imposition."

"You won't be. Besides, you need time to recuperate." Joss turned to Seamus for support. "Doesn't she?"

Talk about awkward. The physician in him agreed with his hostess. Those dark circles under Megan's eyes and her bone-thin appearance demanded more rest, more care. But he recognized a kindred spirit as well, one whose entire world had been gutted and bled out by the selfish act of another. Trust would be a long time returning in Megan's life even if she felt guilty for doubting the very people she'd turned to for help.

He compromised, knowing neither woman would be happy, but it really wasn't his problem.

Rather than see the disappointment in Megan's eyes, he focused his attention on Joss. "She needs another twenty-four hours to make sure there aren't any lasting side effects from the medication I gave her. But barring complications, there's no reason she shouldn't set up housekeeping by herself."

Megan stepped in front him, forcing Seamus to acknowledge her presence. "In case you didn't notice, Mr. Fitzhugh, *she* is right here, and *she* can and will speak for herself. I'm not an idiot nor an invalid. If I didn't think I could take care of myself and my daughter, I'd say so."

He had to admire her courage, facing down a vampire who outweighed her by a good eighty pounds. Males of any of the three species didn't take well to someone getting right in their face, but vampires were especially prone to attacking if provoked. He ignored the faint pain of his fangs running out and his body's predictable reaction to an attractive female's challenge.

"Don't put words in my mouth, Megan." He fought for control. "I didn't say you were an idiot or incompetent. I said, *medically* it would be better if you took it easy one more day. That's all."

She stared up at him for several seconds, her own fangs slipping down far enough to show. Finally, she nodded. "Okay. Twenty-four hours."

Then, remembering they had an audience, she pasted a bright smile on her face. "Joss, Rafferty. I don't mean to sound ungrateful, but I've been on the move for a while now. It will be a relief to begin to build a stable home again."

An hour later, Rafferty pulled up in front of a squat building, obviously designed for function rather than style.

"Here's your new place of business." He tossed Seamus a set of keys. "Check it out, and let me know what you think."

"You're not coming in?" Which would be a relief.

Rafferty shook his head but kept his eyes trained on the building. "I'm going to catch up with Joss and Megan. Despite what she said earlier, I'm thinking both Megan and her daughter will be ready for some rest."

Then he turned to face Seamus, his green eyes hard as jade. "I'm willing to cut you some slack for a couple of reasons. One, you saved the life of someone who is important to my wife. And two, we need a medic on-site.

"Having said that, I will be keeping a close eye on you myself until Conlan gives you a clean bill of health. He's an obnoxious jerk, but he is thorough. If there's something that's likely to bite you on the ass, you'd be better off telling me now, especially when it comes to your ability to take care of my people."

Seamus should tell the bastard to take his job and shove it, but that would be counterproductive. He settled for righteous indignation. "I'm qualified, with primary emphasis on our species, but with enough experience with the other two to do the job."

"That's more than I had hoped for in a medic." Rafferty gave Seamus a short nod. "Go ahead and look the place over, especially the supplies we stocked. Make a detailed list of what you'll need to set up shop. Divide it up by what you *have* to have and what you'd *like* to have. When you're ready, we'll talk budget and set up an inventory system to automatically replace what you use."

"I'll work on it tonight." Seamus reached for the door handle, needing more than ever to get away from his new employer.

But the vampire wasn't done with him. "One more thing. There's an attached apartment for your use. It was stocked with only the basics, too, but I've set up an account for you at the supply depot."

Rafferty looked away again, his eyes focused on the distant horizon. "You're not the first one to show up on my doorstep with little more than the clothes on your back. Don't let pride keep you from taking what you need."

"I don't like charity." Especially Rafferty's.

"Then consider it an advance against your wages." Rafferty's mouth quirked up in a small smile. "And believe me, as the only medic on the place, you'll earn every dime I'm paying you—and then some."

It was all he could do to nod. This time, when he started to open the door, Rafferty let him escape but rolled down the window.

"When you're done, call the house. The number's by the phone in the office. One of us will come for you."

"Sounds like a plan."

Seamus waited for Rafferty to pull away in a cloud of dust before unlocking the door of the clinic. Once inside, he leaned against the wall and closed his eyes. Maintaining control around his enemy was a bitch, but then he hadn't planned on having so much direct contact with the vampire.

Of course, if he convinced Rafferty he could be trusted, it would make it that much sweeter when he finally carried out his plan. But there was one other thing he hadn't counted on—actually liking the older vampire or at least respecting what he was trying to do here on his estate. Their impromptu tour of the grounds had revealed a well-run, burgeoning enterprise.

Most of the humans who made up the majority of the workforce had retired to their homes for the night. Many had waved and smiled as Rafferty's transport had passed by. Odder yet, both Joss and Rafferty had waved back, often calling to people by name. Seamus was pretty sure his late father would've been hard-pressed to name more than a handful of humans by name. It was probably only a ploy to make the cattle work harder for less pay, but it obviously worked.

Speaking of working, he'd better get started

himself. He flipped on the lights and got his first clear look at his new temporary place of employment.

Megan looked around the cottage; there had to be something that demanded her attention—a dirty dish that needed washing, a towel that needed folding—anything at all. She and Phoebe had been living in the place for only just over a week, not enough time to make much of a mess. Besides, she'd cleaned the place thoroughly the day before. And the day before that.

Now that her energy levels were improving, she needed something to keep her busy. Anything to keep from thinking too hard about the mess her life had become. Cut off from friends and family, she was now surrounded by nameless strangers.

Well, except for Joss and her husband, but she couldn't claim to really know either of them. It had been years since she'd spent much time with Joss, and she'd only just met Rafferty. Of course, there was Conlan, the gruff chancellor security officer, but he was some distance away at the gate. And finally, Seamus Fitzhugh, new to the estate himself. She wanted to trust someone, anyone, but for Phoebe's sake she had to be careful. Her daughter's life depended on it.

Rather than think about that or the troublesome circumstances surrounding her new job, she double-checked the supplies she'd put together for Phoebe. Right now her daughter was sound asleep in her crib, so peaceful, so pretty, so blissfully unaware of the dangers that inhabited their world. If it were up to Megan, Phoebe would remain innocent and unscarred by life for as long as possible.

To that end, she fully intended to stay within the electrified fences and walls of Rafferty's family estate, no matter who showed up at the gate demanding that she surrender her daughter to their care. Both of the O'Days had been remarkably supportive during the time she'd been there, not to mention patient. She knew she should share the truth of her situation with them, but she'd grown too accustomed to living a secret to make confiding in someone easy.

For Phoebe's sake, eventually she'd confess all to Joss in order to take legal action naming her cousin and Rafferty as Phoebe's guardians, just in case something happened to her—say, like being poisoned. Once again, the medic came to mind. She owed him her life. If only he weren't a vampire—but he was, and she'd never risk involvement with another one.

There was nothing left to do but stare at the clock until the sun went down. Once it did, she'd be on her way to her new job. And her new boss—Seamus Fitzhugh.

The soft purr of a well-tuned engine caught her attention. She turned on the outside lights and slid open the peephole as a transport slowed to a stop in front of the cottage. As soon as she recognized Joss climbing out of the driver's side, she leaned down and gave her daughter a quick kiss.

"Okay, little girl. Here's where the whole trust thing gets started."

Bracing herself for separation anxiety, she opened the door and stepped outside. "Joss, come in. Are you sure you don't mind watching Phoebe for a couple of hours?"

"Not at all. I live to spoil her rotten." Her cousin grinned. "In fact, Rafferty will be along in a minute to help with that."

"You didn't come together?"

"Nope. We wanted to leave one of the transports here for you to use, so we drove separately. There he is now."

Joss held out the keys. "So here, and don't

protest. We keep a fleet of vehicles for everyone to use. It's part of the whole package."

Megan wasn't sure she believed that, but she was willing to accept the small lie. "I appreciate all of your help."

"You'd do the same for me. Now trade me my favorite little girl for these keys. You don't want to be late for your first night on the job."

It hurt to hand off her daughter, but she did her best to hide it. "Mr. Fitzhugh said he'd only need me for a couple of hours tonight."

"I know, but anytime you need a break, all you have to do is ask." Joss's expression turned fierce. "And Phoebe will be safe with me and Rafferty."

Tears burned her eyes. "That means a lot, Joss."

"We'll handle whatever comes, Megan, up to and including toxic diapers." Rafferty joined them. He smiled down at Phoebe before meeting Megan's gaze. "You know if there's anything else we can help you with, all you have to do is ask."

She'd been expecting the offer. She forced herself to face the vampire. "I know. I'll think about it."

"Do." He softened the order with a wink. "I promise you and your child will be safe here."

"Thank you, Rafferty." Her eyes burned, but she was done crying. "Now, I'd better get to work. Wouldn't want to anger my new boss on the first day."

"Good luck!"

She drove away while she had the strength to do so. Starting from the minute she'd found out she was pregnant, it had been just her and Phoebe. Now, being separated from her daughter was ripping a hole in her heart. Even if she'd only be gone a short time to go over her new duties with Seamus, it was still hard. Once she knew more what the job entailed, she'd have to make arrangements for Phoebe's care.

She absolutely hated that, but she couldn't live on Joss's charity, either.

The infirmary was only a short distance from her cottage, close enough that she could've walked. She was just as glad to get there and get this first encounter over with. She still wasn't sure how, out of all the people on Rafferty's estate, she came to be working with Seamus Fitzhugh. It wasn't as if she had a medical background, but evidently he needed her computer skills. Time to get moving.

A transport pulled up out front. Seamus set down the list he'd been staring at for the past fifteen minutes as he waited for his new co-worker to arrive. Technically he supposed he was her boss since Rafferty had put him in charge of the clinic. Since he had no desire to be in charge of anything, much less Megan Perez, he'd show her what needed to be done and then concentrate on his own duties. Maybe their paths wouldn't cross all that often.

Megan was going to build the database for the estate's medical records. When he and Rafferty had gone over the inventory, the discussion had turned to the logistics of providing adequate care for the various inhabitants of the estate. It came as no surprise that Megan Perez wasn't the only one who would prefer not to update her official records with the North American Coalition anytime soon.

At Rafferty's suggestion, Seamus was to see the patients as needed and make note of any treatment rendered. At some point in the future, should they ever get a licensed physician, then they'd decide what to do about the regulations that demanded that all doctors report to the Coalition Medical Department.

It was splitting hairs when it came to compliance with the law. At best, the North American Coalition was a loosely organized governing body whose main function was to oversee any interactions where the three races crossed paths. As long as no one complained about their records being incomplete, the Coalition wasn't likely to care one way or the other.

But in any case, Rafferty would be the one to take the heat, provided the vampire lived that long.

With that happy thought, Seamus opened the door for Megan just as she was reaching out to ring the bell, startling her. For the space of a heartbeat, the two of them stood frozen, her hand reaching out, his eyes locked on hers. Finally, she jerked her arm back. He retreated a step. Both of them drew a deep breath.

He finally found his voice. "Sorry, Ms. Perez…Megan. I didn't mean to startle you. Please come in."

She sidled past him in the hallway, only stopping when she'd reached the more spacious waiting room. He took his time locking the door, needing that short break to get himself back under control. He'd thought over the past week that his memory had exaggerated his body's powerful reaction to the skittish chancellor. But no, one look into those pretty, but worried, eyes had his adrenaline pumping hard.

He joined her in the reception area, careful to keep his distance. Her face looked softer, more rounded than he remembered. Good, she was definitely on the mend.

"How are you?"

She managed a small smile. "Are you asking as my medic or making polite conversation?"

He laughed, the tension between them easing. "Both, I guess."

"Better and fine. Phoebe and I have settled into the cottage that Joss picked out for us." She frowned. "Where are you staying?"

"There's an apartment attached to the clinic here. It was intended to be used for whoever is on call. But since I'm it for medical staff right now, I'll be living here."

He hated knowing the food he ate and the roof over his head came straight from his enemy, but there was no way to avoid it here in the middle of O'Day's family estate. Something of what he was thinking must have shown on his face because Megan gave him a sympathetic look.

"Feels like charity, doesn't it?" She pretended an interest in the design of the receptionist's desk. "Joss says I'm being silly, but I'm used to earning my keep."

"Is that why you took the job working here at the clinic? To earn your keep?" What had he expected? That she'd chosen this particular job in order to spend time with him?

She gave him a rueful grin, one that revealed a small dimple in her right cheek. How had he missed seeing that before? He realized, while he'd been staring at her, he'd missed what she was saying.

She didn't seem to notice as she continued, "Of the open positions, this one was the closest fit to my skill set. I've designed record systems before for a variety of businesses. I don't have a medical background, but I figured you could help me with that."

"Out of curiosity, what were your other choices?"

Megan's serious expression was belied by the twinkle in her eyes. "Right now I could be driving a tractor, baling hay or learning to be a transport mechanic. Can you imagine? All those possibilities, and yet I chose to work here."

"Amazing. What were you thinking?" he asked, enjoying the banter far more than he should. "Instead of being out in the bright sunshine, you get to spend your time in a back office here in this lovely concrete building. Or as I've come to call it, the bunker."

The teasing light died in her eyes. "That was a big part of the attraction."

Because she didn't want to risk being seen by the wrong person. "Well then, let me show you around and then I'll introduce you to your new domain."

It didn't take long for Seamus to show her the clinic. When they returned to the reception area, he ushered her into the office she'd be using.

"I downloaded a copy of a Coalition medical records form for you to use as a template but with some minor changes. It's all there in the folder by the computer. I'd also like a color-coded filing system for the hardcopy of the patient charts based on species."

She nodded. "Any preference on colors? Like red for the vampires, white for the humans, and pink for the chancellors since we're somewhere in between."

He raised an eyebrow. "I assume that was a joke."

"Not much of one, since you didn't even smile." Not that she even tried to look apologetic.

"All right. It was cute, but I'd still prefer something like blue, green and yellow."

"Okay, one boring filing system coming up." She walked around the desk and sat down.

Seamus finally smiled. "I'll be directly across the hall if you need me. I thought you might want some time alone to get settled in and maybe make a list of any supplies you require. That's all we needed to talk about tonight. The clinic opens for business the day after tomorrow at four in the afternoon."

Four o'clock? But he was a vampire. The vampires she'd known usually didn't work while the sun was up. "You'll be working during the daylight hours?"

"It's not a problem for me. When I was in training, they varied our hours all the time to acclimate us to different sleep patterns. We're going to start with being open from late afternoon until midnight, which should be fine for all three groups. Since the humans work the day shift, they can come in at the end of their day. Same for most of the chancellors, although their schedules seem to be more erratic. Any resident vampires can take the later appointments. I'll handle emergencies as they arise."

How odd. In her experience, the vampires she'd known had expected the other two species to change schedules to accommodate their preference for the night hours. Back when she thought she and Banan had a future together, she'd actually traded a job she'd loved for a lesser one because he'd demanded it. What a fool she'd been. She should have known then that he was all take and no give.

Seamus picked up on her mood change. "Is something wrong?"

She forced a smile. "No, sorry, my mind wandered off."

"And not to a happy place, judging by the expression on your face."

Darn, he was far too perceptive. "No, it wasn't. Now, I've already taken up too much of your time. I'll make that list for you."

She walked into her office. *Her* office. It was amazing what a mood lifter that simple expression was. She looked around, surprised at the spacious feel of the room, despite the lack of windows. The furniture was pragmatic rather than fancy, but the computer was top-of-the-line. Rafferty obviously spent his money where it counted.

She jotted down both a supply list as well as some questions for Seamus about what kind of records he wanted to keep. It occurred to her that neither he nor Rafferty had mentioned anything about billing for the services rendered. She'd have to ask about that. Maybe they planned to hire a bookkeeper, but until the clinic got busy, she should be able to handle that, as well.

Satisfied with the start she'd made, she crossed the hall and knocked on the door frame before entering. "Got a minute?"

"Sure. By the way, no need to knock if the door's open. I'll close it if I need privacy." Seamus looked up from his computer screen. "Have a seat. I'll be with you in a second."

While he finished up, she looked around his office, noting there was barely room to walk between the single bookcase and his desk. Then there were the piles of books on the floor along the wall. Why was he holed up in such a cluttered space while her office was so roomy? Even his name plate on the door was held on with tape. How odd.

When he stopped typing and sat back in his chair, she asked him, "Shouldn't you have the bigger office? All I really need is a place to set a computer while you have all this to deal with." She waved her hand toward the stacks of books piled around the room.

His eyes slid to the side. "I liked this one better."

"Right, everybody wants to run into an obstacle course whenever they walk into their office." What was he trying to hide? "Want to try that again?"

A look of anger flashed across his face. "Okay. I thought you'd need room for a crib and a changing table for Phoebe. This office isn't big enough for all of that."

Had she heard him right? "You want me to bring my daughter to work with me?"

"You mean you don't?" He looked both surprised and a bit defensive. "I thought you'd worry more if she wasn't with you."

Her eyes burned. This vampire was little better than a stranger, and yet he'd known without asking how hard it would be for her to leave Phoebe. What could she say to that? "That's very kind of you."

"I'm not being kind at all. I'll get more work out of you if you figure you owe me." He definitely looked more grumpy.

Obviously he didn't handle gratitude well, so she changed the subject. "Here's the supply list you wanted. I guess I should add a crib and changing table."

"I already ordered them. They'll arrive tomorrow. I'll get them assembled before you're due to arrive."

"Thank you, Seamus."

"It's nothing." His pale skin flushed. "Back

to your duties. We're it as far as staff goes. Rafferty is on the lookout for a receptionist and a medical assistant for me."

"And a billing clerk?"

He shook his head. "Rafferty's not charging his people for medical services. He says it's all part of the benefit package, which he hopes will entice more highly trained applicants to move to the estate."

Why did that look as if it left a sour taste in Seamus's mouth? As long as he was being paid by Rafferty, why did he care?

"Would you mind if I take the computer home with me to study the programming?"

"No, that's fine, although I don't expect you to take your work home with you on a regular basis. I meant what I said about your needing time to rebuild your strength. I respect your need for independence, but if you find the hours are too much, say so. We'll work around it."

"And I said I'm feeling fine." If she sounded defensive, too bad.

He wasn't buying it. "Do I have to remind you that it's only been a week since you almost died? Don't push yourself. You won't do either of us any good if you have a relapse."

She stood up and glared down at him, her hands clenched in fists. "And this isn't the first time I've had to remind you that I'm the best judge of what is and isn't good for me."

He stepped around the desk to loom over her. "And was it your good judgment that got you poisoned in the first place?"

That did it. She'd never slapped anyone in her entire life, but his arrogance shattered her control. His vampire reflexes kicked in, enabling him to catch her wrist before her hand made contact with his face. Her temper flamed hot as she struggled to pull free of his grasp. Instead of letting her go, his other arm snapped around her and yanked her up against his chest.

"Seamus."

She meant to yell his name, to protest his rough treatment of her. But the single word came out as a whisper, almost a prayer as his lips touched hers and their burning anger changed into a whole different type of heat.

Chapter 5

She tasted honey sweet with just a hint of hot spice.

He'd wondered about that; now he knew. Her tongue mated and danced with his, both of them lost in the moment. Touches were tentative, gentle. A brush of fingertips there, a slow caress tracing a curve, a slight squeeze. How long had it been since someone had touched him at all? He couldn't remember. Their bodies shifted and aligned perfectly, her softness against his hard strength.

Warmth, all delicious temptation, slid through his veins, running out his fangs and making him want to savor far more of this woman than a simple kiss. Her blood called to him, arousing his craving to taste life in its purest form. He broke off the kiss and nibbled his way along the elegant curve of her jaw and down her neck. There, he found it—the soft flutter of her pulse running so enticingly close to the surface.

He gently raked the tips of his fangs across her skin, asking permission without words to take this exploration one step further. But instead of offering herself up to him, she gasped as if in pain and shoved him backward. The unexpected move, combined with her chancellor strength, caught him off guard. Once again his vampire reflexes saved him.

The chill in Megan's eyes left no doubt that the moment had passed, leaving only their original anger hovering between them. Despite his disappointment, he had to admire the way she stood her ground, refusing to cower before a fully aroused, fully enraged vampire male. He fought hard to bank his temper, his frustration and the powerful need to take her right there amidst the clutter on his desk.

They remained frozen in place, both breathing hard as if running a race. Finally, he blinked and stepped back, breaking the spell. More distance would be needed if he was going to resist the urge to touch her again.

"Go home, Megan." He forced the words through the tightness in his throat.

"But..."

He held up his hand to stop her. "I know. We can't. We won't." When that didn't seem to satisfy her, he added, "Hell, Megan, if anyone ever asks, I'll even swear we didn't. But you need to leave. Now."

She nodded as she backed toward the door. "I'll tell Rafferty to find someone else."

That would probably be the smart thing to do, but right now he wasn't feeling all that intelligent. "No, you won't."

To his amazement, rather than blow up again over him trying to boss her around, she laughed. "Wasn't your trying to issue orders what got us into this position?"

This wasn't the position he wanted to try out with her. In fact, he could think of several, but in that direction lay madness. If she could lighten up, so could he, even if it killed him.

Forcing a great deal more good humor into his words than he actually felt, he said, "Okay, Ms. Perez, let me rephrase that. I would most humbly appreciate it if you would not demand Rafferty find you another job."

"Why? It's not like you have a lot invested in my training or anything."

"This might be the only job where you can bring Phoebe with you. I'm the only one who knows there's a very real threat to both of you. That is, unless you want to come clean with Rafferty or Conlan and tell them somebody wants you dead."

His words hit her hard, making her flinch. He didn't regret saying them, though. He'd saved her life once, but that was no guarantee he'd be able to again.

"What if your vampire lover tries again? I might not get to you in time if you're working days or on the other side of the estate. What if he goes after Phoebe the next time?"

"That won't happen because he wants her. It's me he's finished with." He could tell that admission cost her a lot. She shrank in on herself, once more looking like the desperately ill woman she'd been when he first met her. Then her shoulders snapped back, her spine ramrod straight.

"I'll keep the job, Seamus, but only if you promise this won't happen again. It was nice. Actually way beyond nice, but I've learned my lesson. I won't risk getting involved with another—"

She stopped midsentence, unable or at least unwilling to continue, but they both knew what she'd been about to say. She wasn't willing to get involved with him because he was a vampire, just like Phoebe's mysterious father. That was all right. He couldn't afford to get involved with anybody, regardless of species. He had his own agenda to follow.

"We'll write it off to a momentary weakness that won't happen again. We'll make sure of that. Do we have a deal?"

She reluctantly nodded. "All right. I'll be back tomorrow afternoon with Phoebe. If you change your mind before then, call. I'll understand."

"I won't change my mind."

"Unless there's something else, I'll go pack up the computer and leave."

"I'll walk you out." He braced himself for the argument sure to come.

Once again, she surprised him. "All right, but just this once. After all, Rafferty is very careful about who he lets in. We're safe here on the estate."

Seamus knew for a fact Rafferty hadn't been all that careful. After all, he'd let Seamus in, hadn't he? But wisely, he kept that little bit of information to himself.

It didn't take long for Megan to gather up her computer, the file and her keys. Seamus waited for her by the front door of the clinic, not wanting to crowd her. Even more, he didn't want to test his control around her. When she was safely tucked into her transport, he stood in the doorway and watched her drive away, not wanting her to feel like he was hovering.

As soon as she was out of sight, he changed into shorts and a T-shirt. He'd already established a routine of taking a late-night run, using his need for exercise as an excuse to learn the layout of the estate. So far, he'd taken a different route each time, but made sure to pass by Rafferty's home at some point.

Unlike the infirmary, which had no windows in the walls, Rafferty's house was definitely more high-tech. Heavy-duty shutters protected the vampire leader from sunlight during the day, but they opened at night to allow in the evening air. Each pass through the area netted him more information, learning the behavior patterns of the locals, including Rafferty and his wife. As he ran, he noted whose dogs barked, where the vampires lived, whose lights went off early.

Once he started official office hours, his chances to scope out the estate would become more restricted. So tonight, he'd take the long way around, and if his route took him past a certain cottage on his way, so much the better. It wasn't as if he was hoping for another glimpse of Megan Perez. He just wanted to make sure she'd gotten home safely.

Yeah, right.

Damn, Conlan could really learn to hate that bell. It was petty on his part, but he continued to ignore the summons until he finished reading the report from one of his operatives. Once he'd signed off on it, he took his own sweet time stepping outside. The security lights were on, bathing the latest stray in stark relief.

Vampire, judging by his size and the time of his arrival. Conlan drew his weapon and walked toward the gate.

The jerk flashed his fangs with a hiss. "It took you long enough. I'm sure your boss won't appreciate knowing how incompetent his lackey is."

Charming. So not only vampire, but one from a top-level clan. It didn't matter which one, the behavior was always the same: arrogant, demanding and a pain in the ass.

Well, two could play that game, too. "Sorry. You don't have an appointment. Next time, call before you decide to show up unannounced."

He smiled, showing off his own impressive set of fangs. "Now if you'll excuse me, I have things to do. You know, important lackey stuff."

Back inside, he counted down the minutes until either the bell started up again or his phone rang. It didn't take long. As tempting as it was to ignore the phone, he knew better than to ignore Rafferty O'Day.

He kicked back in his chair and put his feet up on the desk. "Hi, Rafferty. What's up?"

"Shea, why am I having to make this call?"

"Because I'm not supposed to allow questionable characters onto the premises. That's my job description."

Silence. Conlan smiled and started a mental countdown until the explosion. He only got as far as eight, a new record.

"The only son and heir of the Delaney clan is not a questionable character."

"Sorry, boss, but he didn't identify himself. Had I known, I would've let him in. Honest."

"Go do it now. Offer him something to drink while he waits in your office until I can get there to pick him up."

"Will do, boss. Immediately, boss. Is there anything else, boss?"

"Conlan—" Rafferty paused, drawing a slow breath as if praying for patience.

"Yes, boss?"

"Be grateful Joss likes you so much."

"Oh, believe me. I am." Sometimes he even felt guilty about it. "See you in a few minutes, sir."

Then he hung up and headed outside to open the gate. Rather than wait for the vampire, Conlan walked back inside without a backward look, saying without words that the fool was beneath notice and no threat. Coming from a chancellor, the Delaney heir would recognize the implied insult. Conlan stopped short of closing the door, although the temptation to make the vampire wait outside on the porch was strong.

He was already back at his computer working when his guest sauntered in, all arrogance and anger. *Bring it on, punk, and you'll find out why chancellors are employed to keep both vampires and humans in line.*

Opening the fridge, he pulled out a blood pack and tossed it on the desk. "Here. Enjoy."

"I suppose warming it first would be too much to ask."

Conlan kept his eyes firmly on the computer screen. "The kitchen's through that door. Knock yourself out."

The blood pack came flying back across the

desk as the young vampire sneered. "Do you have any idea who I am?"

Conlan tossed the pack back in the fridge. "According to Rafferty, you're one of the Delaney clan."

"I'm the heir."

Clearly he expected Conlan to be impressed. He wasn't. "Congratulations or else condolences, depending on how you feel about that."

"Does O'Day have any idea how insufferably rude you are to his guests?"

"You'll have to ask him yourself. Now if you'll excuse me, as I said, I have work to do." He saved the report he'd just downloaded from his operative and then fired back a list of follow-up questions.

The young vampire leaned back in his chair and propped his feet up on the corner of Conlan's desk. "You might want to update your résumé while you're at it. When Rafferty finds out how you've treated me, I'm sure you'll be needing it."

Actually, that might be true, but Conlan wasn't going to worry about it. Right now he was going to do some quick digging to see why someone of Delaney's status would come knocking on Rafferty's gate unannounced. Ever since Rafferty had married Joss Sloan, his relationship with the upper echelons of the vampire community had been chilly at best. They couldn't shun him completely; his money wielded too much power for that to happen.

But for the heir of one of the snootiest families to show up like this warranted checking into. He'd keep his inquiries low-key rather than risk setting off a major feud between the two clans. Rafferty really would fire his ass for that, but watching out for possible threats to the estate was Conlan's job, after all.

It was always possible Delaney had a good reason for being there. But Conlan's instincts, finely honed after years of sifting through the bullshit to find the truth, were screaming that something was off about this visit. Punks like Delaney usually traveled first-class and with an entourage. Conlan was still trying to make sense out of the scant details in Seamus Fitzhugh's portfolio, but that would have to wait. Right now, he had other fish to fry.

"Well, today's the day."

Seamus didn't bother to check his appearance in the mirror. He might need every scrap of energy he could muster to get through the next eight hours. Even so, he straightened the collar of his lab coat and patted his pockets to make sure they were stocked with the usual stuff—pencil, pen, notepad and some silly stickers for any younglings who came in.

The sound of the front door opening echoed through the building. Time to go. Megan had insisted on coming in early for the official opening of the infirmary. She said it was to give Phoebe time to settle into her new surroundings, but he suspected Megan had picked up on how nervous he was about all of this. Even though he'd used his medical training merely as the means to get through the gate, he found himself wanting to do the job right.

In fact, sometimes he actually forgot about his real reason for being there. Then something would make him think of his sister Petra and all the grief and anger came rushing back to remind him that he had a higher purpose than merely dispensing medication and doing physicals. If his clan was destined to disappear, he insisted on taking his enemies with him.

But it wasn't time for that. Not yet, but soon. Definitely soon. The more time he spent in this charade, the easier it would be for him to forget the debt that was owed, the price that must be paid. And spending hours in the company of Megan Perez and her sweet daughter weren't helping any.

Not for the first time, he wondered what kind of coldhearted bastard not only cast Megan aside, but tried to kill her. A man lucky enough to have Megan in his life should've cherished her. And to be doubly blessed to create a child together? That was such a rarity among his kind.

"Seamus? Are you in there?"

"Coming."

Megan waited for him in the short hallway that led to both of their offices as well as to his private quarters. They'd been careful in their dealings with each other since that kiss two nights ago in his office. Even so, the memory, the potential of it, seemed to hover over them whenever they were in the same room. Maybe if they'd actually carried the encounter through to its logical end, they would've been able to write it off to nerves or proximity or even just plain need.

Instead, they maneuvered around each other, careful not to touch, careful not to linger, careful not to get too close. However, all that their careful dancing accomplished was to emphasize the temptation and his secret hope it might happen again. But now definitely wasn't the time for such thoughts.

"Hi, you ready for this?"

Megan smiled. "As ready as I can be. I'll do my best to funnel the patients through to you in the right order."

"First come, first served…"

"Unless there's blood involved." She finished for him, smiling.

He'd explained the basic principles of triage to her, but that pretty much summed it up. "That is, if we get any customers at all."

He followed Megan into her office where she settled Phoebe into her crib. "Oh, I wouldn't worry too much about that. Have you looked outside lately?"

"No. Should I?"

"Follow me."

She led the way back to the front entrance and slid open the peephole in the door. He leaned in over her shoulder to look outside, doing his best ignore to the twin distractions of the rapid trip of Megan's pulse and the scent of her skin. He closed his eyes briefly to force himself to focus and took a look outside. Then he blinked twice and looked again.

He stepped back to put more distance between him and temptation. "The line goes all the way to the road."

"I know. It's even longer now than when I came in."

A familiar surge of adrenaline simmered in his veins. "Guess we'd better get ready."

"I'd better give Joss a call. She said if it looked like we'd be busy, she'd come by and take care of Phoebe for me until she goes down for the night."

The last thing he wanted was one of the O'Days underfoot right now. Things were bound to get hectic with that many patients on his first night. On the other hand, it was doubtful he could play a triple role of receptionist, nurse and medic by himself. If Joss could free Megan up to work with the patients, things were bound to go more smoothly.

"That's a good idea." He closed the peephole after taking one more look. "I guess they really did need a medic on the estate."

She smiled on her way to the reception desk. "Looks like. Joss and Rafferty will be more glad than ever that you're here."

Not if they suspected his real reasons for being there, but now wasn't the time for such thoughts. He waited until Megan called Joss before unlocking the door to invite the first patient of the night through the door.

Megan's back ached and her feet hurt, but it was a good tired, the kind that came from a job well done. Other than a couple of small glitches, the past nine hours had flown by. Starting from the initial onslaught, they'd never had more than a ten-minute break between patients all night long. They'd planned on closing at midnight, but around ten o'clock a pair of chancellors had carried in a human with a nasty gash on his leg.

As Seamus had said, blood took priority. Taking him ahead of everyone else who'd been waiting barely caused a stir. In fact, several offered to come back the next night, but Seamus had insisted on seeing each and every patient. If they were willing to wait, he was willing to see them.

She could only imagine how tired he must be. She saw the last patient out and then locked the door and turned off the outside lights. She really wanted to take Phoebe home, but not before she knew Seamus was all right. As far as she knew, he hadn't had a chance to feed or eat all night. Rather than ask, she pulled three packs out of the refrigerator and put the blood in to heat.

He wasn't in his office, so she went on a hunt. He was in the lab looking at a slide with a microscope.

"Seamus, can't that wait?"

He made some notes and then set the slide aside. "That's the last one."

"Good. You've done more than enough for one night. Surely anything else can wait until tomorrow. Come on, I've got blood warming for you."

He gave her a dark look but followed anyway. "Your job description doesn't include waiting on me."

"And I don't plan on making a habit of it." She blocked his office door. "No, you don't need to spend the rest of the night at your desk. Go sit in your living room and I'll bring it to you."

"Megan…"

"Seamus…" she echoed, with a smile. "Look, just go sit. The faster you do what I tell you, the faster I can go home."

He clearly wanted to argue the point, but she walked away before he could. When she returned with the packets, she found him sprawled on the sofa, his head tipped back and his eyes closed. It was the first time she'd crossed the threshold into his private quarters and wasn't sure if she should. Both of them had worked hard the past couple of days to establish a strictly professional relationship.

Feeding him in his home was definitely on

the other side of the line they'd drawn. But it would have taken a much harder heart than hers to see how tired he was and not want to help.

"Seamus," she called softly.

When he didn't answer, she tried again, this time reluctantly reaching out to shake his shoulder.

His eyes popped open as soon as she touched him. "I'm awake. I'm awake."

"Sure you are. Here, take this." She handed him one of the packets and put the other two within easy reach before backing away.

When he didn't immediately feed, she resorted to nagging. "Seamus, that's going to get cold."

He inverted the packet a couple of times to mix it. "I was waiting for you to leave."

"I've seen a vampire feed before. It doesn't bother me."

"Maybe it bothers *me*."

Before she could ask why, Phoebe made her own demands known. "Okay, I hear my name being called. I'll leave you to it."

Joss had taken care of Phoebe as Megan worked the reception desk, staying far longer than they'd originally planned. She'd sworn she didn't mind because Rafferty was out giving an unexpected visitor the grand tour. Once Phoebe settled into sleep, she'd gone home.

"Hey, there, little one. I'll bet you're hungry." Normally, Megan would've preferred to take her home first so she could put Phoebe back to bed after she'd been fed. But right now, it would take too long to pack everything up and haul it out to the transport.

After changing Phoebe's diaper, she took her out to the waiting room and sat down in one of the chairs. These quiet moments spent nursing her daughter were always the best ones of the day. She found the time soothing, the physical connection between them almost spiritual. She brushed Phoebe's wispy hair and smiled.

"Hey there, little one. I love you."

Tears stung her eyes. Maybe because she was tired, but the reason didn't matter. Sometimes it hit her hard how much she'd gone through just to get where she was, safe and with her daughter in her arms. No matter what she'd given up, she didn't regret her decision to keep Phoebe.

This might not be the life she'd envisioned for herself, but she had few regrets. A slight noise caught her attention. Seamus was standing in the shadows across the room, watching the two of them with such stark hunger in his expression. Yeah, she had regrets, but meeting Seamus Fitzhugh wasn't one of them.

If only he was a chancellor, but he wasn't. All the more reason to keep some distance between them.

"Don't let us keep you, Seamus. I can let myself out."

"Not going to happen. I'll make sure you get home safely."

"But—"

He leaned against the wall and closed his eyes. "Megan, we're both too tired to argue. If it weren't so late, there'd be enough people still out and about to make it safe for you to be on your own. So either I take you home or I'll follow you. Either way, you're not going to be alone."

She suspected that he'd find another excuse tomorrow night, but she really didn't want to fight about it. Phoebe had already fallen back asleep; they could go now. Tomorrow would be soon enough to get this matter settled once and for all.

"I'll get my things."

Conlan had picked up the phone half a dozen times in the past two hours. Rafferty hadn't spoken to him since Delaney's arrival two nights ago. If there'd been any problems with the vampire heir's surprise visit, surely Conlan would've heard.

Even so, he couldn't quit thinking about the young vampire's unexpected appearance. Maybe it was just the inborn arrogance of a vampire scion that had gotten under Conlan's skin, but he didn't think so. It was more the kid didn't fit the profile of the usual applicants for residency on the O'Day estate, which made him a bit of a mystery.

Conlan hated mysteries.

"Screw it."

He gave in and punched in Rafferty's number. No answer. He slammed the receiver back down and considered his options. His assistant had arrived, so Conlan could go poke around the estate himself and see what he could find out.

As he waited, he thumbed through the stack of files on his desk. The third one down belonged to Seamus Fitzhugh. So far, all the information matched what the young vampire had given them. Oddly enough, that's what bothered Conlan. It was too perfect. Next, he'd send one of his operatives to quietly interview anyone who might have really known Seamus. But as far as Conlan could tell, Seamus had left behind no friends, no family, no nothing. Hell, he hadn't even had a parking ticket.

Oddly enough, despite his misgivings, Conlan realized he very much wanted to approve the file. He'd liked the young vampire, but that wasn't why. Watching Seamus fight for Megan Perez's life had been like watching a highly trained warrior go into battle, armed with little more than his courage and determination that no one would die on his watch. That kind of heroism deserved to be rewarded.

Unlike the egotistical jerk who'd shown up the other night, Seamus deserved a chance here on the O'Day estate. Maybe he'd drop in on young Fitzhugh at the infirmary. Before he made a final decision on Seamus's future, he wanted to look the young medic in the eye one more time.

History had proven Conlan's judgment wasn't infallible, but right now, it was all he had to go on.

Chapter 6

Seamus set a stack of patient files on Megan's desk. The brightly colored folders represented the impressive amount of work they'd accomplished on their first night in business. Tonight could be just as busy. In the past, Rafferty had made arrangements for emergency care for the residents of the estate, but that was all.

Much of what Seamus had done last night was routine care—immunizations, medication renewals, minor infections. The one injury had been bad enough, but nothing that couldn't have been evacuated to a trauma center if necessary. He'd stitched the leg wound closed easily enough. The guy would have an interesting scar, but no lasting damage.

Seamus found himself looking forward to what the night's patient load might bring. He wasn't sure how he felt about that. It had been a long time since he'd actually had anything at all to look forward to. In medical school, the heavy workload pretty much insured that all he and his fellow students had time to think about was getting through each shift, grabbing a few hours of sleep and then starting all over again.

How long had it been since he actually had some control over how he spent his days—or nights? Too long. And he was only fooling himself that he did now. He had one goal, one last duty to carry out, and to consider anything else was a waste of energy. He needed to hold the people he met at arm's length, but that was so much harder to do than he'd expected.

It didn't help that the air in Megan's office was rife with her scent coupled with Phoebe's sweet baby smell. There was also a taste of Joss O'Day mixed in, but that was beneath his notice. It hadn't taken long for Megan to make the room her own. The woman definitely had some control issues. She'd given him very specific instructions where to put the files as he finished with them. He had no doubt that she'd even double-check to make sure he'd input the information correctly before putting the patient files away on the shelf.

He couldn't wait to see how she did it. If it were up to him, they'd be filed by species first and then alphabetized by last name. He was betting she'd do the same. But however Megan set up her filing system, she'd be able to lay hands on anything he wanted with easy efficiency—one more thing he liked about her.

Which was the last thing he needed.

He allowed himself one more deep breath of Megan-scented air before leaving her office. There was much to be done to get ready for tonight. But as he headed across the waiting room, intent on restocking the examination rooms, there was a sharp knock at the front door of the clinic. He veered in that direction, his pulse already kicking into high gear to deal with whatever crisis awaited his attention.

When he threw the door open, there was obviously no emergency. Instead, Joss O'Day gave him a bright smile and shoved a picnic basket toward him.

"Hi, Seamus. I figured you'd be up and might appreciate a meal you didn't have to cook for yourself. Megan said you had a heck of a first night on the job."

His hand automatically closed on the basket's handle, despite the strong temptation to refuse the gift. He had no desire to accept any more handouts from O'Day and his wife than was absolutely necessary. On the other hand, the better he knew his enemy, the better his chance to strike hard when the time came. The two of them had played loose with the rules of their society, with no regard for the fallout their games had caused. They would soon learn that such carelessness would come back to haunt them.

"Would you like to come in, Mrs. O'Day?" he asked, forcing a note of friendly curiosity into his voice. When she frowned, he added, "I mean, Joss."

He preferred to use her married name, to maintain that much more distance, but she'd already insisted on him calling her by her first name. Neither of the O'Days stood much on formality, a definite anomaly among the vampire clans. Another was their willingness to take in strays, although he doubted they would appreciate him calling their people that. It was true, though. Rafferty had made it clear that his estate offered a new start for anyone willing to work hard, with few questions asked other than Conlan's initial screening of all applicants.

Seamus stepped back into the shadows of the

doorway as he waited for her to decide. Even so, there was still too much sunshine for comfort.

Joss didn't hesitate. "If you're sure you don't mind."

He led the way into his office, wanting the solid presence of his desk between them. "You timed this perfectly. I was going to restock the exam rooms before grabbing a bite to eat. We used up a lot of supplies last night."

And he was babbling. To keep his hands busy, he opened the basket. The rich scent of tomato and basil filled the air.

"I hope you like spaghetti and meatballs," Joss said with a smile. "It's one of Rafferty's favorites, so I thought you might like it, too."

"I'm sure I will."

"Go ahead and eat while it's hot."

"Will you join me?"

"No, I'm fine. In fact, while I'm here, I think I'll put together some more patient files for Megan. She showed me how last night, and it will give her a head start. Rafferty is still sleeping because he had a late night with an unexpected guest, and I'm restless."

He would rather she didn't stay, but knew he was fighting a losing battle. Instead, he concentrated on eating, figuring he'd need all his strength to get through what could be another stressful night.

The meatballs were just as he liked them—spicy and no garlic. Back in the day, before the present system of government evolved to allow the three species to coexist side by side, humans thought that garlic would protect them from vampires. The truth was, his species just didn't care for the taste. He wondered if the same was true for chancellors.

Before he could take another bite, he heard something. Was that someone else knocking at the door? Before he could get up, Joss poked her head in.

"You eat. I'll see who it is. If you're needed, I'll holler."

Who else would it be for? He was the only medic in the region.

He set his fork down and listened. He could hear Joss's voice as well as a deeper male one. It was too early for any of the vampires on the estate to be out, so that left the humans and chancellors. As the voices drew closer, recognition kicked in. What was Conlan Shea doing here?

Joss led the security officer straight into Seamus's office. "Seamus, you must be special for Conlan to come calling, especially considering he's turned down every invitation I've made since he hired on."

Conlan's face flushed red. "Sorry, Joss. I've been busy."

"Yeah, right. Well, since you're here anyway, you *will* show up at my house this evening at midnight to eat with Rafferty and me." She gave him a narrow-eyed look. "You wouldn't want to hurt my feelings, would you?"

Judging by Conlan's expression, he really wanted to refuse, but knew he was trapped. "All right, Joss, I'll be there. But shouldn't you ask Rafferty first?"

"You let me worry about him." She smiled, clearly unafraid of her vampire spouse. "Good, that's settled. Now I'm going back to work in Megan's office with the music turned up so I can't hear what the two of you have to gossip about. See you tonight, Conlan."

"All right." The chancellor waited until she closed the door before quietly adding, "I'm sure Rafferty will be thrilled."

"I heard that!" Joss called just before the music started playing.

Seamus fought to hide a smile, but then gave up and grinned at Conlan. "I take it you're not Rafferty's favorite employee."

"True, but the fact that he's not my favorite employer sort of evens things out."

Conlan leaned forward and sniffed. "Did Joss make that?"

Seamus recognized hungry when he saw it. "Yeah. If you want some, come with me."

Without waiting for Conlan to answer, Seamus gathered up the food and put it back in the basket. "We'll have more room next door in my quarters."

Conlan followed him, not bothering to hide his curiosity about Seamus's home. "Nice place. You settling in all right?"

Figuring the security officer rarely asked idle questions, Seamus considered his words carefully before answering.

"Yesterday was our first night to open the infirmary. It was a madhouse, but I liked feeling useful."

"Yeah, I get that." He accepted the plate of spaghetti and salad. "It's probably rude of me to invite myself to lunch, but I love Joss's spaghetti. She makes great lasagna, too."

So Conlan knew her well enough to know her cooking skills. Interesting. "How long have you known her?"

"Since our days as arbiters for the Coalition negotiating agreements between the three species. She was one of the best before she resigned."

Seamus wasn't surprised by that. In fact, Conlan would be surprised to know exactly how much Seamus did know about Joss's time as an arbiter for the Coalition. After all, her actions during that time had set in motion the events that had brought destruction raining down on Seamus's sister.

For that, Joss and her vampire husband would pay. But now wasn't the time for such thoughts. Not with a sharp-eyed chancellor sitting across the table from him.

"She definitely has a way about her."

"That she does." Conlan cut himself another slice of bread. "I understand Megan's working here at the infirmary, too. That's convenient."

Seamus glared at Conlan. "What's that supposed to mean?"

The chancellor shrugged. "Nothing. Just that since she's the only person you knew here, it was nice that you ended up working together. I assume her health has improved."

"That it has. Good thing, too. Try telling her to take it easy and you'll get your head handed to you."

Conlan didn't exactly smile, but his eyes warmed up. "Can't say that it surprises me.

Toughness must run in their family. As sick as Megan was, I'm still amazed she made it all the way to the gate. Good thing she did, and better yet that you happened to be there at the right time."

He leaned back in his chair and gave Seamus a hard look. "I'm due to make my final recommendation on your application to live here. Is there anything you want to tell me before I send my report to the boss?"

"Not that I can think of, but if you have any specific questions, I'll try to answer them." Seamus made himself meet Conlan's direct gaze head-on. He hoped like hell that the chancellor was on a fishing expedition and not really expecting to catch anything.

"Do you like living here?"

"Yes." At least he could be honest on that point.

"Why?"

How to answer that? The real truth was out of the question. He picked up his dish and set it in the sink and thought about how he would have answered if he were the man he was pretending to be.

"I won't deny that I've made my share of poor choices, but I'm good at what I do. Most of the patients I saw last night were routine cases, but that doesn't mean the care I gave them was unimportant. The residents here on the estate need somebody with my particular skills."

He turned back to face Conlan. "I'd like to stay."

"Glad to hear that, considering I've already sent your file through with my recommendations that we accept you, Seamus. But make no mistake, if I find that my trust was misplaced, I'm a bad enemy to have."

So was Seamus, but Conlan wasn't his target. "Thank you, Conlan. I don't want to disappoint you."

But he would, and he hated knowing that.

"Well, I've got to go. Thanks for sharing your lunch with me. I've other business to take care of before I have to be at Joss's at midnight." Conlan still didn't look pleased about what was essentially a command performance.

Seamus followed him to the front door. "Look on the bright side. Maybe Joss will make lasagna."

"Even that won't make dinner with Rafferty any more palatable. Especially if his guest is still hanging around. I don't know why that vampire is here in the first place."

Seamus let a little bitterness seep into his

voice. "You mean he's not broke and running from his past?"

Conlan clapped Seamus on the shoulder. "Now, listen, Joss prefers that we think of our residents as running toward their future, not from their past. But to answer your question, this guy is the sole heir to his family's fortune, definitely not the kind of vampire we usually have show up at the gate, especially alone."

Seamus's mental alarms went off. "Did he say why he's here?"

"I can answer that."

Neither of them had noticed the music had been turned off. Joss joined them at the door. "Banan Delaney says that he's heard about our more progressive ways of doing things and wanted to see them for himself. He claims he's been butting heads with his family over how to get the most work out of their human and chancellor employees."

Conlan nodded, as if her explanation confirmed something for him. "Sounds like you don't believe him."

"It's hard to take him seriously when he spends most of his time drinking up our blood supplies and looking bored. If he's asked one intelligent question, I haven't heard it. And there's something off about him when we do show him around."

"How so?"

Joss frowned as she considered her answer. "He seems more interested in who we have working for us than how the work is being done. If he's wanting to change things on his own estate, it should be the other way around. It's almost as if he's hunting for somebody."

For the first time Seamus saw the warrior side in the two chancellors. Both radiated strength and determination, their fangs showing, although not fully extended. If he were this vampire heir, he'd be treading carefully around these two. Ever perceptive, Joss picked up on Seamus's own tension.

"Seamus? Do you know something about Delaney I should know about? Have you met him before?"

Joss's question jerked his attention back to her. "No, no I haven't. I'm afraid I wasn't exactly listening. I've got a lot to get ready before we open again tonight."

Joss seemed to accept his explanation. He wasn't so sure about Conlan, but then the chancellor was paid to suspect everyone and everything.

"Thanks again for bringing lunch, Joss."

"You're welcome. We'll get going so you can get something done."

Seamus locked the door after they left, intending to restock the exam rooms. However, he couldn't concentrate as the conversation played over and over in his mind. An irritating visitor was hardly his concern, but something about Joss's description of the vampire's actions prodded at him.

Was the vampire looking for someone specifically? If so, then the question was who? A chill danced down his spine. As Conlan had pointed out, quite a few of the estate residents had their own secrets to protect, but he knew one in particular who had a vampire in her past.

It was huge leap in logic, but they all suspected that Megan had been running from someone, and most likely that person was a vampire. But what Joss and Conlan didn't know was that she'd been systematically poisoned. If Delaney was indeed Phoebe's biological father, he could be here to try to finish the job and reclaim his daughter.

Seamus's own fangs ran out fully at the perceived threat to Megan. If the vampire tried to harm either female, Seamus would kill the bastard. And it wouldn't be an easy death, not if the vampire dared to threaten Megan. Seamus had dragged her back from the edge of death, and that made her his woman now.

His.

And that realization ricocheted around in his head as he tried to make sense of it. What was he thinking? Megan wasn't his. Never would be. But on a gut level, he knew that didn't matter. There was a connection between them that was forged that first day and had only strengthened with each minute he'd spent in her company.

She and her innocent daughter deserved to live in peace, not be haunted by a specter from her past.

There was no way to know if this Delaney fellow was really the villain in this affair, short of asking Megan point-blank who the father of her child was. Even then, she might not answer. While he admired her desire for independence, he wouldn't let it stand in the way of her safety.

He checked the time. She'd arrive for work in just over two hours. He'd put the time to good use and do some snooping of his own. The news media loved to cover the social circles a vampire heir like Delaney ran in.

It was a long shot, but it might just give him enough information to confront Megan with.

* * *

Banan checked his messages and cursed under his breath. So far, his mother, his father and two of his four grandparents had seen fit to send him e-mails. Each and every one of them contained the same demand for an update on his progress. He could sum it up in one word: *none*. He considered sending out a blanket message to that effect, along with a request that they leave him the hell alone, but that wouldn't be smart.

Right now, his relationship with the higher-ranking members of his clan was dicey. If he were to push back too hard, it would be just like them to cut him off without a dime. According to his mother's mother, he'd had more than enough time to pick a nice vampire female from an appropriate family to marry. Not only that, the clan needed an heir to solidify the clan's future and right now his bastard daughter by a chancellor was their only option.

More and more the vampire clans were finding it harder to produce a new generation to carry on the family name. Humans and chancellors, on the other hand, had no such problem. They bred herds of young like the cattle they were. The only plus was that their mixed genes meant chancellor women were capable of producing a pureblood vampire.

When he'd culled Megan Perez out of the herd to breed with, he'd known the odds and rolled the dice. First time out, they'd produced a healthy vampire female. Custom demanded that Megan give the child up to her father's family to raise.

Where he'd gone wrong was that he'd also chosen Megan for her intelligence, not just because she was pretty. Who could've guessed that such a stubborn nature existed under that pleasant facade? Under increasing pressure from his family, he'd resorted to extreme measures to get the child away from her. She should've died from the poison he'd given her. Instead, she'd disappeared.

He ripped open another blood pack and poured it into a glass. It was insulting that Rafferty didn't provide humans for Banan to feed from, but that didn't mean that Banan would stoop to sucking his meal from a plastic bag. He took a long drink and waited for the familiar buzz of the rich liquid to hit. Unfortunately, the packaging process diluted the effect, forcing him to drink more blood to get the same energy from it.

At least his host kept a well-stocked supply of even the rarer types, although he suspected Joss O'Day was growing tired of playing hostess. Too bad. Even though Rafferty had all but severed any ties with the vampire hierarchy, he couldn't afford to alienate them completely. So as long as Banan didn't break any of the household rules, such as direct feeding, Rafferty would allow him to stay.

Because of the sprawling size of the O'Day family estate, it was taking longer to search for Megan than Banan had planned on. It would help if he could access the records on Rafferty's computer, but they were password protected. Before coming to the estate, he'd even paid someone to hack into the Coalition medical files but with no luck. If Megan had received any medical treatment, it hadn't been reported anywhere.

Not for the first time, he wondered if he'd actually succeeded in killing her. While that would save him the trouble of having to try again, that didn't answer the question about where his daughter might be. It wasn't as if he knew for certain that Megan had sought out her cousin Joss for sanctuary, but he'd already exhausted all the other logical possibilities.

Certainly her parents hadn't exactly welcomed her back into the fold. Most chancellors preferred to see their young stick to their own species, increasing the likelihood any resulting children would also be chancellors. And if they gave birth to either a full-blooded human or vampire, the expectation was that the child be given up to their own kind to raise, a fact Banan had been counting on.

However, in a surprise move, Megan had defied both him and her parents by insisting that she be the one to raise Phoebe. Personally, he wouldn't have given a rip if Megan lived or died, but unless he found his daughter and soon, his whole life was going to implode. And that was simply unacceptable.

At last the sun was going down outside. He'd indulge himself with one more blood pack and then take off by himself. As long as he returned by midnight for the requisite meal with his host, he was free to wander the estate. Maybe he'd have better luck this time. Once he knew for sure that Megan was living on the estate, he'd leave.

Back in the civilized comfort of his own home, he'd make plans for the best way to repossess his daughter. Megan would never willingly give Phoebe up to him, even though it was the sensible thing to do. Her rash actions had already caused him great inconvenience and threatened his comfortable lifestyle.

The more he thought about it, it was clear

Megan would have to die, regardless of how it happened. A better man might feel bad about that, but he certainly didn't. She'd brought this disaster on herself. After all, cattle shouldn't expect to have any rights. If she'd surrendered his daughter like any reasonable chancellor would have, neither of them would be in this fix. And according to his parents, his failure to control this one chancellor female cast doubt on his ability to rule the clan. Time was running out for all of them.

Megan reached the clinic less than an hour before they'd have to open the door to patients. She fumbled for her keys and hurried inside, ignoring Phoebe's fussing over being jostled. After flipping on her office lights, she set Phoebe down in her crib and patted her daughter on the cheek.

"Give me a second to get settled, little one, and then I'll take care of you. What do you say to that?"

When she turned back to her desk, she about jumped out of her skin. "Seamus! You startled me."

He tried to look sorry, but gave up and grinned. "Sorry, but I was on my way by and heard you talking. I wanted to see if Phoebe answered."

Her pulse continued to race, although not because of Seamus's unexpected appearance. No, the disconcerting effect on her libido was strictly due to his high-wattage smile. When it dimmed a bit, she realized that she'd been staring at his mouth for several seconds, very possibly with her own hanging open and drooling a bit.

Time to get her head back on straight. "I wanted to get in early to catch up on the computer stuff before the onslaught starts again."

He held up his hand to stanch the flow of words. "Don't worry. You're fine. Get your daughter settled and do what you need to. If there's a line at the door, I'll pass out forms to everyone to fill out. That will keep them occupied until we're ready."

Which reminded her. "Files! We're almost out. That's why I meant to come in earlier." She started to reach for the box of empty files, but spotted a stack already assembled and sitting in the middle of her desk.

"Never mind, we seem to have plenty." She eyed him suspiciously. "Did you do this?"

"Nope, not me. Joss stopped by earlier with lunch for me and looking for something to do."

When he reached for the files, his fingers brushed against hers, sending a rush of warmth dancing over her skin. By the way he quickly stepped back, putting more distance between them, she suspected he'd sensed the connection, too, and didn't much like it.

Rather than dwell on it, she cranked her smile up a notch. "I should be ready shortly."

"No rush, and I should warn you that I suspect Joss is going to come by again. I think she enjoyed being here last night." He sounded a bit bewildered by that.

She wrinkled her nose and grimaced. "I'll talk to her. If I can't do my job and take care of Phoebe, it's not right to expect Joss to step in."

"I don't mind her being here. After all, she owns the place, or at least Rafferty does."

"True, but it's your clinic."

He looked decidedly uncomfortable with that idea. "Not really. One of these days, Rafferty will find a physician to take charge."

"That wouldn't be fair, not after you've gotten everything up and running."

"There's a lot about life that isn't fair, Megan." Then Seamus made a show of checking the time. "I'd better get moving. Come along when you can. No rush."

Then he was gone, leaving her staring at the

empty door and wondering if she'd offended or embarrassed him. Okay, so maybe she wasn't exactly neutral on the subject, but it was clear that Seamus had worked hard to make the clinic opening go smoothly. From what she had seen, he treated each patient with calm, professional courtesy. Despite the crowded waiting room, he hadn't acted rushed, taking the time to make everybody feel important.

He did the same thing to her sometimes when he turned that powerful intelligence in her direction, listening to each word she said as if she were about to utter the wisdom of the ages. Or maybe she just liked to think that she mattered in even that small way to him.

Now wasn't the time for such thoughts. She needed to get to work. After a quick check to see that Phoebe had settled in, she started to head for the reception desk. Before she reached the door, though, Seamus was back and looking worried. Really worried, in fact.

"Seamus?"

"Megan, I just got a call from Rafferty. He's had a vampire visiting the estate this week, evidently checking out the innovations Rafferty has made in how he runs things around here. This guy has been making the rounds with the boss, but he's out on his own right now. There's a chance he might stop by here tonight."

"And you're telling me this why?" Although she couldn't keep the fear from her voice. It couldn't be Banan. It just couldn't. In all the time they'd been together, he'd never shown any interest in where his family's money came from. His talent was in spending money, not making it.

"Don't play coy, Megan. Now's not the time."

He was right. "Did Rafferty mention any names?"

Seamus's eyes gleamed with anger and his fangs flashed as he said, "This vampire's name is Banan. Banan Delaney."

Chapter 7

Megan heard Seamus's words, but they held no meaning. From his worried expression she knew he was telling her something, probably something important. But as she struggled to make sense of them, her head filled with a deep swirling darkness, and she could no longer feel her legs beneath her. Suddenly, she was sitting down at her desk with Seamus's hand on the back of her neck and shoving her head forward.

"Damn it, Megan, put your head down and breathe."

Despite her confusion it registered in the back of her mind that although he was angry, he kept his voice pitched low and calm to avoid disturbing Phoebe.

She managed to choke out, "Sorry, I don't mean to be a bother."

"But you are that," he grumbled, but softly as if he didn't really mean for her to hear his words.

She concentrated on regaining control. When the world quit spinning she pushed herself back upright. Her first thought was to take Phoebe and run, but she immediately rejected the idea as futile. She had nowhere else to go, and now wasn't the time to let fear rule her decisions. Her life and that of her daughter could very well depend on what she did in the next few minutes.

When she attempted to stand up, Seamus backed away to give her room to move but stayed close enough to catch her again. Bless the man, he might not like being a hero, but he was one right through to the core. If she hadn't sworn off vampires, she'd be seriously tempted to… No, she wouldn't go there. There was too much at risk.

"Sorry, Seamus. You always seem to be in the right spot when my life goes into meltdown, although you might not think that's a good thing."

She moved past him to stand over the nearby crib where her daughter was sound asleep, sucking on her fist. It was time for some painful truths.

"You're suspicions are right on the money. Banan Delaney is Phoebe's biological father. We were lovers for a few months."

She tucked Phoebe's blanket in around her and then stepped away from the crib. "I guess that much is obvious, though, isn't it? Either way, I was a fool. I thought he loved me, that we had a future together."

Seamus's big hand came down gently on her shoulder. "A vampire of his status would never marry outside of his class, especially when he's the heir to the family fortune."

"I know that now, but at the time I didn't." Was it bitterness or fear leaving such a sour taste in her mouth? "He didn't explain the facts to me until I was into my second trimester."

"I'm guessing he feared you'd end the pregnancy if he told you sooner." Seamus's voice was as grim as death.

"Then he didn't know me very well. Phoebe is everything to me and has been since the first day the doctor told me I was pregnant." She sat back down at her desk. "I was so happy. I went rushing home and fixed a fancy dinner—candles and everything. I wanted everything to be romantic and perfect."

She looked up at Seamus, hoping to see something in his expression that hadn't been there in Banan's that night. There was something there all right. It might have been pity rather than sympathy, but even so, he nodded as if urging her to continue.

"I thought he'd propose, we'd plan a wedding and build our lives around our new family. Oh, make no mistake, he acted happy enough. But after that night there was a new distance between us. I kept hoping things would change, but they didn't. A few months later he announced that his parents would be adopting the baby to raise."

"What did your family say?"

"They agreed with Banan's parents. I think they would have preferred that I go into seclusion, hiding my pregnancy from their friends."

When tears streaked down her face, Seamus shoved a handful of tissues into her hand and backed away. The gesture made her smile. The man could face blood and guts without hesitation, but a few tears were obviously scary stuff.

She sniffed and wiped her face. "Sorry, Seamus. I don't mean to dump all this on you."

"I have a suspicion you've needed to unload."

She considered that. "Oddly enough, I do feel better. Or I would, if I knew for certain that

Banan wouldn't find me. He tried to kill me once. I can't give him another chance."

"He won't get one." Seamus knelt down to her eye level. "I can keep you and Phoebe out of sight in my place tonight. He might have permission to check out the clinic, but he has no business poking around in my personal quarters."

"Won't he be able to detect our scents?"

"Let me worry about that. For now, let's move the crib and changing tables into one of the exam rooms so they look like they're here for my patients to use. Then we'll get you settled in the apartment."

"But how will you handle the patients alone?"

"I'll call Joss and tell her that I sent you home because we thought Phoebe might be developing a cold. She'll be glad to cover."

"Are you sure you want to get sucked into the mess my life's become?"

"No one deserves to have their life ruined, or ended, by the cruel, homicidal actions of another, Megan."

As he spoke, his eyes turned chilly, his expression hard, belying the gentle touch of his hand on her face. In a surprise move, he pressed a quick kiss on her lips before stepping back.

"Now get your things together. Time's short."

* * *

Damn it, Seamus knew better than to let himself "get sucked in," as Megan had put it. But he couldn't live with himself if he didn't do everything he could to prevent Banan Delaney from finding Megan and her daughter. And that's how Seamus thought about Phoebe—she was Megan's daughter. That Banan happened to be the sperm donor was but an unfortunate accident of fate.

If the bastard didn't value Megan, he didn't deserve the child they'd created together. But with the minutes ticking down until the clinic needed to open, now wasn't the time to be considering how best to destroy another selfish vampire scion.

At least Joss was on her way. He was convinced Megan had to trust her secret to more than just Seamus. He'd fight to the death to defend her, but he couldn't provide around-the-clock protection for her and still do his duties—or seek his own revenge.

Again, no time for that right now, either. They'd finished rearranging the crib and baby table in one of the exam rooms, and Megan was safely tucked away in his bedroom with her daughter. Satisfied with how things looked, he had one last detail to take care of. He took the lid off a bottle of rubbing alcohol and headed for Megan's office. Then, oops, he dropped it. And clumsy him, he dropped it again in the lobby. It took quite a while for him to get it all cleaned up.

The pungent odor of the alcohol should mask any remaining traces of Megan and Phoebe, unless Delaney's sense of smell far exceeded that of the average vampire. Next he hurried back to the crib and table and wiped them down with an antiseptic with a strong medicinal odor.

Showtime. He washed his hands, grabbed his lab coat and headed for the front door. He let in a handful of patients, handing each one a blank chart to fill out as they filed past him. By the time the last one was seated in the waiting room, a very worried-looking Joss arrived.

He needed to head off the discussion until they were somewhere more private. "Mrs. O'Day, can I have a moment of your time?"

She followed close on his heels as he led the way into Megan's office. Joss noticed the absence of the crib immediately.

"Seamus, what's going on? How sick is Phoebe? Is it what Megan had?"

He placed a finger over his lips and waited until he closed the door and turned on the stereo before answering.

"Megan and Phoebe are both fine. They're in my apartment right now."

Gone was the concerned friend, replaced by the fierce warrior. "Why? What's happened?"

Where to start and how much was his right to tell? "It probably won't surprise you to learn that before coming here, Megan was being pressured to give up her baby by her parents as well as Phoebe's biological father and his family."

There was no mistaking the anger that flashed through Joss's expressive eyes. "The idiots. It's that kind of stupidity that Rafferty and I are hoping to put an end to here on the estate. Just because it's the way things have always been done doesn't make it right. We hope to make things better for our people."

She slammed her fist down on the desk. "How can they think that anyone else would be a better mother to Phoebe than Megan?"

Now wasn't the time for Seamus to tell Joss what he thought about the changes she and Rafferty had made. It all sounded altruistic of them, but it was still their own self-centered needs that started it all. They might be happy, but others had paid dearly for their selfishness. But right now, this wasn't about him—or his need to avenge his sister.

"Here's what's going on. Your houseguest

lied about his reasons for his visit. Banan's here hunting for Megan and Phoebe. Before she came here, I'm convinced he even tried to poison her, but I have no way to prove it. Right now, she needs to stay out of sight."

"I'll throw that sniveling bastard out on his ass." Joss's fangs would do a full-blooded vampire proud. "That is, if Rafferty doesn't stake him first after I tell him and Conlan what's going on."

"You'd both have to get in line behind me, but I'm not sure it's the best idea. If Delaney doesn't find her soon, maybe he'll decide she didn't come here after all and leave. If we attack, he'll bring the weight of all his clan down on us."

Joss's eyes turned frosty cold. "The Delaney clan be damned. They have no jurisdiction here. That's the law. Even the Coalition's authority is limited within the borders of the estate."

"Maybe, but you and I both know that the law doesn't always protect the innocent, especially when there's enough money involved. Then the advantage goes to the highest bidder."

The words slipped out before he could stop them. Damn it, he could only hope that Joss thought he was talking in generalities. His control was slipping badly. They needed to move on to safer topics.

"Look, we can talk later. I have patients to see. Can you cover the desk out front? All you need to do is have any new patients sign in and give them a chart to fill out. I'll take them in order unless an emergency comes in."

Her eyebrows had snapped back down after her reaction to his last comment, but she let it pass. "Okay, and if Banan does show up, what do you want me to do with him?"

"Let him look around, as long as he respects the privacy of my patients. If we try to control his movements, it will only make him more suspicious. I don't plan on making him feel welcome nor will I keep my patients waiting to answer any fool questions."

He softened the remarks with a smile. "There, do I sound arrogant enough to be a real doctor?"

Joss tipped her head to the side and studied him. "Yes, I do believe you do."

"Good. We'd better get moving. We've got patients waiting."

Banan flexed his hands and forced his fangs to retract. One more day. That was all he had left to find the bitch who'd kidnapped—no, stolen—his daughter. His mother had sent him a reminder that the annual meeting of the hierarchy in the Delaney clan would be held in just over a week. One of the agenda items would be a review of his role in the family businesses. His spending habits had already undergone a close scrutiny, resulting in a tightening of his access to clan funds.

He had to show up at the meeting with his daughter, the clan's first member of the next generation. Without her, he could very well be replaced by one of his distant cousins as the presumptive heir.

More than ever, he wished he'd choked the life out of Megan Perez with his bare hands even if poisoning her with an iron supplement had been a safer choice. After all, everybody needed a certain amount of iron in their diet. Who could have guessed that a healthy chancellor would've had such an adverse reaction?

But instead of dying, she'd fled the city. Her parents were more angry than concerned. He'd quietly hired an investigator to dig into Megan's life to see who she knew that might offer to help her. The file had been remarkably fat, which only emphasized how little he'd really known about her. One by one, he'd contacted her friends and coworkers, expressing his heartfelt concern, and almost gagging on the words. Most of them clearly had no idea where she was, but he was convinced at least a couple had been lying to him.

Unfortunately, he couldn't leave a trail of dead or damaged humans and chancellors in his wake as he continued his search. Once he'd eliminated all the possibilities in her more common haunts, his search had expanded to the areas outside the city. In the end, that had led him to Rafferty O'Day's estate. There was no indication that Megan had been in contact with her cousin Joss, but he suspected she'd grown desperate enough to risk the trip.

If she'd taken refuge here, though, he'd yet to find anyone who would admit to having seen her. Granted, Rafferty's lax standards had attracted a lot of new residents, making it easier for a recent arrival to blend into the crowd. His gut instincts were screaming he was on the right track.

So tonight, he'd visit a few more possibilities. Being limited to the night hours was a problem, but he'd do what he could. He stopped in front of a squat, ugly building—the infirmary. Before making his approach, he watched several people walk out of the building.

Even though the new medic was a vampire, he'd set his office hours to accommodate all three species. How noble of him. It made Banan sick to see one of his own kind catering to the needs of the two substandard species. A vampire should have more dignity than to play nursemaid to humans and chancellors.

But Banan couldn't afford to let his disdain show once he stepped through the door. He rolled his shoulders to ease the tightness that came from too many days away from the comforts of home with nothing to show for it. As ready as he'd ever be, he'd walk through the door and flash his practiced smile at the receptionist. With luck he'd be able to charm her into letting him have a peek at their record-keeping system on the pretext of seeing how it was set up.

That idea tanked as soon as he walked in the door. What was Joss Rafferty doing working at the infirmary? Charm wasn't going to work with her.

Without looking up from what she was reading she held out stack of forms. "Here, have a seat and fill these out."

When he didn't immediately take them, she looked up. "Oh, Banan, sorry about that. Thought you were another patient. You're not, are you?"

"No, I'm not." He smiled and glanced around

the crowded waiting room. "Seems like a popular place."

She nodded. "This is only the second night the clinic has been open, so our medic has a lot of catching up to do for even the routine stuff. I'm here to help with the crush. Once we know more what the real demand is, we'll know how to staff the clinic."

"I was hoping to look around." Especially in any areas they were reluctant to let him see.

One of the humans approached the desk to hand Joss his papers. "Here you go, boss lady."

Joss grinned at the man. "Thanks, Will. It shouldn't be much longer."

"Tell the doc to take his time. I don't mind sitting on my backside for a couple of hours."

"Well, it is one of your better talents."

Both Joss and the human laughed. Their easy familiarity was offensive. Something of his thoughts must have leaked into his expression, because Joss was staring up at him with her own dose of disapproval. It was a good thing he planned on leaving at sunset tomorrow. His welcome here was clearly coming to an end. Charm wouldn't work with Joss, so he went for businesslike.

"I know you're busy. Would you mind if I

just poke around? If your medic has time, I'd love a chance to talk to him."

"As long as you don't interfere with the flow of patients." She shot a look across the small room to where Will sat, his head tipped back and his eyes closed. "And just so you know, Banan. According to Rafferty, Will over there hasn't missed a single day's work in ten years except when he broke his leg saving the lives of three young vampires."

Her fangs showed over her lower lip. "So, if the fact that I treat him as an equal and a friend offends you, too damn bad."

A human hero. Big deal. It was only right the fool sacrifice himself for the benefit of his superiors, but now wasn't the time to share his opinion on that subject. "If I've offended you, I apologize. I also promise not to get in the way while I look around."

"Fine. The hall to the right leads to Seamus's office and the one designated to be used for the office manager and as the record room. To the left are the exam rooms, the operating room, lab and X-ray. Seamus can tell you more about that area when he has time."

She smiled, but it wasn't at all friendly. "*If* he has time. By the way, the door past his office leads to his private quarters, which are off-limits. We respect the privacy of our friends."

Which he took to mean humans and chancellors as well as the vampires on the estate. Yeah, he couldn't wait to get back to his home where the stench of humanity knew its proper role in the world.

He checked out the office with Seamus Fitzhugh's name plate taped on the door, and crookedly at that. How could the man breathe amidst such clutter? Every horizontal surface was piled high with papers and books, including the floor. The office across the hall, on the other hand, held nothing more than a desk, a chair and a couple of empty shelving units.

Once again his sense of propriety was sorely offended. Why would a vampire accept such inequity? Especially when he was in charge of the clinic. It wasn't as if the space in the other office was being used. And what was that smell? It went way beyond the usual medicinal smell he associated with a doctor's office.

He wandered into the manager's office and looked around. Normally, his sense of smell told him a lot about who had been in a given area, including their species. But the acrid odor that permeated this room interfered with that.

Interesting. The spill may have been accidental, but it could also have been a deliberate attempt to hide something—or someone.

There were also faint scratches along the wall, as if another piece of furniture had been there. Also very interesting.

"Oh, there you are."

Banan whipped around to find a vampire standing just inside the doorway. "You must be the medic. I'm Banan Delaney."

"Seamus Fitzhugh." He immediately backed out into the hallway. "Joss said you'd like a quick look around the infirmary. I've got a few minutes right now, but that could change any second. It's the nature of the business."

Without giving Banan a chance to respond, Seamus walked away. As Banan followed him back toward the waiting room, he heard a noise coming from behind him. Or at least, he thought he had. He stood listening with his eyes closed to focus all of his attention on the locked door at the end of the hall. But all he heard was a heavy silence.

Reluctantly, he followed the medic as he considered just what it was he'd heard. It could have been nothing or it could have been the muted cry of a youngling. For the first time, his predator instincts went on full alert.

* * *

Seamus clenched his teeth and silently cursed Delaney and his whole family. There was no way Banan's vampire hearing would've missed that soft cry coming from Seamus's apartment. The damage was already done. Short of throwing the bastard out on his ass, there wasn't much Seamus could do but pretend it hadn't happened and continue on with the tour.

He led the way into one of the exam rooms with the unwelcome vampire. "We have regular examination rooms, but also a fully equipped surgical suite."

If Banan was truly interested in how Rafferty was managing his estate, it didn't show. Right now, Banan was staring at Seamus rather than looking around.

"Do you have any questions?"

"What brought you to Rafferty's door?"

Not exactly the question he expected Banan to ask, or maybe he should have. "The turbo, same as most of the people who come here."

Banan's laugh sounded forced. "Sorry, it was rude of me to ask. You're entitled to your privacy."

Banan trailed his fingers across the counter, picking up one of the scopes and holding it up to his eye. "What's this for?"

As if he'd never had his ears or eyes looked at by a doctor. "To check for ear or eye infections."

He held out his hand for the instrument. Banan handed it to him and moved on to study the chart on the wall that showed the comparative bone structure of the three species side by side. Studying medicine quickly stripped away any illusions about the nature of the three species. Although Banan probably didn't care, only a very few differences at the DNA level separated them. Granted, those variations in genetic makeup gave vampires their superior strength, their extended lifetimes, but also their dependence on blood.

The chancellors got the strength but also inherited the humans' ability to tolerate a wider variety of climates, not to mention daylight. Most folks thought the humans got short shrift, but Seamus wasn't so sure. They could live anywhere, under even the most extreme conditions, including freezing cold as well as the burning heat of the midday sun.

Banan turned back toward Seamus. "How late do you plan to work tonight?"

Where was he going with that question? "Office hours officially end at midnight, but I stay until the last patient is seen. Why?"

"I was wondering if you'd like to have dinner with me at the O'Days'. I'm sure they'd hold the meal long enough for you to get there."

"I wouldn't like to impose on their hospitality." True enough. He was having an increasingly harder time socializing with his employers.

"I'm sure they won't mind. I'll be leaving soon, and I'd like more time to talk to you about your plans for the clinic."

Banan's smile looked so sincere. If Seamus didn't know the truth about the aristocratic vampire, he might have actually believed that the man really wanted to spend time with him. If they had met in Seamus's prior life, they might have even been friends, but he'd like to think not. What kind of bastard tried to murder the mother of his own child?

Personal honor should count for something, especially among their kind. Their lives were too long, their memories too sharp to allow for lax morals. Even a hundred years from now, Seamus would still want to hold Banan accountable for his actions against Megan. When grudges could carry on for centuries, one had to be extra careful in the decisions that were made.

Seamus was aware that Banan was still

waiting for an answer. "If they have room for me, I'd be glad to join you for dinner."

"Perfect. I'll talk to Joss on my way out." Banan immediately walked away, all pretense of interest in the infirmary gone.

More than ever Seamus was convinced the vampire had heard Phoebe's cry, and that could lead to disaster. He'd finish his rounds as expected, but then he'd have to talk to Megan. She might not like it, but she was going to have to stay in his apartment until Banan left the estate.

If somehow he planted someone to watch the infirmary to see if Megan and her daughter came out, Banan could attack before they could stop him. At the very least, if he knew Rafferty was harboring them, his influential family could cause the O'Days a great deal of trouble. Ordinarily Seamus would've been all for that, but not at Megan's expense.

Once again, he found himself siding with his enemy against a common foe. Of course, as long as Rafferty and Joss thought that Seamus was firmly on their side, his ultimate betrayal would be that much sweeter.

Or so he hoped.

Three hours later Seamus let himself into his apartment. He was not looking forward to breaking the news to Megan that she was under lockdown for at least another twenty-four hours. She was likely to tear into him but good for making a decision on her behalf without consulting her first.

She was waiting in the living room. He'd hoped that she would've dozed off so he wouldn't have to talk to her, but that was cowardly. Besides, she needed to know what was going on.

"Did Banan leave?"

"Yes, but I'm supposed to have dinner with him at Joss's in a few minutes."

"So it's safe for us to go home now?"

"Not exactly."

He headed for his bedroom to grab a clean shirt. Phoebe was curled up in the middle of his bed surrounded by pillows to keep her from rolling off the side. Megan had followed hard on his heels.

"What's that supposed to mean?" Even though she whispered because of Phoebe, her anger came through perfectly clear.

"I'm afraid he heard Phoebe when he was sneaking around in your office. If so, he might very well watch this place to see if you come out."

"So I'm supposed to hide in here until *you* decide that it's safe for me to leave?"

"Joss thought it was a good idea, too, especially after I told her he'd poisoned you." Oh, yeah, that really helped. Now she'd think they were ganging up on her.

"Megan, I don't like this any more than you do. But we can't risk Banan finding you. If I knew a way to get you home without impacting your safety, I would do it in a heartbeat."

"Sorry to inconvenience you so much." She retreated to the living room.

Damn it, that's not what he meant. "Megan, that came out wrong. I don't want to see you hurt by him. It's only twenty-four hours, give or take. Surely we can handle staying here together for that long. You and Phoebe can have the bedroom. I'll take the couch when I get back."

"Fine. You do that."

He didn't have time to talk her down off the emotional ledge she was on. He was holding up dinner as it was.

"We'll talk more when I get back."

It was hard to tell if she heard him. She was too busy closing the bedroom door in his face.

Chapter 8

The atmosphere around the dinner table had been brittle, as if the wrong word, the wrong look would've shattered the peace. Joss had made a valiant effort to keep the conversation rolling, but the four males had definitely failed to hold up their end of things. Finally taking pity on his hostess, Seamus had launched into a description of how his first two nights at the clinic had gone. He aimed his remarks toward Banan, but he showed remarkably little interest in anything Seamus had to say on the subject.

Considering the clinic was the reason that Seamus had been invited to dinner, the motives behind the Delaney heir's visit to the O'Day estate were even more suspect. Judging by the hard looks Conlan shot in the vampire's direction, the security officer had his own qualms about the vampire.

Seamus made his excuses right after dessert was served. He'd walked to dinner, wanting the chance to see if he was followed on his way back. It was an iffy proposition because of the risk of Banan offering to accompany him, especially given the vampire's habit of roaming the estate at night. There was no way Seamus could refuse, but he'd make sure that Banan understood that Seamus was heading home to his bed.

His bed. Where right now Megan was probably curled up sleeping. Damn, that was not an image he needed in his head at the moment.

Definitely time to get moving. "Dinner was great, Joss, but I need to get back to my quarters. It's been a long couple of days."

Rafferty followed him out onto the porch. "Thanks for coming, Seamus. I was glad to hear Conlan gave you his approval, and I've heard great things from Joss about the job you're doing over at the infirmary."

"I appreciate their vote of confidence."

"Well, I sleep better knowing you're here for our people. We'll still have to evac anything major, but they'll get the right care beforehand when each minute counts. The wrong decision can cost lives."

Yeah, there were lots of ways lives were lost when people made the wrong decisions, just like when Rafferty had broken his word to Seamus's sister. He stepped down off the porch. "I'd better get going while I still have the energy to move."

"I can run you home, if you'd like."

He wanted no extra favors from his employer. "That's all right. I can use the exercise as well as the fresh air."

"It's a nice night for it. Don't be a stranger."

Seamus walked away, forcing himself to take it slow and easy no matter how badly he wanted to put some distance between himself and Rafferty. It was getting too easy to forget that this wasn't his real life, that Rafferty was the villain, and that being a medic where one was desperately needed wasn't where Seamus was supposed to be.

As soon as he was out of sight of Rafferty's house, he cut across country. He'd circle back when he reached the cover of the trees to see if Banan followed him. So far there was no sign of Delaney, but then vampires didn't have to depend on their superior night vision. Their sense

and sound. Images flashed through his mind: Megan close to death, dragging herself step by step to get her daughter to safety; Phoebe, so pretty and sweet, almost an orphan; Banan's snooping through the infirmary, looking for the two females. Hatred, pure and clean, sent Seamus's aggression level skyrocketing.

He landed a solid punch to Banan's jaw and another to his gut. Fist fighting was the stupidest thing a surgeon could do with his hands, but right now Seamus wasn't thinking as a doctor. No, the potent blood of his ancestors, predators all, overrode both caution and rational thought. The world narrowed down to a blinding rage that demanded the blood of a fool who'd tried to destroy the precious gifts that life had given him, who yet continued to threaten the two females.

"You don't know who you're messing with," Banan hissed, his fangs bared, his hands scrambling for purchase as he tried to ward off Seamus's furious attack. "Let go of me."

"Hell, no! I'd rather make you bleed or, better yet, die."

Banan danced back out of reach. "What did I do to you?"

Seamus circled to the left, trying to trap Banan back against the wall of the clinic.

Before his maneuver had a chance to work, he was blindsided by another male and sent sprawling to the ground. Banan didn't hesitate to bolt, immediately disappearing into the darkness. Meanwhile, Seamus ended up flat on his back with Banan's unexpected ally's hands wrapped around his neck and choking off his breath.

"Damn it, Seamus! It's me, Conlan. Knock it off before I hurt you."

"Not going to happen." Seamus pitched and rolled, trying to break free. "Get your hands off me!"

"Stop fighting me, and I will."

Slowly Conlan's words got through to Seamus, but that didn't keep him from struggling to break free from the chancellor's hold. He finally managed to drag Conlan's hands off his throat and shoved against the chancellor's chest, tossing him backward to land hard some distance away.

Seamus immediately surged back to his feet before Conlan quit bouncing. He fought an uphill battle for control while every synapse in his body fired hot and screamed for blood—Banan's, first and foremost, but with Banan out of the picture, Conlan's would do. Hell, better yet, Rafferty's. It didn't matter as long as somebody bled.

At least Conlan had the good sense to lie still. By going totally passive instead of aggressive, he gave Seamus the chance to regain control. Gradually, when some of the adrenaline burst had worn off, he stepped forward and offered Conlan a hand up off the ground.

"Didn't anybody ever tell you not to break up a fight between vampires?" His voice sounded as if he'd been chewing glass. The bruises from Conlan's choke hold would fade by morning, but right now they hurt like a bitch.

Conlan rubbed his shoulder and tested the mobility in his arm. "Normally I know better, but what the hell were you doing fighting with Banan, anyway?"

"At first, I didn't realize it was him sneaking around." Okay, so that was a lie. Better to derail that line of conversation. "Are you all right? Lucky you, the infirmary takes emergency patients."

Conlan laughed. "I'm fine. Besides, I deserve a few bruises for not getting to you sooner."

"So what were you doing lurking outside my clinic?"

"I was walking back to my transport from Joss's house when I spotted someone sneaking around in the woods. Figuring as security was my job description, I followed him, especially considering what Joss told us about him and Megan after the two of you left."

"That was me you saw."

"No, it wasn't because I saw you go by first. It was that bastard Delaney. I waited to see what he was up to, but he caught wind of me and took off running. By the time I caught up with him again, you two were already swinging fists."

Seamus froze, listening to make sure they were alone. If Banan was still lurking in the area, the young vampire was far better than he should be at hiding his presence. It was almost a shame he was gone. Between Seamus and Conlan, they could have done a bang-up job of convincing the vampire that he was unwelcome.

"He's definitely gone."

Conlan waited until Seamus once again focused his attention on him. "I'm pretty sure he'll hightail it back to Joss's house, and Rafferty will make sure he stays there. I don't trust that punk vampire and can't wait to see the last of him. If I had hardcore proof he was the one to poison Megan, I'd execute the bastard myself and damn the consequences. He's leaving tomorrow whether he wants to or not because I made his turbo reservations myself. Sending him back to his family all bruised up may cause a few ripples, but too bad."

"Tell Rafferty I'm sorry."

"But not Delaney himself?"

Seamus flexed his hands, wishing he had them wrapped around Banan's neck. "Hell, no. I defend what's mine. He had no business sneaking around the infirmary. If he was here to see me, he should've announced himself rather than hiding."

Conlan gave a noncommittal grunt, leaving Seamus unsure how much trouble he was in. On the other hand, his fighting instincts were still running high. Once his energy burn was gone, exhaustion might kick in. Right now he was ready to defend his actions, with his fists if necessary. It was definitely time to get inside. Rafferty might forgive an attack on an unpopular guest; trading punches with his security officer not so much.

"If you're sure you don't need pain medicine or an X-ray, I'm way overdue for some downtime."

Conlan tested his shoulder again. "No, I'm good. I was going to drive back out to my quarters, but I'll hang around until tomorrow night to escort Delaney off the property myself with a warning not to return anytime soon. If you want me for anything, give me a call."

"Thanks, I will. Good night."

"Same to you. And, Seamus—"

"Yeah?"

"Thanks for watching over our two friends. We'll all sleep better knowing they're not alone right now." He rubbed his shoulder one last time. "Especially now that I know what kind of punch you're packing."

Seamus didn't know how to respond. He settled for a mumbled, "It's nothing. Anybody would do the same."

"That's where you're wrong. Most people wouldn't. See you around."

Then the chancellor disappeared back into the darkness, leaving Seamus staring after him. Feeling out of sync by the whole encounter, he pulled out his keys and let himself inside the clinic.

Although there was no reason to think Banan had broken into the infirmary, Seamus wouldn't sleep easy until he checked all the rooms. Normally, he would've also spent time writing up the last few reports on the patients he'd seen, but he was still too revved by the fight to concentrate. He'd never get to sleep if he didn't find a way to burn off this excess energy.

Which brought Megan Perez to mind. Somehow he doubted she'd be interested in helping him out with that particular problem.

Even if she thought she owed him for saving her life, he didn't want to bed her only because she felt grateful. With that unsettling thought, he turned the lights off in the clinic before retiring to his own quarters.

He'd hoped Megan was already asleep. Instead, she was curled up on his couch pretending to read when he walked through the door. He couldn't imagine she'd find a treatise on the blood disorders of ancient vampires riveting enough to keep her up this late, which meant she'd been waiting up for him but didn't want him to know.

He dropped his keys on the table and gave the book a pointed glance. "So which treatment would you recommend? Transfusions?"

"Leeches, I think."

Okay, he hadn't expected that. "You actually read it?"

"No, not really." She closed the book and tossed it aside. "Mainly I looked at the pictures. Nothing like close-ups of blood cells to stir the imagination."

He couldn't help it. He laughed. "Sorry, I didn't have anything better around for you to read. I'm still trying to organize the medical books Rafferty bought for the infirmary."

"That's okay. You weren't exactly expecting to have overnight company."

She studied her hands. "So, how did dinner go? Was Banan as charming as ever?"

"Not particularly. He'd invited me specifically to talk about the clinic, but yet didn't ask a single relevant question. Conlan was there, too, but didn't particularly want to be. Rafferty was quiet, too, so poor Joss had to do most of the talking."

Talking about Megan's former lover did little to further calm Seamus's fight-or-flight instincts.

Megan toyed with a loose thread on his couch. "So now that your dinner party is over and the sun will be up soon, can I go home?"

He might not want to have this discussion, but didn't see how to avoid it. "I won't stop you, but I wish you wouldn't because Banan could still be out there somewhere. Right before I came in, I could feel somebody watching me and jumped him. Conlan broke up the fight before I could corner Banan long enough to learn why he was hanging around in the dark."

To lighten the moment, he added, "I thought Conlan was on Banan's side and tangled with him, too. Fangs all look alike at night, you know."

His attempt at humor fell flat. Megan sounded fierce when she asked, "Banan's not going to give up on finding us, is he?"

Seamus shrugged. "I'd say not, but the good news is he's leaving the estate tomorrow night. Conlan made the turbo reservations himself, but right now he's on the loose. Banan has failed to endear himself to anyone around here, but without proof of anything, all they can do is shove him out the gate."

Megan sighed. "I should have told Rafferty and Joss myself, so you didn't have to. Obviously ignoring the problem didn't make it go away."

"So you *will* stay tonight." It wasn't a question, but a statement of fact. He really didn't want to force the issue, but if he had to, he would.

"Okay, but I'll take the couch." Again that stubborn chin came up.

"It'll be crowded with both of us sleeping on it. Last time I looked, Phoebe was hogging the middle of my bed." He flashed Megan a teasing look. "Let me get you something to sleep in and dig out an extra toothbrush for you. I'm sorry, I should've thought to do that before I left."

"That's okay. Do you have a drawer I can

borrow for Phoebe to sleep in? That worked great when we were at Conlan's."

"Not a problem."

He dumped out his sock drawer and carried it out into the living room along with one of his undershirts and a pair of running shorts for Megan. He stood back and watched as Megan gently carried in her sleeping daughter and settled her into the padded drawer.

As Megan leaned down to adjust Phoebe's blankets, her hair fell forward over her shoulders and hid her face. Damn, he wanted to kiss the back of Megan's neck, to taste her sweet-smelling skin with his tongue and then with his fangs. And the rounded curves of her backside would be exactly perfect to cushion a lover's thrusts when he took her.

He had to get away from her before he acted on the fantasies playing out in his head. It had to be the leftover aggression from his fight with Conlan driving his libido. He knew better than to get involved with anyone right now, but especially Megan. She'd already suffered enough at the hands of one of his kind who wouldn't share his future with her. Even if Seamus wanted to, he had no future to offer.

When she started to look up, he ducked into the sanctuary of the bathroom to give them both some space. As he started up the shower, it occurred to him that it had been years since he'd shared living quarters with anyone. He would've expected it to make him feel crowded, especially in a small apartment. But instead, it felt…right somehow. As if Megan belonged not only in his home, but in his bed, and maybe even in his heart.

Now that was a scary thought.

Megan stared at the bathroom door wondering why Seamus had suddenly bolted from the room. Just before he'd disappeared, she'd sensed a change in his mood. What was up with him, anyway? She hoped he wasn't hiding an injury from his altercation with Banan. Neither man seemed like the type to do their talking with their fists, but then they were vampires. Their species hadn't developed all that physical strength for nothing. All she knew was that she always felt safe when Seamus was around, perhaps for the first time in months.

While he was out of sight, she quickly changed into the shirt and shorts he'd brought her. Their size swamped her, but they'd be more comfortable than sleeping in her own clothes. While she waited for her chance at the bathroom, the muffled noises Seamus made in there as he got ready for bed sounded homey and surprisingly soothing. Despite her intimate relationship with Banan, he'd never slept at her place nor had he invited her to stay over at his. Maybe that should have told her something, but she'd been blind to anything but his charm.

Seamus might lack some of that high-gloss surface polish that Banan took such pride in, but she found that reassuring. With him, what you saw was what you got. He had his own secrets, she had no doubt. But inside, where it counted, he was honorable. It was there in the way he approached his patients, as if each and every one deserved his full attention and the best care he could offer.

As much as it frightened her to admit it, she would have been dead without his intervention. She owed him far more than she could ever repay.

The bathroom door opened and Seamus stepped out in a cloud of steam from the shower he'd taken. Bare-chested and wearing flannel pajama bottoms, he looked ready for bed—and she didn't mean as in going to sleep. Without his lab coat and stethoscope to hide behind, he looked more approachable, more powerful and masculine. She noticed the shower had left his smooth skin damp. What would he think if he realized how badly she wanted to lap up those small droplets of water, to taste his essence with her tongue?

But, no, she shouldn't be having these thoughts. Not about a vampire. Not again.

But what she should do and what she wanted to do were two very different things. Her eyes traced the well-defined muscles of his chest down and down until she saw exactly what kind of effect her scrutiny was having on her host. As her own powerful mating instincts kicked in, her fangs dropped down. She licked her lips, the tip of her tongue tracing the point of one of her canines.

Seamus's gaze locked on her mouth. "Megan?"

She rose to her feet. "Seamus?"

Despite the distance between them, the sizzling heat in his eyes caressed her body as if he held her in his arms. Instead, he hovered in the doorway across the room as he waited…for what? Then they both took a step forward at the same moment, forever shattering the last bit of control she had.

This might not be about love. It definitely wasn't about happily ever after. It was about trust. She could lose herself in his arms for a few hours, taste his passion, share hers with him and know that he would shelter her from the world outside. It had been so long since she'd last felt safe and cared for. Seamus had given that back to her with his fierce determination to save her life and to protect her daughter.

His arms wrapped around her, holding her secure against the warm wall of his chest. Her head tucked in under his chin, his erection pressing against her belly. She shimmied against its hard length, wanting nothing more than to be skin-to-skin, to brace herself for the power he'd bring to their lovemaking. Tension coiled deep within her, leaving her hovering on the precipice with just his embrace.

His breath teased her skin as he whispered near her ear, "Megan, God knows I want this, I want you, but are you sure?"

Even as he asked, his hands were already roaming, learning the curves of her body and how sweetly she fit against him. He closed his eyes and awaited her answer, his conscience hoping she'd back away and his soul praying that she wouldn't.

She raised up far enough to bring her lips to cover his. "Yes," she murmured, her eyes half-closed and dreamy.

"I want this," she said between the small kisses she gave him, her hand slipping down between them to make sure he knew exactly what she was talking about.

"I want you." She smoothed her hand up and down the length of his erection. He'd been aroused before, but now she definitely had his full attention.

He caught her jaw with the tips of his fingers, angling her face to deepen their kiss. His tongue swirled in and out of the sweetness of her mouth, testing the sharpness of her fangs, imagining the feel of them against his throat, piercing his skin.

Just the thought was enough to send him to his knees. It was time to take this to his bed, right where he'd been imagining Megan. With no warning, he swept her up in his arms and carried her into his room, kicking the door closed, shutting out the rest of the world. For these precious few hours, this would be about them, two lovers with no past, no future, no regrets.

He knelt on the edge of the mattress and gently laid Megan down, right where she belonged. Her eyes were huge as she stared up at him, watching and waiting for him to make the next move. Where to start?

He needed to go slow, to savor the experience. Stretching out beside her, he propped his head up on his right hand and considered the possibilities. Finally, he laid his palm at the hem of her shirt, moving his hand upward, tugging up the soft fabric along in its wake to uncover inch after luscious inch of her skin. He paused long enough to trace the pattern of her ribs before moving on to feather his fingertips across the sensitive peaks of her breasts.

"Perfect," he whispered as he leaned down to kiss and nibble his way around the full curves and then teasing her nipples.

Megan arched up off the bed as she tangled her fingers in his hair, pressing him closer, asking for more. He broke away long enough to help her peel the shirt off over her head. When he tossed it on the floor, she raised up and pushed him over onto his back.

"My turn."

She straddled his hips, settling the full weight of her body against his erection. He was pretty sure his brain was going to explode from the incredible sensation. He loved having her pretty breasts right there for him to knead and kiss as she rocked back and forth, the friction setting them both aflame. He couldn't remember a more perfect moment in all his life, and it was only going to get better when they finally shed the last layers of clothing between them.

Megan then moved farther down his legs

and leaned over to kiss his cock, the warmth of her breath feeling incredible as she nuzzled him from top to bottom. He groaned when she reached through the fly to stroke him. Megan definitely had a talent for doing exactly what would drive him crazy.

"Keep that up and this party will be over way too soon."

Grasping her wrist, he pulled her hand up his mouth to place a warm, wet kiss on her palm. At the same time, he slid his other hand inside the waistband of her shorts to tangle in her damp curls. He kissed her throat, loving the syncopated beat of her pulse just below her skin.

"Oh, yes," she moaned as he eased one, then two fingers deep inside her slick heat. "Seamus, please!"

It was too soon in their relationship for him to feed from her vein unless she offered, but he could taste her in other ways. He withdrew his hand and journeyed down the length of her body to remove first her shorts and then his own flannels. Her eyes widened with appreciation as she reached out to cup him with one hand and explore his length with the other.

The woman definitely knew what she liked and what she wanted. But he was running too close to the edge to take her yet, not if he wanted to please his lady as much as himself.

He moved back out of the reach of her busy hands. "Open up for me, Megan."

She froze, unsure what he meant. To show her, he wrapped his hand around her ankle and tugged it toward him. "I need you to make room for me."

Cautiously, she slowly spread her legs apart, watching him as if she would bolt if he moved wrong or too fast. He knelt between her feet and then stretched out, as she watched his slow approach with her eyes wide and her breath coming in shallow pants as she waited in anticipation.

He drew in her scent, making it part of him, knowing he'd never walk away from this encounter unchanged. Then he kissed her, tasting the sweet flavor that was hers alone. Her head kicked back on the pillow as her legs opened wider in surrender. He lifted her knees up onto his shoulders, feasting deeply and long until she keened out her release. He gave her but a short reprieve before relentlessly driving her up and over the edge again and again.

"Seamus! Enough, take me now!"

She'd never had such an unselfish lover, one so determined to pleasure her before seeking his own release. Now, as good as it was, she wanted more. She wanted to bear his weight, to feel the solid strength of him deep in the very heart of her, to know the power of his body.

This time he heeded her demand and rose up to settle the tip of his cock against her, and then with one powerful thrust, buried himself fully inside her. He paused, holding himself still with obvious effort, to give her body time to accept him. His consideration for her was stunning in its generosity. She scraped her nails gently across his shoulders and then down his arms.

"Seamus, I'm so ready for this." She lifted her hips up to meet his. Then she arched her head up and to the side, "And this."

Her twin offers snapped his control. He began thrusting, his hips working hard to seat himself deeply within her with each stroke. The tension built with each pounding beat, spiraling tighter and tighter until it shattered. As spasms of brilliant-colored pleasure ripped through her, the pulse of Seamus's own release shuddered deep inside her.

Then in a lightning-fast move, his fangs pierced the side of her throat, and a second wave of ecstasy flooded through them both in a warm gush of blood.

Chapter 9

Banan walked into his room and fought against the urge to slam the door. He'd already drawn Joss's unwanted attention when he'd stormed into the house and stalked right by her without saying a word. She'd had a lot to say, though, ending with ordering him to remain in his room. He was so damned enraged right now, he couldn't be sure that he wouldn't attack her.

Worse yet, he wasn't sure he'd actually win against the chancellor. She'd enjoyed a fearsome reputation in her work as an arbiter. More than one vampire had learned the hard way not to cross her.

Safe in his room, he stopped in front of the

mirror and forced his image to appear. Still badly rattled, it took him several attempts to bring it into clear focus. Leaning in for a closer look, he stared at the purplish bruise spreading out across his lower jaw and up toward his eye. His hand gingerly pressed against his stomach, testing the extent of the bruising there, as well.

He knew one thing for sure: Seamus Fitzhugh needed to die—painfully and begging for mercy.

How dare that clanless low-life vampire lay a hand, much less a fist, on a Delaney? Anywhere else but here on this backwater estate, Banan would've summoned the chancellors to drag the medic away in chains. Even that wouldn't be enough to assuage Banan's wounded pride.

No, he wanted Seamus staked out where the morning sun would find him. He played the scene out in his head, savoring the imagined screams and the scent of smoke as the scum slowly caught fire, smoldering at first and then burning brightly until his lungs exploded and the dying vampire could scream no more.

Oh, yeah, that would be so sweet, however unlikely. Gone were the days when the vampires could execute their enemies without due process. He doubted the North American Coalition would think that a few well-placed punches would warrant a death penalty. However, money in the right hands could still purchase justice. He added that to the list of things he needed to take care of once he got back to civilization.

To that end, he pulled out his duffel and began packing so that he could start for the gate as soon as the sun set. Once that was done, he popped open a few more bags of Rafferty's blood supply, concentrating on using up the rarer, and therefore more expensive, vintages. The extra pack or two would go a long way to healing his injuries while he slept.

As he turned out the lights and stretched out between the cool sheets, he thought back through the day's events. He was almost certain he'd heard a baby cry at the infirmary. Better yet, the noise had come from the direction of the medic's private quarters, not from one of the examination rooms.

It also occurred to him that Seamus's attack had been over-the-top savage if all Banan had done was startle him. Normally, a vampire didn't succumb to such blind rage unless he was defending something that really mattered to him. As a recent addition to the estate, it didn't make sense that the vampire would be so territorial about that hideous clinic.

Which meant what?

The answer was obvious. If Seamus wasn't

defending *something,* he was defending *someone.* It wasn't too much of a leap to guess that that someone had to be Megan and the baby. Why else would Seamus not mention he had a mate and a child? That wasn't exactly something he could have kept secret from Rafferty and Joss, either, so they were in on it. The obnoxious security officer had to be, too, so add him to his enemy list.

It infuriated him to know Megan had gone straight from his bed to that of a no-name lowlife like that medic. Not that he had any interest in bedding the bitch again. Had the two crossed paths before they'd come to Rafferty's estate? Maybe Seamus was the one who'd helped her escape. He'd known all along she wasn't smart enough to elude his efforts to find her this long all on her own.

Interesting, though, that Seamus was the only one who'd dared to openly attack him. Why? Joss was Megan's cousin and a warrior in her own right, not to mention Rafferty being one of the most powerful vampires around. They must suspect that he was hunting for his daughter, but not that he'd actually tried to kill Megan to simplify his life.

Seamus, on the other hand, had somehow figured it out, making him the only immediate danger to Banan's plans. The only question was what to do about him. The ache in Banan's jaw made it difficult to concentrate, especially with the sun rising in the east and with it the pressing need to sleep.

He'd leave as ordered, but he'd be back. And then there would be hell to pay.

She was cold. Why? Where had all the warmth gone? Megan rooted across the bed, unconsciously looking for that living wall of heat, which had sheltered her so sweetly as she slept. Slowly, she awoke feeling confused and alone.

Where was she? And Phoebe! Bolting upright, the sheets pooled around her waist, making her aware that she was naked. She never slept in the nude. Fear and confusion washed through her mind until she heard the muffled murmur of a familiar voice coming through the door.

Seamus Fitzhugh. Her hand immediately went to her throat, testing for soreness there and finding it. The memories of the time the two of them had spent in this bed, starting in the middle of the night and at least twice more after that. A tentative touch, a gentle kiss and then the passion would ignite again.

What had she been thinking? Her conscience forced her to give the honest answer to that question: she'd been thinking how right it had felt to welcome Seamus into her arms and into her body. Making love with him had been… perfect.

And what a terrifying thought that was! Before she could decide how to react, the bedroom door quietly swung open revealing her lover with her daughter cuddled in his arms.

"I was just going to wake you. Phoebe's finally decided I'm not the one she needs right now."

As he approached the bed, Megan tugged the sheet back up to cover herself, although it was a bit late for that, especially considering Seamus's excellent night vision. She gave up and held out her arms for Phoebe. The sweet baby smell immediately soothed her.

"I'll scrounge us some breakfast. Take your time, though."

He started to lean toward her, but then backed away when she flinched. Guilt washed over her. He'd been nothing but considerate, and here she was treating him so badly. Although he was already on the wrong side of the door, she knew he could hear her, anyway.

"Seamus, I'm sorry. I'm not used to…well, any of this. I've never slept through the day with anyone, not even Banan. I'm not sure how to act."

His voice was muffled by the door, but she suspected he was smiling. "Me, either, if that's any comfort."

Amazingly, it was. For the moment, she concentrated on nursing her daughter, losing herself in the familiar routine. She whispered to Phoebe, telling her the sorts of things that mothers had been saying to their younglings forever. That Phoebe was pretty, that she was loved, that everything was going to be all right.

She could only hope that last part was true.

Seamus listened to Megan talking to Phoebe. He didn't mean to eavesdrop, but vampire hearing made that difficult. He loved the sweet tone in her voice and knew firsthand how it felt to be held close and warm in Megan's arms. He'd hated leaving his bed when Phoebe woke up and demanded attention. However, because of him, Megan hadn't gotten much rest during the day and he figured she deserved to sleep as long as possible.

He grinned as he set the table. Megan wasn't the only Perez female who was a heartbreaker. Little Phoebe definitely had her mother's expressive eyes and pretty smile. And both females brought out every protective instinct he had. Sure, he'd promised her that she could go back to her cottage as soon as Conlan escorted Banan Delaney to the turbo. That didn't mean he wanted her to go.

He began cracking eggs into a bowl as he pondered what he should do about that idea. The obvious answer was nothing. One vampire had already betrayed her trust and come close to killing her. There was little doubt that Banan was still out there, still trying to find her in order to take Phoebe away.

Seamus would do anything he could to prevent that from happening, but his own motives for being on the estate wouldn't stand up to close scrutiny. He was living a lie, one that was a direct threat to Megan's cousin and her husband. Granted they were the true villains, their actions directly responsible for the disaster that loomed over their heads. That they also stood the best chance of keeping Megan and Phoebe safe here on their estate was beside the point.

Right? His sister's image popped into his head. Petra had been much older, but she'd been good to him in her own way. She'd been so beautiful; everyone said so. And now, now she was dead and buried, leaving him alone, broke and clanless. It went against his nature to lie to anyone, especially someone he cared about. After all, Rafferty's lies to Petra had resulted in her death.

Unless he wanted to be guilty of the same crimes as both Rafferty and Banan, he had to reestablish emotional distance between himself and Megan. One night of passion had only whetted his appetite for more of the same, but his hypocrisy had limits.

The bedroom door creaked slightly, warning him that he was no longer alone. He whipped the eggs and poured them into the skillet.

"Can I help?"

"You can pour the coffee."

Between the two of them, breakfast was served up and ready in a matter minutes, another reminder of how well they worked together. He so didn't need that right now.

"Think I'll be able to go back to my cottage long enough to change clothes and pick up a few things for Phoebe before time to start work?"

He mulled over that idea. "Let me give Conlan a call first and see when he plans on shoving Banan out the gate. Once we're sure he's gone, it should be fine."

"Good. We've imposed on your hospitality long enough." She carried her dishes over to the sink.

Last night had been anything but an imposition. It had been incredible.

While Megan washed the dishes, he dialed Conlan's number. He smiled at the gruff response from the other end of the line.

"Conlan, it's Seamus. I was wondering where you are."

"Glad you called, Rafferty. I'm already back at my place, but I'll be out of touch for a while. Delaney here needs a ride out to catch the turbo. I figured you'd like me to play nice and give him a lift."

So Conlan didn't want his guest to know who was calling. "I don't suppose you could put him under the turbo rather than on it."

A bark of laughter carried back across the line. "Good one, boss. Remind me never to get on your bad side. Gotta go now or we'll be late."

"Thanks, Conlan. I owe you."

"Don't worry about it. I'll be sure and collect next time I'm there."

The phone went dead. Seamus hung up. No more excuses for keeping Megan sequestered in his apartment or sharing his bed. He wished he could be happier about that.

"Is he gone?"

He schooled his features to hide his disappointment. "Yeah, Conlan pretended he was talking to Rafferty in case Banan was close enough to hear his end of the conversation. They're on the way to the turbo station. Conlan will make sure Banan really does leave."

"Good. I'll go change back into my own clothes, and then Phoebe and I will get out of your way."

He caught her arm. "You're not in my way, Megan."

Damn, he was going to kiss her again. So much for reestablishing any distance between them. She met him halfway, her lips parting in invitation. His tongue savored the velvet texture of hers. She tasted like dark roast coffee and sexy female, a combination that rivaled the richest vintage of wine. He pressed closer, letting her know without words the powerful effect she had on him.

When they came up for air, he rested his forehead against hers. He wished he had the right words to describe how she made him feel, even if these were the last moments he dare share with her like this. When they wouldn't come, he kissed her again, starting with a series of quick licks at the pulse point on her neck where she'd let him feed.

Oh, God, if he kept that up, she was going

to come right there. She arched her head to the side, offering him free rein. He worked his way up the curve of her neck to her ear. That talented tongue of his traced the shell of her ear, the sound of his ragged breathing making her ache for far more than they could share standing in his living room fully dressed.

Earlier, at breakfast, she'd thought he'd been a bit cool, distancing himself from her and what they'd shared during the long hours they'd spent in his bed. Right now, though, they were only seconds from either trying out his couch or maybe even the floor. She couldn't wait to find out which it would be.

"Megan, honey, we shouldn't…"

Not what she wanted to hear. "That's not what you said last night when I did this." She really loved the soft slide of flannel over something so deliciously hard.

His voice grew rough. "But Phoebe…"

"Is asleep. We've got time, Seamus, although it might make me a little late to work." She cupped him with a gentle squeeze.

His breath went out in a rush. "Maybe I can have a word with your boss."

Then he scooped her up in his arms and headed for the couch. When Seamus gently laid her down, she scooted toward the back of the couch, making room for him to stretch out beside her. His knee pushed between her thighs at the same time his mouth found hers. She wrapped her arms around him tightly, relishing the sensation of once again being sheltered by his powerful body.

This time it seemed that neither of them wanted a slow exploration, maybe because they both knew the world outside wouldn't leave them alone for much longer. She worked her shorts down off her hips as Seamus continued to kiss her senseless. When he realized what she was trying to do, he helped her.

After shifting her onto her back, he settled in the cradle of her body. He pushed his own pants down only far enough to free his cock. And then with a couple of sharp thrusts, their bodies were joined again. He guided her ankles high up around his hips.

"Hold on tight, honey. This is going to be fast and furious."

She rocked against him and smiled. "Go for it, big guy."

He grinned down at her response, and then put all his considerable strength into his powerful claiming of her body. She'd never been the focus of such an explosive experience. What was there about this particular vampire who brought out such intensity in her?

Seamus dragged the tips of his fangs across the veins that ran along the side of her neck. He didn't break the skin, but it was still enough to send her rocketing toward ecstasy. When he offered her his vein, she bit down hard. With a shout, he poured out his own release.

Before either of them could do more than lie there in boneless bliss, the world came rushing back accompanied by a loud rapping on Seamus's door.

"Megan? Seamus? Sorry to bother you, but it's an emergency. Rafferty's been hurt."

With a muttered curse, Seamus immediately pushed away from Megan, his eyes bleak. "Get in the bedroom. I'll see what's going on."

She was perfectly capable of getting back up off the couch by herself, but a hand up would have been nice. However, it was clear that Seamus had lost all interest in touching her. With her eyes burning, she picked up her shorts and stalked into the bedroom, her pride the only thing holding back her tears.

Maybe she was overreacting. There was no reason she should feel embarrassed if Joss figured out what she and Seamus had been doing. They were both adults, after all. But as she closed the door, she'd risked one more look in Seamus's direction. She'd never seen him look so grim, so unapproachable. Gone was her smiling lover.

In his place stood a cold-eyed vampire with death in his eyes.

What a screwed-up mess! Seamus heard the click of his bedroom door, well aware that he'd managed to hurt Megan without meaning to. They'd both known they were running out of time.

Joss pounded on the door again. "Seamus, they'll be here with Rafferty in a few minutes. He's going to need surgery, but he's bleeding too badly to wait for the med techs to get here. He needs help now."

Or he could just let Rafferty die. But Seamus kept that particular thought to himself as he yanked the door open.

"What happened?"

"Witnesses said his transport veered out of control and plowed into a tree." Joss was pale, her hands shaking.

"Have them take him to the first exam room."

"Thanks, Seamus. I can't tell you how glad I am you're here for him."

Not if she knew the truth. "I'll be right there."

Joss ran back toward the front door of the clinic, leaving him to deal with his other guests. He knocked on the bedroom door.

"Megan, I'll be out in the clinic with Rafferty."

She opened the door as he stepped away. "I'll join you as soon as I change clothes."

He wanted to tell her to stay away, not wanting any complications until he figured out what he was going to do. He wanted his revenge, but he hadn't expected an opportunity like this to drop in his lap.

"All right."

He ducked into the pre-op to grab a set of scrubs to put on. No time to shower, so he washed up at the sink instead. By the time he was done, he could hear voices out in the waiting room. His breakfast churned in his stomach knowing the next hour could very well be the last one of his life. If he let Rafferty die, and Joss figured out it was deliberate, she'd stake him.

He'd thought he was ready to face that possibility, but evidently his will to live was stronger than his need to punish the vampire who'd destroyed his world. And he knew who he could thank for that—Megan Perez. No one could experience what the two of them had shared and think one day like that was enough. But if he was going to die, at least he was going out on a high note.

Joss was hovering over her husband as they carried him in on a makeshift stretcher. She looked like hell and Rafferty looked worse. It didn't take a medical degree to see why. His right leg was bent at an unnatural angle and jagged bone shards jutted up through the fabric of his jeans. Blood pooled and dripped off the board they'd strapped him to. If he'd been bleeding that badly for long, it might already be too late.

Joss knew it, too. It was there in her terror-filled eyes. "We called for an emergency evac, but they said it would be thirty minutes to an hour before they can get here."

False comfort wouldn't help anyone. "He can't wait that long."

Rafferty needed immediate help if he was to survive. Even with medical intervention, success was far from a sure thing. Seamus weighed his options. After studying the possibilities, he chose Megan on several levels.

He sought her out in the crowd. "Megan, go put on scrubs. I'm going to need an extra set of hands."

She backed away. "You need someone who knows what they're doing."

"Do you see anyone who meets that description around here?"

They both looked at the cluster of humans, all farmers judging by their attire and the dirt caked on their boots. Megan obviously came to the same conclusion because she handed Phoebe off to Joss.

Seamus nodded in approval. "Okay, we need to get moving. We don't have all night."

While he waited, he checked Rafferty's pulse. It was thready and weak, but the vampire's eyes opened and looked around until he spotted Seamus. Dazed and wracked with pain, he struggled to talk.

"Don't waste your energy, Rafferty. You don't have any to spare."

Still the vampire fought to speak. Seamus leaned down to listen, knowing his patient wouldn't give up until he said his peace. Rafferty finally whispered one single word. "Petra."

Suddenly, Rafferty wasn't the only one who was having trouble breathing. Seamus stared down at his patient. Their eyes met and held as they both came to terms with their shared truth.

Finally, Seamus nodded. Evidently satisfied they'd reached an understanding, Rafferty gave in to the pain and passed out, leaving Seamus wishing he could do the same.

Chapter 10

Seamus pegged one of the farmers with a hard look. "Call Conlan and tell him to get his ass back here. He may be out of range for a while, but keep trying until you reach him. Tell him what's happened."

"Sure thing, Doc."

"I'm not a doctor." Although he really was. "Now let's get Rafferty into pre-op. We've got to get that tourniquet off before it causes more damage."

"What do you mean by 'pre-op,' Seamus?" Joss blocked his way. Every inch of her vibrated with the protective nature of a warrior. "You're just a medic. Do what you can to stabilize him. That's all."

Seamus stared at the bloody mess in front of him. Yes, he could continue this farce of pretending to be less than he was, which would even play into his desire for revenge. It was doubtful that Rafferty would live long enough to make it to the trauma hospital. Without lifting a finger, Seamus could simply let his enemy die.

But that wasn't going to happen. Somewhere along the line, these people had come to mean something to him. Not just Megan and Phoebe, but also the O'Days themselves and the people who depended on the vampire for their living, for their homes, for the second chance Rafferty had offered all of them.

His decision might come back to haunt him, but his vow to do no harm outweighed his vow to avenge his sister. Time to get moving.

"They can't get here fast enough, Joss. He's already lost too much blood. If that doesn't kill him, the trip will. Let me take care of him. Now, before it's too late."

The indecision looked out of place on the chancellor's face. "He's all I have."

"I know, Joss. And if you don't get the hell out of my way, you won't have him for long." Brutal, but it was no less than the truth.

For the second time in less than a minute, he reluctantly made hardcore eye contact with someone and made a promise. "I can do this, Joss. Trust me."

She drew a shuddering breath and jerked her head in a sharp nod. "What can I do to help?"

"Take care of Phoebe." Which would give her something to concentrate on besides her husband.

Next, Seamus dragged Megan along in his wake on the way to the pre-op. "Scrub up and put some gloves on. Then start cutting away Rafferty's jeans while I'll get him medicated."

Megan tried one last protest. "Seamus, what if he..."

"There'll be no *if* about it unless we get moving." He realized he was barking at her and softened his voice. "I'll point at what I need. I just need an extra pair of hands. You'll do fine."

Then he glanced at his patient. "You both will."

With Megan's help, Seamus had Rafferty stripped, prepped and medicated for surgery in a matter of minutes. Even with his untrained helper, he was able to get IVs started and a unit of blood dripping into Rafferty's vein. Their species could survive almost any wound as long they didn't bleed out completely. With transfusions and the right drugs, the older vampire stood a good chance for a full recovery.

Once the bleeding was under control, the

next hurdle would be to get the bones realigned quickly enough. Seamus could still try to stabilize Rafferty enough for transport and let someone else take it from there. But left on their own, the bones would solidify as they were, leaving Rafferty permanently crippled. Even if Seamus got them even partly back in place, it would make it easier for a surgical team to try realign them correctly, but as bad as the break was, it was unlikely they'd succeed.

That left one more option. Seamus could come out of hiding and do the complete surgical repair himself. As soon as the thought crossed his mind, his decision was made. Time to get started.

Megan studied their patient's face. "His color looks better."

"That's the blood doing its work. Now we need to get him into surgery."

Together they maneuvered the gurney into the next room and positioned it by the surgical table.

"On a count of three, we'll lift him over. Are you ready?"

When she nodded, he counted, "One, two, three!"

It was a good thing Rafferty wasn't awake for that because jarring his leg that much had to hurt like a bitch.

"What next?" Megan kept her eyes focused on Seamus's face, clearly not wanting to look at the torn flesh and shattered pieces of bone that used to be Rafferty's leg. He draped the site with sterile dressings.

"Now, we pretend this is a particularly challenging jigsaw puzzle and get to work."

He pulled the tray of sterile instruments over within easy reach. "Luckily, I've always been good at puzzles."

God knew how many hours later, they were finally done. Megan's back ached, her head pounded and her eyes stung from sweat. Even so, there was no place she'd rather be than watching Seamus Fitzhugh perform his magic.

She'd known firsthand that he was good at what he did, but watching him put Rafferty's leg back together was like watching an artist in action. Piece by piece, stitch by stitch, what had been a hideous mishmash of blood and bone fragments became whole again. Right now Seamus was slowly sewing the long incision closed, his tiny black stitches tidy and neat.

"You were amazing." In so many ways, although right now she meant his gift for healing. "I didn't know that medics could do something like this."

Seamus glanced up at her. After a second, he said, "They can't."

"But—"

"They also don't have the training to dispense the kind of medicine that saved your life. Not legally, anyway."

He went back to his work, leaving her confused about what he was trying to tell her. If medics didn't do surgery or dispense the medicine he gave her, then that meant…what exactly?

"Come on, Megan, you're smart. You can figure it out." Seamus snipped the last thread and dropped the small curved needle back down on the instrument tray.

The truth hit her hard. "You're not a medic at all, are you? You're a doctor, and a surgeon at that."

"Half right. I finished medical school and should have been licensed to practice medicine. However, I lack a few weeks of training to finish my residency in surgery." He bandaged Rafferty's leg and then checked his patient's vitals.

After making several notes in the chart he'd started, he covered Rafferty with a warmed blanket.

She stepped back from the table. "Why pretend to be somebody you aren't?"

"My reasons are my own." He adjusted the flow of the IV a bit. "Go tell Joss that her husband came through with flying colors. He'll be asleep for a while, but she can come sit with him until he wakes up."

It was clear she wasn't going to get any more information from Seamus. Whatever was going on in that head of his, he wasn't ready to share, not even with her. That hurt, plain and simple. She'd seen every impressive inch of him during the past twenty-four hours, but right now she was having a hard time recognizing him at all.

"I'll go get her."

The waiting room had filled up since the last time she'd been out there. As soon as Megan appeared in the doorway, both Joss and Conlan were up and moving in her direction. As tired as she was, she let them come to her.

"Is Rafferty—"

When Joss couldn't go on, Conlan finished the question for her. "Is Rafferty ready to go? The evac chopper landed twenty minutes ago, but we held them off waiting for Seamus to get him ready to transport."

When Megan started to shake her head, Joss blanched and staggered back a step. Conlan immediately wrapped his arm around his friend's shoulder while Megan hastened to correct herself.

"No, Joss, Rafferty is doing fine. Seamus did an amazing job of putting the pieces of his leg back together. He sent me out to get you so you can sit with Rafferty until he wakes up. Come on, I'll take you back."

Conlan followed hard on their heels, his face grim. When they filed into the small surgical suite, Seamus was waiting for them.

"Glad you're here, Conlan. We need to move Rafferty out of here so I can get the room cleaned up and restocked. I could use your help lifting him."

"But what about the helicopter? They won't wait forever."

"Let them go. They can't do any more for him than I have and being jostled right now could actually make things worse. If the ride got rough enough, they'd have to operate again. Thanks to his age, Rafferty's tougher than most. That doesn't mean he's invincible."

The security officer crossed his arms over his chest and blocked the door. "Fine, I'll call them, but then we need to talk, *Doctor*."

That definitely sounded like a threat to Megan, but Seamus only looked resigned.

"No arguments on that count, Chancellor, but not right now. Let's get your boss situated, and then I need to check if any of that crowd out there is waiting to see me. Once I've seen to my patients, I'll surrender peaceably."

"Can we trust you with their care?" Conlan kept his voice low, probably out of consideration for Rafferty, but still managed to sound belligerent.

Seamus's smile didn't reach his eyes. "Right now, I'm all you've got."

Joss studied her husband's pale face and then the bandage on his leg. "Let him, but I want you with him every minute. I'll stay with Rafferty. Once he's awake, we'll decide what to do."

Then she got right up in Seamus's face. "And if he doesn't wake up, you're dead. Painfully, permanently dead."

Megan tried to shove her way between Joss and Seamus. She wasn't sure what all the undercurrents to this conversation meant, but she wouldn't let them raise a hand to hurt Seamus. No matter what else he'd done, he'd saved her life and Rafferty's, too.

She dragged her cousin back a couple of steps. "Joss, back off. I know you're worried and upset. But in case you've forgotten, he just saved Rafferty's leg, not to mention his life!"

Her cousin leaned in close and sniffed Megan's skin. "Just because you spent the night in his bed doesn't mean he's trustworthy, Megan. We both know your taste in lovers is questionable at best."

Seamus shoved Megan out of his way. "Okay, that's enough, Joss. What happened between me and Megan is none of your damn business. You want to rip into me, fine, have at it. But you don't say another word to her or your husband won't be the only one bleeding in here today."

"*Shut up,* all of you!" Conlan roared. "Joss, you might want to remember that Megan just helped save his life, too. Focus on Rafferty and leave Seamus to me."

Then he turned on Seamus. "As for you, take care of your patients, including Rafferty. I'll stay with you because Joss asked me to, not because I don't trust you to do your best by them."

His face gentled when he finally got to Megan. "Strip off that bloody gown because I suspect that's your daughter calling for you."

Conlan was right. Phoebe was her priority, but still she hesitated. "Seamus?"

There was exhaustion in his stance and great sadness in his face. She instinctively reached out to him, despite everything needing to offer him some kind of comfort. When he flinched and stepped back out of reach, her heart hurt.

"Go on, Megan. I'll be…here."

She left. And if anyone noticed the tears streaming down her face, they didn't say so.

"Boy, when you decide to screw up, you don't mess around."

Seamus opened an eye and stared across the exam room at his unwanted companion—or warden. He wasn't sure which Conlan was at the moment and didn't really care. He figured he was only hours away from being dead or thrown out on his ass. He was too tired at the moment to worry about anyone but himself.

Well, except for Megan. Right now he'd give anything to be back in his apartment, pretending that the hours they'd shared there were more than just a momentary lapse in judgment. He'd known better than to involve her in his problems, and yet he'd managed to drag her right down into the muck with him.

Evidently ignoring Conlan wasn't going to work because he sat up straighter and tried again. "Are you ready for that talk?"

"Does it matter whether I am or not?"

"Not really."

He stood up. "That's what I thought. Let's

take this party back to my quarters. I'd kill for a cup of coffee."

"Fine. Let me tell Joss where we'll be."

Seamus walked through the clinic and was glad to see the waiting room was empty. Once he'd gotten Rafferty taken care of, he'd had a steady stream of patients requiring his attention. Conlan had kept his promise to Joss and stayed with him every step of the way, stepping out only when the patient was female and required a physical examination.

As Seamus headed for his quarters, he was surprised to see the light on in Megan's office. He quickly learned there was a good reason for that.

"Megan, what are you still doing here?"

She looked up from the file she'd been reading. "I work here, remember? Unless that's changed."

A rush of unexpected warmth gave him a new surge of energy. "I wasn't sure you'd want to."

"Make no mistake, you've got some explaining to do, mister, and not just to me." She frowned. "I swore never to let another vampire into my life, but it seems I must trust you on some level. If I didn't, I wouldn't have spent all those hours in your bed."

She picked up her pen and began making

some notes, leaving him standing there staring at her in bewilderment. She still trusted him?

When he didn't immediately leave, she asked, "Was there something else?"

"Uh, no."

"Okay then." Then, she closed the file and reached for the next one on the pile. "And, Seamus, don't make me regret last night. Life doesn't offer many gifts like that."

What could he say to that? He'd never been anyone's gift before, and now was sure as hell the wrong time and place for it. He let himself into the apartment and started raiding the refrigerator. Since it looked as if he'd survive the day, he might as well eat something.

By the time Conlan strolled in, Seamus had thrown together a couple of sandwiches, but he had to take care of one more thing before he sat down.

"Go ahead and eat. I'm going to check Rafferty's vitals and give him another dose of medicine." He left without waiting for Conlan to respond. If the chancellor still wanted to babysit him, fine.

Joss looked up from her magazine when Seamus walked into the room. "What are you doing now? Where's Conlan? I thought he was told to stick with you."

"He was. He did. Right now I'm going to check on my patient and give him something for the pain."

A hoarse voice entered the conversation. "I'm done being a pin cushion, Fitzhugh."

Joss and Seamus both turned to see Rafferty blinking up at them. Although clearly still feeling the aftereffects of everything that had been thrown at him, the vampire looked coherent.

Joss hurried to his side. "God, Rafferty, you ever scare me like that again, and I'll operate on you myself—and without drugs."

When the vampire laughed, he winced in pain. Seamus offered them his back as he filled a syringe with Rafferty's medicine, to allow the couple a private moment.

A few seconds later, Joss cleared her throat. "Uh, Seamus, you can turn around now."

He walked around to Rafferty's other side and swabbed his arm with alcohol. The older vampire glared at the needle.

"Is that necessary?"

"Yes, it is. But on a happier note, barring unforeseen complications, it should be the last dose through a needle. You can take pills after this if you need them."

"Good. Now when can I go home?"

"With luck, the day after tomorrow you'll

be out of that bed and hobbling around on crutches." He quickly injected the meds and covered the spot with a cotton ball. "When you can manage to walk from here to the front door without hurting yourself, you can go home."

"Why not tonight?"

"Because I need to keep an eye on your surgical site, and Joss needs to get some sleep. She'll need all the energy she can muster to wait on you hand and foot once you're back home."

"I like the sound of that." Rafferty gave his wife an evil look. "And how long can I milk that for?"

"As long as you feed regularly, making it fresh blood whenever possible, you'll be completely healed in a couple of weeks. So take advantage of every minute you can." He winked at Joss.

"Hey, he's hard enough to live with as it is, Seamus. Don't encourage him," Joss protested, although she was smiling down at her husband.

He needed to put some distance between himself and them, both physical and emotional. "Conlan wants to talk to me, and then I'm going to get some sleep. After that, I'll sit with Rafferty so you can go home, Joss."

Before Seamus reached the door, Rafferty spoke again. "Seamus?"

"Yes?"

The vampire struggled to lift his head up so he could glare at him. "Thanks for saving my leg and, most likely, my life. That doesn't mean I'm not going to kick your ass for you once I'm off the crutches."

He could feel the cold steel in Rafferty's gaze from across the room. "Fair enough."

It was too much to hope that Conlan would've given up and gone home. But no, he was firmly ensconced on Seamus's couch, his feet propped up on the coffee table. Memories of how that couch had been put to use flooded through Seamus's mind as he picked up his sandwich and dropped down on the opposite end from Conlan.

At least Conlan held off on starting his inquisition until Seamus had devoured everything on his plate as well as two packs of blood. By now, he was well past caring if Conlan or the whole damn world watched him feed. When the second pack was empty, he tossed it aside.

"Okay, the condemned man has had his last meal. Fire away." Not that he was in the mood for answering questions.

Conlan shifted to face Seamus. "So it turns

out you're a doctor, and not just a medic after all."

There was no use in denying it. "Yes, I've finished medical school, but I was asked to leave before I completed my surgical residency. I was specializing in orthopedics, but had extensive practice in general surgery before starting my last round of training. The school refused to grant me my credentials, so the part about being licensed as a medic is true. They didn't even want to give me that much."

"Want to tell me the rest of the story? I'll find out one way or the other."

"Do you really think confession is good for the soul, Conlan? Because no matter what I say, I'm guessing you'll toss me back out the gate and probably in broad daylight. However, for Rafferty's sake, you might want to wait until I take the stitches out."

"Don't be a smart-ass." Conlan was clearly not amused. "As much as I'd like to oblige your death wish, I'm not the judge nor the jury around here. Rafferty and Joss will decide what happens to you from this point on. None of us take well to being lied to, no matter what the reason. I might think the boss is a pompous jerk most of the time, but I do respect what he's trying to accomplish here."

His right hand flashed out and caught Seamus

by the collar, jerking him halfway across the couch. For the first time, as he got in Seamus's face, the chancellor let his anger show, along with his powerful fangs.

"You bastard, I actually *liked* you. Hell, I gave my approval on your application even though I knew there was something off about your story, that you were hiding something. The only reason you're not bleeding right now is because you've saved the lives of two people I care about."

Seamus instantly responded with all the belligerence of an irate male vampire in his prime. He broke Conlan's grasp on his shirt and shoved the chancellor back to his own end of the couch.

"Yes, I lied, but at least I was actually more qualified than I claimed to be. I've never used my medical skills to do harm."

True enough, although he'd been damn tempted. Frustration and something that felt an awful lot like shame had him wanting to punch something. Or somebody.

Before he gave in to the urge, he lurched to his feet to put the narrow distance of the small living room between them. Both he and Conlan were breathing hard, the inborn aggression native to both species hard to contain.

Finally, Seamus forced himself to speak. "I had my reasons for why I lied, Conlan. Reasons that have nothing to do with you and everything to do with Rafferty. That's all you need to know."

"That's where you're wrong, boy! Everything around here is my business. I won't rest until I know the truth. The sun's already up, so I know you're not going anywhere for a few hours. I've got a couple of my men and the transport mechanic checking over Rafferty's vehicle. If I find out there's more to this than a simple accident, you'd better hope you've got a watertight alibi."

The anger faded into shock. "You suspect it was sabotage?"

"I don't know yet, but I'm not ruling it out." Conlan cracked his knuckles out of frustration. "But Rafferty's transport was practically new. That the brakes would fail in the one vehicle that he drives all the time might be a coincidence, but I'm thinking not."

Who else would've had it in for Rafferty? Banan, but he was out of reach at the moment. "Let me know what you find out."

"Oh, believe me. You'll be the first to know."

Now wasn't the time for this. Until they

knew for sure if the wreck had been an attempt on Rafferty's life, there was no reason to try to convince Conlan that Seamus hadn't been involved.

"Look, I told Joss I'd catch a couple hours of rest and then send her home. You're welcome to sack out on the couch or in one of the exam rooms if you want to stay close by. We'll all think better when we're not running on empty."

Which reminded him, Megan was long overdue to be heading back to her cottage.

"Banan Delaney's gone, isn't he?"

"Yeah, he had just boarded the turbo when I got the call about Rafferty. Why?"

"I wanted to make sure it was safe for Megan to go back home."

Conlan's expression turned sour. "Yeah, and that's one more reason I want to kick your ass from one end of the estate to the other. I shouldn't have been the last one to learn about the poison. I'm still sorry I didn't throw the bastard *under* the turbo as you suggested."

He took a step in Seamus's direction, his fists clenched. "Megan's a nice woman and deserves someone who'll treat her right. You understand me?"

Seamus agreed on both points. "No arguments from me."

"Tell her I'll take her home and check the place out for her if she'd like me to."

"I'm sure she'll appreciate the offer."

As Seamus headed out the door to tell her, he realized that for the first time he regretted being a vampire rather than one of the other two species. At least if he were a chancellor, or even a human, he would be the one to escort Megan and her daughter safely back home.

Instead, despite his superior strength, he was stuck inside and unable to keep his lover safe from harm.

The sound of Seamus's door echoed down the hallway. Megan immediately put her hands back on the keyboard to look busy. The last thing she wanted was for Seamus to catch her daydreaming, especially about him. She'd meant what she told him about still trusting him, but that was true only up to a point. He had some serious explaining to do. After that, she'd make up her mind how far her faith in him would extend.

Her traitorous body clearly had no such reservations. As soon as he appeared in the doorway, all she could think was how much she wanted to brush his hair back off his forehead and how good that stern mouth had tasted when he'd kissed her.

"Hi, there."

"Hi, right back to you."

She shut down the computer and stood up as she was hit with a powerful urge to walk straight into his arms. "Was there something you needed?"

"Conlan has offered to see that you and Phoebe get home safely."

Conlan, but not Seamus. Okay, so much for those daydreams.

As if sensing the direction her thoughts had taken, he added, "The sun's up."

"Oh, then, that makes sense. It will feel good to get out of these same clothes."

Seamus's smile changed from friendly to something far hotter. "I wish I could go along and help with that."

So did she, despite everything that had happened, but she couldn't give in to temptation. Not until she knew more about what was going on. And Seamus knew it, too. His smile disappeared and the blue of his eyes turned icy.

"Seamus, I can't…"

"I see. That's okay." Although it clearly wasn't. He retreated back into the hallway. "I'll get Conlan for you."

And coward that she was, she let him walk away.

Chapter 11

The smart thing would be to let him walk away, to rebuild that wall of caution between them. Maybe it was because she was so tired, but she wasn't feeling all that bright at the moment.

"Seamus! Come back!"

She sensed him still out in the hallway, trapped between his apartment and her office and unsure which way he wanted to go. He wasn't going to make this easy for her.

"Please."

He reappeared in the doorway but made no move to come back into the office.

"What now, Megan?"

He sounded so tired her heart ached. She

came around the desk and walked straight toward him. At first he only watched her, but at the last second, he held out his arms. God, it felt so good to be gathered in close to the strength of his chest, to let his warmth engulf her.

"I'm sorry, Seamus." She leaned her head back to look him in the eye. "I know you have good reasons for…whatever you've done."

"Call it what it is, Megan. I've lied to Conlan, to Rafferty and to you. And if circumstances hadn't forced my hand, I would've gone right on lying to all of you."

It all came down trust, something she'd had in short supply these days. So what could she say to him without giving either one of them false hope? She had to try.

"I had my own secrets, Seamus. If you hadn't been there when I arrived, I would've died. But even so, I was in no hurry for everyone to find out that I have poor taste in men."

Oops. She dropped her head back down against his chest with a sigh. "Sorry. That came out wrong. I meant to say I *had* poor taste in men. Before coming here. Before I met you."

To her surprise, Seamus laughed. Then he crooked his finger and used it to tilt her face back up toward his. "How about we just admit we're both too tired to be having any kind of serious discussion right now?"

While he spoke, he focused on her mouth, as if waiting for something. Permission, maybe?

"Okay, I'll go along with that idea, provided you figure out something else we could be doing right now besides talking."

"How about this?"

Then he kissed her. At the first brush of his lips across hers, the stress of the past twenty-four hours disappeared. His kiss was everything she wanted and not nearly everything she needed from him. Now wasn't the time to push for anything more.

Slowly, he broke away, saying without words that he regretted having to do so. "Conlan's waiting. Go home. Get some rest."

"I'll be back tonight."

He shook his head. "The clinic's closed tonight, except for emergencies. You've been through a lot. Take it easy and spend some time with Phoebe."

"But…"

He put his finger across her lips. "But nothing. I'll have my own big baby to take care of, or have you forgotten that I've got Rafferty staying in the clinic? How long do you think he'll like being confined to bed?"

She giggled, mainly because he wanted her to. "Okay, but if you need me, call."

"I will. Now get packed up. I'm going to get some sleep so I can send Joss home to rest."

"You're a nice man, Seamus Fitzhugh." She raised up to kiss his cheek.

"No, I'm not, but I'm glad you think so." Then his expression turned serious. "I hope nothing you learn about me changes your thoughts on that subject."

"We just agreed now wasn't the time to get all serious." She gave him a gentle push. "Now tell Conlan I'm ready to go."

He gave her another quick kiss and disappeared, but this time looking a great deal happier. She quickly bundled up her daughter and waited in the hall for Conlan. Seamus was right. She needed to rest, to give herself time and space to get some perspective on the monumental changes her life had gone through in the past few days.

However, there was something she'd already learned. Hope was a precious thing, and she'd had far too little of it for a long time. But with Banan gone and Seamus in her life, she had hope again. And that was a good thing.

The alarm went off, jarring Seamus out of a sound sleep. He slammed the palm of his hand down on the clock to shut off the obnoxious noise. Now if he could just make the rest of the world disappear as easily, he'd be happy.

He pushed himself upright and sat on the edge of the bed for several seconds. Okay, time to get moving. He'd promised to replace Joss at Rafferty's bedside, a chore he wasn't looking forward to, but a promise was a promise. Thinking of his vampire host, he thought it was a damn shame that not everybody felt that way.

On the other hand, he'd never seen his sister's eyes light up at the mention of Rafferty's name nor could he imagine her sitting at the vampire's side as he recuperated from a near-death injury. Rafferty had been betrothed to Seamus's half sister but he'd called the engagement off shortly after he met Joss. Seamus suspected that if Rafferty had married Petra, the two would've both been locked into a loveless relationship forever.

He poked at that idea, trying to decide how he felt about it. Without question, he would prefer Petra were alive—period. Despite her shortcomings, she was his sister, and he'd loved her. But was her pride worth the cost of making not two, but three people miserable for the duration of their long lives? Rafferty wanted Joss. Joss wanted Rafferty. That much was clear.

He knew exactly what Petra had wanted: the status from being married to a vampire male from a higher-ranking clan. All things considered, she'd have found Rafferty's cash to be cold comfort. Seamus had learned the hard way status was a fragile thing indeed. Any friendships and other relationships based on it even more so. Events totally out of his control had taught him that bitter lesson.

Now, here he was in the middle of nowhere, surrounded by people he'd known but a short time. Yet, for the first time, he knew where he belonged, what his role in life should be. Hell, he even knew the woman he wanted to share that life with—Megan. How bizarre was that? His honor still demanded retribution for the death of his sister, but at what cost? And who would pay that price besides him?

This was getting him nowhere. Time to go babysit his patient. Do no harm, that's what he'd promised. He now knew for certain that those were more than idle words, that they defined him as a person. Strip him of friends, family, money and anything else of value, and he still had those words.

Do no harm—the bedrock of his soul.

* * *

Joss crossed her arms and stayed right where she was. "And I'm telling you I'm fine."

Seamus should have known it wouldn't be easy. "Joss, go home. Don't make me get Conlan to help me drag your exhausted backside out of here."

Rafferty opened his eyes, a slight smile playing around his mouth. "I'd buy tickets to watch that. And just so you know, Seamus, even with the two of you ganging up on her, my money would be on Joss."

His wife leaned over to kiss him. "Thank you for that vote of confidence, big man."

Seamus threw up his hands. "Fine, she's the toughest thing around these parts. That doesn't mean she can go without food and sleep. You put me in charge of the health care for everyone on the estate, and that includes both of you."

He glared at the couple and waited.

Rafferty supported him. "You heard the doc, Joss."

She stared at her husband briefly before turning her hard gaze on Seamus. "Can I trust you with him?"

He knew what she was asking. He'd already told her the answer to that before he'd dragged the bleeding vampire into surgery and resented having to say it again. So he didn't.

"Not a problem. He's not my type."

She didn't find his answer funny, but at least Rafferty did. "I'll be fine, Joss. Go."

"Okay, but I'll be back."

As she walked out, Seamus followed her. She made it almost across the waiting room before stuttering to a stop where she slumped against the wall. He'd been expecting the collapse, figuring the only thing keeping her upright was sheer stubborn determination. Joss resisted when he tried to support her, but then gave in as tears poured down her face.

Finally, when the deluge had run its course, she stepped back, wiping her cheeks dry with the handkerchief he handed her. "Oh, God, I almost lost him."

"But you didn't. He's a strong man, Joss."

"But not invincible."

"None of us are," Seamus replied. "Will you be all right?"

"No, I'll be okay." She stepped out into the bright sunshine.

"I know." He hovered back in the shadows and watched until she reached her transport and pulled away before locking the door. Time to go face the music.

On the way, he snagged four blood packs and warmed them. Okay, so as a delay tactic, it sucked, he thought ruefully. At the most, it would slow down the confrontation by only a few seconds. Besides, after feasting from Megan's vein while being held in her arms, taking his nourishment from a plastic bag just didn't cut it.

Rafferty probably felt the same way, but right now processed blood was all either of them had. He carried the peace offering into the other room.

"So I guessed right. You're Petra's half brother." Even flat on his back, Rafferty had a commanding presence.

Seamus sat down in the chair Joss had been using. "Yes, although the *half* part never mattered. She was my only living relative."

He held out two of the blood packs. "Drink these."

Rafferty tried to hand them back. "I don't need to feed as often as you do."

"And you'd prefer your wife's vein. I get that. But right now, you're running several quarts low, and she's already exhausted. Drink that or I'll pump it in through a dull needle. A big one. If I look hard enough, I might even find a rusty one."

"Okay, hard-ass. I'll drink it."

After they'd both finished, Seamus disposed of the empties and then quickly checked Rafferty's vitals. "I'm going to look at your leg now. Want me to sit you up so you can get a look at your handsome new scar? Eventually it'll fade away, but it's pretty impressive right now, if I do say so."

"Sure."

When Seamus cut away the bandage, he stepped back to let Rafferty get a good look at his handiwork.

"Son of a bitch! I knew it was bad, but…"

All the color leeched out of Rafferty's face. "No wonder Joss kept checking to see if I was really breathing. I came damn close to losing that leg, didn't I?"

The vampire was the kind of man who'd want the truth. "No, you almost lost your life. If they hadn't gotten you to me when they did…"

"You probably don't want my gratitude, but you have it." Rafferty covered his eyes with his forearm as he pressed the button to lower the head of the bed.

A few seconds later, he asked, "So, you do want to talk about what happened with your sister?"

Now that the moment had arrived to confront his enemy, Seamus found he lacked the words or even the will to do so. Instead, he concentrated on applying a new bandage to the surgical site.

"I never cheated on Petra with Joss, Seamus. There was one night, but—"

"What you did destroyed my sister, Rafferty. I don't need excuses or details." He added one last strip of tape, amazed he could keep his touch gentle when what he really wanted to do was to punch something.

"No excuses offered. But you need to know the details." Despite his calm tone, Rafferty's fangs showed enough to reveal the powerful emotions he was fighting. "I need you to know them."

"It won't change anything."

"Nothing will, but the truth is better than lies and misconceptions. If we're going to find a way to get along from this point on, Seamus, we need a do-over."

The import of his words sank in. Seamus looked at Rafferty in shock. "You're not going to throw me out?"

"Let's just say, it wouldn't be my first choice. Now, are you going to listen or not?"

"I'll listen. That doesn't mean I'll believe you."

Rafferty smiled and shook his head. "God,

you remind me of me. Joss thinks I'm the only one this stubborn."

Seamus didn't like that one bit, especially considering his low opinion of Rafferty. Although he had to admit, that had changed since his arrival on the man's estate.

"I said I'd listen. I didn't say I'd sit here and be insulted. How did you figure out who I was?"

"Something about how you were acting today reminded me that her brother was studying to be a doctor."

"And you let me operate on you? You had to know I'd be looking for vengeance."

There was real regret in Rafferty's voice. "Had I known what happened…what the fallout had cost you, I'd like to think I would have done something about it."

"Yeah, well, that's easy to say now when it's too late."

"Okay, Doc, do you want the long or the short version?"

"What's to tell? You broke your word to my sister and it destroyed her. I was just collateral damage."

"You're right, of course. I was betrothed to your sister when I first met Joss. But knowing your sister, did you really think our relationship was a love match?"

"No, of course not. I wasn't blind to my sister's faults. She'd already broken one betrothal when she realized that you were a step up for her."

"And I was looking for a female who could handle all the demands our society places on a scion of a highly-ranked vampire clan. It seemed like a fair trade."

"And then you met Joss." He so didn't want to hear this.

"She was the newest arbiter for the Coalition." Rafferty stared up at the ceiling as he lost himself in the past. "I knew from the first minute she was something special."

He rolled his head toward Seamus. "Imagine—a vampire of my age and experience falling that hard and that fast. Not that I had any intention of acting on it. I was a vampire, after all, and she was a lowly chancellor."

He winked at Seamus. "Don't tell her I said that or both of us will be bleeding."

Seamus didn't want to be charmed by Rafferty's embarrassed admission, but he was. And for some inexplicable reason, Megan Perez's pretty face drifted through his thoughts, yet another "lowly" chancellor who possessed both incredible strength and beauty. He hated knowing he and the older vampire had that much in common.

"Oh, boy, you've got it bad, too." There was a great deal of sympathy in Rafferty's voice. "All the more reason for us to get past this."

"Keep talking."

"I fed from Joss one time while I was still betrothed to Petra. That's all that happened, but we'd crossed the line and we both knew it. Joss resigned as an arbiter as soon as the Coalition session ended. I went back home and broke off the betrothal."

He sounded tired, by now his voice barely above a whisper. As Petra's brother, he needed to hear more. But as Rafferty's doctor, he needed to make his patient rest.

"We can finish this discussion later, Rafferty. Get some sleep."

The vampire shook his head. "Don't think I can do this again. There's not much more to say, anyway."

"All right."

"Petra didn't take it well. If I'd left her for another vampire, one she saw as her social superior, she would have understood. Or if she'd found another male who was easier to manipulate than I was, but my social equal, she wouldn't have hesitated to dump me. Unfortunately, she visited me while the Coalition was in session and met Joss."

Rafferty rubbed his eyes. "I was so damn careful, but Petra had a real talent for reading people. She knew I was leaving her for a chancellor, and *that* she couldn't tolerate."

That rang true to Seamus. "She would have seen that as insult of the worst sort, especially if her friends found out. She would've never lived it down."

"I planned to wait a while before contacting Joss. To give Petra time to move on, so that no one would make the connection between our breakup and any subsequent relationship I was able to establish with Joss. The nobility of that sacrifice was lost upon your sister."

For the first time, he sounded bitter. Too bad. All of this was still Rafferty's fault. Their society might have overlooked him having a chancellor mistress, but he doubted Petra would have, especially when it was clear that Rafferty felt far more for Joss than he had Petra.

"Then all of a sudden, I was charged with murdering a human, one I was known to have had difficulties with in the past. I was duly convicted, the main evidence being my knife was found wedged in the bastard's chest."

Rafferty sounded so disgusted, Seamus found himself smiling. "Imagine! What were they thinking?"

"Like I would've ever been that stupid. I don't know how familiar you are with the law when a death sentence is involved, but the Coalition grants the prisoner the right to have one of their chancellors review the case. If the evidence holds up, the chancellor executes the prisoner by any means they choose. If the chancellor finds inconsistencies, they have the authority to set aside the judgment. I chose Joss to hear my case."

"And big surprise, Joss set aside your conviction. You managed to walk on a murder conviction, and married your lover. Everybody lives happily ever after. Well, except for Petra."

A fresh wave of bitterness washed over Seamus, leaving him aching. He lurched up out of his chair, kicking it out of his way.

The vampire didn't flinch in the face of Seamus's fury. "No, actually Joss wasn't the one who cleared me. I knew I didn't have a chance in hell of being exonerated, but at least Joss would make my death painless. Not all chancellors are that considerate. But when Joss reviewed the file, she realized your sister had put a lien against my estate, hiding behind a corporation name. Instead of handling the final dispensation of the case herself, Joss called in Ambrose, her boss."

Seamus stood up straighter. This part he hadn't heard. If Ambrose was involved, it changed everything. The honor of the top chancellor for the Coalition was beyond reproach. No one among the three species was held in higher regard.

"What did Ambrose find?"

"He brought Petra in and confronted her. She admitted to having framed me. By law, she was tried, convicted and given the same sentence I was. I know it's cold comfort, but Ambrose saw to it that it was mercifully quick."

A heavy silence settled between them. After a bit, Rafferty stirred restlessly. "I can't tell you how sorry I was that it came to that, Seamus. I may not have loved Petra, but I never wanted her dead. Hell, I even understood why she did what she did."

There wasn't anything Seamus could say to that. He'd known all along that there was more to the story than he'd been told. As soon as it became known that his sister had been executed as a murderer, his scholarships had dried up, his residency canceled and his world came crashing down.

"I'm going to sleep now."

Rafferty tugged his blanket up higher on his chest and closed his eyes. He didn't immediately fall asleep, but the pretense allowed both males time to deal with the emotions that the painful story had stirred up.

Seamus rubbed his chest, as if that would make the pain in his heart would go away. Damn Petra, anyway! If she'd come to him, told him what was going on, maybe he could've helped her find a way to get past Rafferty's betrayal.

But she'd thrown the dice and lost, leaving Seamus alone and struggling to find his own way. He hated that she'd been that bitter and unhappy, but hadn't he meant anything to her at all? Obviously not enough to make any difference. As furious as he was with Rafferty, he was just as mad at Petra. God, the whole thing left him tired straight through to the bone. Catharsis might be good for the soul, but it burned a lot of energy.

Conlan had said Joss preferred that those who came to the estate were running toward their future rather than from their past. Right now, he wasn't up to running anywhere for any reason, but he could walk. And if Rafferty meant what he said about wanting Seamus to stay, he'd eventually pick up speed toward a future that held something good, like hope or friendship.

Or maybe even love, added a quiet voice in the back of his mind. And with the memory of Megan's sweet kiss, he dozed off.

Traveling by turbo left Banan filthy, exhausted and more determined that ever to wrest control of the family fortune by any means necessary. By fair means or foul, it didn't matter. And speaking of foul, he wondered if Rafferty discovered the little surprise he'd left behind. Or maybe it was Joss who'd learn the hard way that the brakes on their favorite transport were about to fail. That would be all right, too. It was the perfect gift to show his appreciation for their piss-poor hospitality.

Which brought him back to the misery of the turbo ride. He could've called for an airlift pickup when he left the O'Day's estate, but maintaining a low profile was more important than comfort. Money also played into his decision.

God, he hated having to conserve funds. As heir, he should have had unrestricted access to the family bank accounts, but showing an improved sense of fiscal responsibility was part of the total image package he was presenting to the older generation. If he'd managed to retrieve his daughter, that alone would've been enough to cement his future role of head of the family. But until he got his hands on her, he had to pretend to comply with the family's expectations.

He'd gotten off the turbo at the first town past Rafferty's stop long enough to make a few phone calls. As luck would have it, one of his distant cousins was up for a little adventure. Riley had long ago burned any chance of ingratiating himself with the current senior generation.

Riley might not be overly smart, but he was greedy. With the promise of money and power, Banan reeled him in with almost no effort. Fool! As if Banan would ever trust anyone whose loyalty could be purchased so cheaply.

Banan checked the time. He had hours left to be cooped up in this metal cage as it rattled along on the track. He couldn't wait until he checked into a decent hotel. One with room service, the kind where they kept willing humans on hand who would offer up their vein for the right price—and their bodies as well, for a slightly higher fee.

Of course, he'd have to be careful not to do any permanent damage. He'd always been hard on his toys, and right now he couldn't risk drawing unwanted attention to himself.

When Riley arrived, they'd make plans for his next visit to the O'Day estate thanks to one of his shady friends who could fly them in and out of a remote section of the estate. From there, they'd have fun checking off all the things he had on his special to-do list. A few drained-until-dead humans would be the perfect start to this particular adventure.

With luck, they'd lay all the blame right at Seamus Fitzhugh's doorstep when they found Megan Perez's body dumped in the woods near the infirmary. Seamus would be lucky if Rafferty staked him before he offered him up to the noonday sun.

And this time, when Banan left the O'Day estate behind, he wouldn't be leaving empty-handed. His parents would be so proud of their granddaughter. They'd hire the best of nurses to take care of her until she was capable of civilized behavior. Say, around age twenty or so. It was, after all, a family tradition.

Chapter 12

Stress was running high in the room. Megan couldn't control the slight trembling in her hands, so she kept them out of sight in her lap. Conlan shot her a sympathetic look, no doubt picking up on her tension despite how hard she was working to hide it. He sat with his leg crossed over his knee, his foot keeping time to a rapid beat only he could hear while Joss methodically tore a paper napkin into small pieces.

Seamus, on the other hand, sat rock still, his mouth a straight slash except for the slightest hint of fang showing. He looked like he'd been through hell and barely lived to tell the tale. Joss and Rafferty had called this meeting to discuss his future, although so far only Joss was seated at the table.

Seamus clearly didn't appreciate anyone having that much control over his life, but the truth was the estate was theirs to run as they saw fit. All decisions were final, but at least they'd invited her and Conlan in on the session, perhaps to ask their take on the situation.

It had been less than a week since Rafferty's brush with death. Without Seamus's quick action and superb medical skills, they'd have been gathered to bury the scion of the O'Day clan. Instead, they had other business to attend to.

She still didn't know what had brought Seamus to the O'Day estate, but it had been bad. Surely he wouldn't have lied about who he was and what his intentions were without good cause. But then her judgment when it came to men wasn't always trustworthy.

Obviously his path had crossed Rafferty's at some point in the past. Other than Seamus himself, only Joss and Rafferty knew for sure and they weren't talking. The only consolation was that Conlan looked as frustrated at she felt.

Finally, she heard the clomping steps of Rafferty making his way toward them. He came around the corner, awkwardly trying to manage his crutches and his injured leg while not dropping a file folder. After maneuvering himself into his own chair, he looked around the table. "Sorry to keep you waiting. Things took longer than they should have."

"Did it come?" Joss nodded toward the file folder.

"Yeah, but I had to grease a few palms to get those greedy bastards moving." He shot a hard look across at Seamus. "I thought the vampire clans had cornered the market on power plays and manipulating people. Those bastards you studied under could teach even the oldest of us a few lessons."

Seamus frowned. "Why were you talking to them? I already told you the reason I didn't finish school."

"Yeah, let's say I hate anyone being backed into a corner through no fault of their own." He reached for the cup of coffee Joss had poured for him. "Dusty work, but it's done."

"What work?" Conlan asked as he reached for a couple of cookies.

Megan watched both of the O'Days, trying to guess what was behind the looks they exchanged. Finally, Joss nodded as Rafferty tangled his fingers in hers, presenting a united front.

"Seamus, here, lied to us about his reasons

for coming here. After a long and private conversation on the subject, we've come to terms with the circumstances that made that necessary. The details are not mine to share."

Rafferty waited until Seamus nodded in agreement before continuing. "Our official policy has always been to permanently expel anyone who has misrepresented themselves to us, no excuses accepted."

Megan gasped, ready to protest, but Seamus wasn't acting either surprised or upset. Why?

"In this case, however, there are extenuating circumstances. We're prepared to overlook the misrepresentation for a variety of reasons."

Joss interrupted, "Not the least of which is that he saved Rafferty's life."

Conlan shot Seamus a conspiratorial look. "Which may show a lack of good judgment on Seamus's part."

"Bite me." Rafferty flashed his fangs at his security officer before returning his attention to Seamus. "So, Seamus, we're officially offering you the chance to remain here on the estate. We'd like to think you've found the work to your liking and have good reasons to want to stay."

No one looked in Megan's direction, but she blushed anyway. Was she one of his reasons? She had to wonder, especially because he'd been avoiding her once everything had blown up in his face.

Rafferty tapped the file he'd laid on the table. "However, we don't want you to stay here because it's the only choice you have. Your school had no right to do what they did, and I've encouraged them to rectify their mistake."

Conlan's eyes opened wide as he grinned. "And how many were left bloody and bruised by your style of hands-on encouragement?"

Ever the predator, Rafferty's own smile showed a lot of fang. "Enough to make it fun."

He pushed the file across the table toward Seamus. "This is only a copy. The originals will be arriving by courier in the next couple of days."

Seamus pulled the papers from the file and stared at them, looking a bit bewildered. He glanced at Conlan for some answers. "I don't understand."

The security officer leaned over and quickly scanned the papers scattered on the table. "It's all couched in the usual legal gibberish and fancy words. However, the bottom line is you are now a board-certified physician and surgeon, free to practice medicine anywhere in the Coalition."

Then he clapped him on the shoulder. "I guess congratulations are in order!"

"We'll second that," Joss said, smiling. "As Rafferty said, we wanted to make sure you had a choice, although we'd really like it if you chose to stay here. What do you think?"

Seamus finally looked up from the papers, his eyes a brighter blue than Megan had ever seen them. He looked at each person in turn, starting with Joss and Rafferty, then Conlan and finally her. She felt the heat in his gaze all the way to her toes. Her heart fluttered in anticipation as they all waited for his answer.

Seamus broke off the eye lock he had on Megan and forced himself to look back down at the stack of papers Rafferty had handed him. His medical degree. He'd given up all hope of ever having it, but there it lay—or at least a facsimile of what it would look like when it was delivered.

Months ago choice had been stripped from his life along with everything that had held any meaning for him: medical school, his sister, his status among their kind. Once his life had veered out of control, he'd been driven solely by his need to avenge his family honor.

He was well aware that everyone was

watching him, waiting for him to respond to the amazing gift that had just been handed to him. It was at once too much to take in and not nearly enough to make up for what he'd lost. But again, this was about beginnings, not what-could-have-beens.

He settled for the simple truth. "I don't know what to say."

As he glanced around the table, he could pretty much guess what most everybody was thinking. Joss was proud of what her husband had been able to do, and Rafferty himself was well aware that the stack of paper would give Seamus back his pride, if not the life he'd lost. Conlan was pleased for Seamus and probably relieved that he wasn't going to have to evict Seamus anytime soon.

There were a lot of thoughts going on behind Megan's lovely lavender eyes, but he wouldn't presume to think he knew what she was contemplating. He'd guess she was relieved in much the same way Conlan was. And like Joss, she was happy that Rafferty had straightened things out for Seamus, although she had no idea why Seamus had run into problems.

And maybe, just maybe, she was hoping he'd stay.

Where else did he have to go? Nowhere.

Who else wanted him? No one.

Did he want to stay? God, yes.

He allowed himself the privilege of reaching over to take Megan's hand in his and gave it a gentle squeeze. He kept his eyes firmly on hers when he announced his decision. "I guess you have yourself a doctor, Rafferty."

Then everyone was hooting and hollering, with Rafferty ordering Joss to fetch the champagne he had on ice in the other room "just in case." She was back in seconds with a tray full of glasses and the wine.

She handed him the bottle. "Here, this is your celebration, Dr. Fitzhugh. You pop the cork!"

Seamus managed to do the job with only a minimum amount of the bubbly stuff spilling onto the floor before Joss managed to catch the rest in her glass. When everyone had some, Seamus held his glass up to make the first toast.

"Here's to running toward the future."

The chime of crystal against crystal rang out as they all bumped glasses.

"Here, here!" Joss said.

Even Conlan managed a small smile as he lifted his glass. "Here's to trust well placed."

The words seemed to solidify and hang in the air between them, sending a chill through Seamus. Yes, for the time being they would trust him, but he had to wonder how strong that newly forged bond really was. But for now, he would sip the wine and enjoy the company.

Tomorrow would be soon enough to start planning for his future.

The night was pleasantly cool. The perfect temperature for walking home, his arm wrapped around a warm, lovely woman. He could see it now—him, Megan, at her front door as she debates whether or not to invite him in. He weighs in on the argument, not with words but with a kiss designed to sway her opinion.

But there was another pretty female who had to be taken into consideration—Phoebe. So rather than holding Megan in his arms, he held her daughter. Not that he was complaining—exactly.

The youngling was wide-awake and happy. If Seamus had to venture a guess, Phoebe was ready to be the center of attention for quite some time to come. He shifted his cheery burden to his other arm and snagged Megan's hand. He liked that her fingers felt so right tangled with his as they walked along.

"If I didn't say so before, I appreciate your being there for me tonight."

"Yes, well, I love my cousin and her husband, but no one should have to face the two of them at the same time without backup." She smiled up at him. "However, you would've done fine on your own. They're smart enough to know that they were lucky to get you."

Luck had little to do with it, but he wasn't going there. "I hope it didn't cost Rafferty too much to get them to issue my credentials."

"You'll probably never know, but he wouldn't have done it if he didn't want to. Either way, it was only fair that the school fixed your records for you. You'd spent years working to become a doctor and surgeon."

"Yes, it's all I ever wanted to do." And would've given it up in heartbeat to get his sister back.

Right now, though, he had an entirely different goal in mind as they turned off the road and walked up to Megan's cottage. She unlocked the door and turned on the lights inside.

"Would you like me to take a quick look around?"

"If you wouldn't mind." Megan looked relieved. "I know it's silly because Banan is gone, but I still worry. I can make tea if you'd like some."

"That sounds good." Well, not the tea, but he'd settle for that just to spend more time in her company.

He started to put Phoebe down in her crib,

but she immediately started to fuss. "Okay, little one, you can take the grand tour with me."

The cottage wasn't much bigger than his apartment at the infirmary, but Megan had somehow transformed it into a real home. There were feminine touches throughout: houseplants, soft pillows, bright-colored curtains. When he stepped into her bedroom, he wished that it was Megan and not her daughter in his arms.

"All clear."

He followed her scent into the kitchen and sat down at the table with Phoebe in his lap. He picked up a string of beads and dangled them just within reach of the baby's tiny hands. She cooed happily as she caught at them.

Megan set a cup a tea within easy reach and sat down in the chair next to him. "Do you want me to take her?"

"No, she's fine." In fact, she'd snuggled in close and was starting to look drowsy.

"You have a real gift with her. She's never that content with anyone else, including Joss." Megan snickered and added, "Rafferty always looks like he's worried that she's about to do something disgusting on his favorite shirt."

Seamus brushed Phoebe's soft cheek with his finger. "Then there's Uncle Conlan. He'd die to protect her, but is terrified by the thought of changing her diapers."

"He caught me nursing her once. I've never seen a chancellor turn that particular shade of bright red before." Megan sipped her tea. "Look, she's already asleep."

"I'll go put her down in the crib."

He slowly stood up and carried Phoebe into the small bedroom that Megan had made into a nursery. The baby stirred slightly and then settled back to sleep. He covered her with a blanket and gently patted her on the back. Not for the first time he realized how much he wished he could lay claim to her.

Banan Delaney was a fool for throwing all this away.

Megan was waiting out in the hallway. He supposed he should head back to his place. Dawn was a little over an hour away. As much as he'd like to stay longer, he couldn't risk being trapped here by the sun.

"Well, I should go. Thank you again for being there for me tonight."

"I had a good time. How does it feel to be officially Dr. Seamus Fitzhugh? I'm so pleased for you." Megan opened the door and stepped outside with him. "Does it seem real yet?"

"Not as real as this does."

He tugged her into his arms and kissed her. She smiled against his lips, teasing him with little forays with her tongue over the points of his fangs as they dropped down.

The sensation was exquisite, making him wish they had hours and hours instead of mere seconds. "You have no idea how much I've been wanting to do this all evening."

He nuzzled her neck, allowing himself the privilege of nipping at her throat right where her blood pulsed closest to the surface. She bent her neck to the side, offering him easier access and encouraging him to continue with a soft moan.

Finally, he stopped for the simple reason he had to, now, before it was too late. With her scent and the heat of her blood driving him crazy, he had to walk away or he'd end up taking both her body and her blood right there up against the door. Or maybe in the cool grass at their feet. Either way, she deserved better.

He rested his chin on top of her head as he struggled to regain control. From the bruising hold she had on his shoulders, she was skirting the edge of control as much as he was.

"I'm going to walk away now, but not because I want to." It took him several more seconds to remember how to actually let go of her and step back. "Your kisses should require a warning label, woman."

When he let go of her, she leaned back against the doorway. "I'll take that as a compliment."

"It was meant as one."

"Um, Seamus, I was wondering. Would you like to have dinner together tomorrow night after we get off work? I know emergencies might interfere, so I understand any plans we make have to be flexible."

"You're a mind reader, Megan. I'd love to have you for dinner." He rolled his eyes. "Okay, that came out wrong."

She giggled, her light-colored eyes gleaming in the moonlight. "Yes, it did. I was talking about a meal with real food."

"Let me try that again. I'd love to have dinner *with* you. At my place."

"Great. I'll see you tomorrow night." She slipped back inside, but before she closed the door, she whispered, "But if you play your cards right, you can have me afterward."

He all but flew home. The sooner he got to bed, the sooner tomorrow would arrive. The whole way, her whispered promise played over and over in his head. Was it too soon to be counting down the hours until he could coax Megan into his bed? Probably, but that didn't stop him.

"So tell me, how does my leg look?"

Rafferty hobbled over to peer over Seamus's shoulder at the X-rays backlit on the screen. Seamus let his patient look his fill. Finally, he turned off the switch, letting the stark black-and-white film go dark.

"Hop back up on the table. I want to check a few things." He kept his expression suitably somber, not wanting to give away anything too soon.

"Why? What did you see?" Rafferty pushed himself back up on the examining table and set his crutches aside. "It looked good to me."

"If you've had experience reading X-rays, why do you need me?" Seamus supported Rafferty's lower leg and helped him flex his knee and ankle. "Does that hurt?"

When the vampire hesitated, Seamus gave him a stern look. "Don't try lying about it. I'll know."

"Okay, fine." He shifted restlessly, probably trying to gauge how much he could get by with.

"I'm not Joss, Rafferty. No need to act invincible in front of me."

His boss grinned. "It doesn't work with her, either. She sees right through the bullshit."

Rafferty drew a sharp breath and winced when Seamus poked and prodded at the damaged muscles. "I can tell you this much—I'm tired of being treated like an invalid. But it hurts when I stand too long, it aches enough to keep me awake and I get tired easily. If I didn't know better, I think I was getting old."

Seamus rolled his eyes. "All normal symptoms. Considering how bad it was, it's healing way better than expected. If you'll take it easy for another week, you should be moving a lot better and able to terrorize everybody again."

Seamus picked up the crutches and stuck them back in the supply cabinet and replaced them with a cane. "Give that a try."

"Really?"

Rafferty immediately stood up on his good foot and gingerly put more weight on the broken leg. Taking the cane in hand, he hobbled back and forth across the small examination room. Seamus made a couple of suggestions to improve his patient's gait and stood back out of the way while he practiced.

"Okay, I'm going to let you go home with that instead of crutches. Your wife has agreed to snitch on you if you abuse the privilege."

"Thanks a lot, Seamus. As if she wasn't already hovering enough to drive me crazy."

"Behave, and she won't have to. You can't expect to be over an accident that bad this quickly. You need to keep feeding more than usual because your body needs it to heal."

"Anything it takes to get me back to normal."

As they walked out, Seamus asked, "Did Conlan ever find out what happened to cause the accident?"

Rafferty's expression turned stone-cold. "Someone messed with both the brakes and the accelerator."

"Any idea who'd do something that stupid?"

"Someone with a grudge against me—or Joss. We both use that vehicle."

Rafferty kept his eyes focused straight ahead, making Seamus wonder if his boss thought that someone might be him. He felt compelled to defend himself.

"I was with Megan from late afternoon that day until they carried you in."

They'd reached the front door. The waiting room was empty since Rafferty had been Seamus's last patient for the day. He unlocked the door and held it open.

"I wasn't accusing you of anything, Seamus."

"Maybe not, but it needed saying. We both know I definitely had an axe to grind. The thought had to cross your mind."

"Well, I won't lie about that, but I dismissed it out of hand. I'm thinking it was more likely a parting gift from Banan Delaney. Conlan would love to have that jerk alone for ten minutes behind a soundproof door. Then we'd know for sure."

"It sounds like something that bastard would do. But either way, thanks for the vote of confidence."

"Confidence had nothing to do with it. I figured when you made up your mind to come after me, you'd make sure I knew it was you taking me down and why. It's what I would do if the positions were reversed. This attack was more Banan's speed—sneaky and cowardly."

"I'm not sure whether to be flattered or insulted."

"Maybe a little of both." Rafferty laughed. He walked toward where Joss waited to drive him home, showing off his new skill with the cane.

Seamus watched until Rafferty made it all the way to the transport without mishap before closing the door and turning off the outside lights. As long as nothing new happened, the vampire was well on his way to being back to a hundred percent.

Right now, Seamus had something far more urgent to attend to, or actually someone. Megan. She was already waiting for him in his apartment. He sniffed the air in the hallway. Hmm.

She wasn't the only hot thing in his kitchen. Whatever she was cooking smelled delicious.

And so did she. Would it be rude to risk letting dinner burn by coaxing her into his bed before they actually ate? Probably. Oh, well, he'd waited this long. He supposed he could hang on for a while yet, but waiting wasn't the only thing that was hard. He'd had that problem all day long every time his thoughts had strayed in her direction, which had been way too often for the good of his sanity.

Did she have any idea how good it felt to know she was waiting for him?

He stepped through the door and closed it behind him, shutting out the rest of the world. Barring blood and broken bones, nothing and no one better interrupt his plans for the evening.

"Hi. I'm in here."

He followed Megan's voice into the kitchen where she was stirring something on the stove.

"How's Rafferty?"

"About as happy as you can expect a big, tough vampire to be when he's hurting. I let him graduate to a cane, though, so that helped improve his mood some."

"Poor Joss! He can't be fun to live with right now."

"Yeah, well, she knew what he was like when

she married him. He's among the most powerful of our kind, but almost dying from something as simple as a transport accident was a real shock to his system."

He paused, thinking about what Rafferty had told him. "Actually it wasn't an accident at all. Someone messed with the brakes and the accelerator."

Megan gasped in shock. "Who would do such a thing?"

"Rafferty figures someone with a grudge against him or Joss—like me, for instance."

She went from concerned to furious in a heartbeat. "He can't possibly believe that's true! You would never do such a cowardly thing."

"Actually, Rafferty agrees with you. Besides, the night it happened I was with you."

He eased up behind her and slid his hand around her waist, moving slowly so as not to startle her while she was so close to the burner on the stove. "As I recall, you kept me pretty busy, both before and after the clinic closed."

He lifted her hair to the side so he could kiss her neck, liking the way she shivered in response. Then he traced the shape of her ear with the tip of his tongue. "The after part was my favorite."

"Keep that up and I'll never finish cooking dinner."

He looked over her shoulder to see what was simmering in the pot. "That smells good. You smell better. Delicious, in fact."

She giggled as he resumed what he'd been doing. Finally, it dawned on him that he hadn't seen the baby. He looked out toward the living room.

"Where's Phoebe?"

Megan leaned back against him and looked up at him over her shoulder. "Seems Aunt Joss wanted to babysit for a few hours. I'm supposed to pick Phoebe up on my way home. You know, sometime around dawn."

Her pretty eyes grew heavy-lidded with promise. "We have almost six uninterrupted hours to linger over dinner…and dessert."

All of his blood rushed south—again. "Perfect. How soon can we eat?"

"In big a hurry, are you?"

He let his hands do a little wandering. "Dessert's my favorite part of the meal, and I've been thinking about it ever since I walked you home last night. I want to make sure we have plenty of time to do any of that lingering you mentioned."

"I thought you might feel that way. Hand me those bowls and I'll get dinner on the table."

"I can't wait."

Chapter 13

Megan refused to be hurried. Yes, they were headed toward Seamus's bed—or maybe his couch, because that was fun, too. But moments like this should be savored, not rushed. Even if it was becoming increasingly difficult to not grab Seamus and drag him to the floor.

But tasting his passion would come soon enough. She'd spent hours putting this meal together, pulling out all the stops. Not that she felt the need to impress Seamus with her culinary skills, but this meal, this night and this man mattered.

Finally, she brought out the dessert, a personal favorite, a light confection of whipped cream and fresh berries. Nothing too heavy, but luscious and bursting with flavor. Seamus's eyes widened at the sight.

"I wasn't kidding about loving dessert," he said as he eyed the bowl she set down between them. "But why only one spoon?"

She scooped up a bite and held it up to his mouth. "I thought we could share."

If his eyes had been caressing her with hot looks before, the temperature simmering between them ramped up geometrically as he accepted the sweet offering. When she leaned in close and licked the small bit of whipped cream off the corner of his mouth, his fangs ran out to full length. That pleased her. He took the spoon and followed her in the dance, gently feeding her a plump berry smothered in cream.

And that pleased her even more.

"How can something so cool make me so hot?" His voice had dropped low, gravelly thick with the promise of what was to come.

And, please God, soon.

Seamus studied her face as he fed her another bite. The berries filled her mouth with a burst of bright flavor.

"This is wonderful, but I'm ready for our real dessert." He set the spoon aside, calmly picked up the rest of their berries and cream and set it in the refrigerator.

How could he think of such mundane details when she was about to melt into a puddle of need right there on the kitchen table? Then he held out his hand for hers, tugging her to feet. She'd thought he was going to kiss her, but instead he led her out of the kitchen, right past the living room and into his bedroom.

"You cannot imagine how much I've been thinking about this moment, Megan."

When he reached out to cup the side of her face, she turned to kiss his palm, tasting the slightly rough surface of his skin with the tip of her tongue. He groaned and brushed his thumb across her lips.

"I want to take this slow, to make it good for you, but I'm afraid my control is a bit shaky right now."

She loved having that much power over him, to know that her kiss and her touch were enough to bring him to his knees. Which she just had. Literally. He knelt in front of her, laying his face against her stomach as his hands swept up the backs of her legs from ankles straight past the hem of her dress and on up to cup her bottom.

Her bones melted. She slowly sank down, straddling his lap as she lowered her mouth to his. As she tongued his fangs, he freed up his hands to start stripping away the layers of clothing that separated them. Her sweater was the first to go, followed by her bra. He paused in his quest long enough to pay homage to her breasts with his lips and tongue and teeth.

Her turn. She unbuttoned his shirt, taking her time, drawing out the process to torment him, only to realize that she was torturing herself at the same time. Finally, he muscled them both back up off the floor in an impressive display of his vampire strength.

"I need your skin against mine. Please."

She'd never deny such a simple request. No other man had ever looked at her with such stark hunger. Stepping back, she quickly finished the job he'd started, letting him look his fill when she stood before him, wearing nothing more than the smile on her face.

"Your turn."

He immediately toed off his shoes, but she pushed his hands out of the way when he reached for the button on his jeans.

"Let me."

She eased the zipper down slowly, too slowly, given the impatient expression on her lover's face. But he didn't complain at all when she removed his boxers at the same time as she stripped the denim down the long length of his legs. In seconds, all was revealed for her viewing pleasure.

All those lean muscles and supple strength drew her like no other lover ever had. She closed the distance between them, taking her time, feeling his heat long before she actually felt the rough slide of his skin against hers. His hands eased her firmly against him, leaving no doubt about how much he wanted her.

"Kiss me, Megan."

He tasted of whipped cream and berries. His tongue enticed hers to join in swirling play as his arms wrapped around her, gentle bands of steel that lifted her up enough that his erection slid between her legs. He rocked against her core; the slight friction had her wanting so much more.

She raised her right leg, wrapping it around his and opening herself up to more of the same. He murmured his approval, but made no effort to take them to the next stage.

As much as she loved his foreplay, it also frustrated her. Finally, she pulled away and gave him a hard shove, sending him sprawling back onto the bed.

His smile promised swift retribution. Perfect. It was just what she wanted.

* * *

He liked Megan's playful side and that she wasn't at all shy about what she wanted. What she hadn't taken into account was a male vampire's dominant nature. He was willing to let her have her way with him—up to a point. He wanted to make a few demands of his own, and that moment had arrived.

He remained motionless, waiting for his lady to join him on the bed. She crawled up on the bed, prowling closer, her fangs showing as she made her approach. When he pounced, she was too startled to do more than let out a short squeak before he'd flipped her onto her stomach. He stretched out on top of her, careful not to crush her, but letting her know that this was how it was going to be.

She immediately bent her head to the side, offering herself up to him. Oh, yes, this was going to be good. He nipped at the nape of her neck and rocked against the sweet curve of her backside.

He'd never had a woman all but purr before, but Megan thrummed with pleasure as he let her feel the length of both his cock and fangs. Her scent filled the air as she arched up against him.

With one hard thrust he took her, giving her

slick heat only seconds to adjust to the sudden invasion before he started moving fast and hard. She chanted his name in counterpoint to the rhythm he established, making him hunger for far more than the spiraling tension between the give-and-take of their bodies.

Finally, when he couldn't wait another heartbeat, he sank his fangs into the rich flavor of her vein. As he drank deeply, she screamed in release, her body convulsing under his. He paused long enough to give her a small window of relief before once again driving her up and up. Suddenly, there was no sense of time or space, just the pounding of two hearts and two bodies, until in a moment of perfect accord, they shattered in a kaleidoscope of colors and sensations.

Seamus wasn't sure he'd actually survived the experience, but at the moment, he was okay with that.

"Wow." Megan reached back to touch his face. "That was amazing. Or maybe incredible. Or both."

He kept his face nestled in her hair, his arm around her waist as they lay spooned in the bed. "I'd say let's try that again, but it might be a while before I can. I'm pretty sure more than just my brain got fried."

When she giggled, he felt the vibration through his entire body. To his surprise, a certain part of his anatomy immediately stirred back to life. He cuddled closer to share the good news with Megan.

She instantly rolled over to face him, a huge smile on her face. "Hey, is that for me?"

"I do believe it is."

"Perfect."

And he did his best to make sure it was.

Seamus opened the driver's door for Megan, reluctant to watch her drive away after the hours they'd spent together.

"Can I ride as far as Rafferty's with you? I'll go on my nightly run from there."

Her eyes lit up. "Sure, but haven't you had enough exercise for one night?"

He climbed in the other side. "Well, I could be trying to impress you with my incredible stamina…or I can admit that I just wanted an excuse to stay with you for a few more minutes."

"Good answers—both of them."

As she steered the transport away from the curb, the headlights hit the trees across the field that backed up on the clinic. For a second there he thought he spotted someone just inside the treeline. "Can you slow down for a second, Megan?"

"Sure. Is something wrong?"

He studied the woods, but whatever he'd seen—or thought he'd seen—was gone now. "No, everything is fine. I thought I spotted someone cutting across country toward the infirmary. I didn't want to take off if someone needed me. We can go now."

As Megan hit the accelerator, he looked back one more time. Still nothing, but he had the strangest sensation that someone had been there, someone who hadn't wanted to be seen. But until he could verify his suspicions, he didn't want to worry Megan.

He'd take a slightly different route on his run and check out that stand of trees. If no one had been there, fine. Maybe his imagination was working overtime. But if someone really had been watching them from the safety of the deep shadows, the real questions were why and, more important, who?

He wasn't worried about himself, but damned if he'd put up with any more threats to Megan and her daughter.

Megan tapped him on the shoulder. "You're looking pretty fierce there."

He'd been so lost in thought that he hadn't

noticed they'd already arrived at Rafferty's house. They both climbed out of the transport, and he looked at her over the roof. "Sorry. I was just thinking maybe that run home was going to be harder than I thought."

She walked around to his side. "I can always drop you back at your place on my way home."

He wrapped his arms around her, pulling her in close. "No, that's okay. I need the exercise. Besides, I've got reasons to keep up my strength."

"Really? And what might those be?"

"Nights like this one." When he kissed her, the flames they'd carefully banked before leaving his apartment threatened to overwhelm them again. Breaking off that kiss and stepping away was one of the most difficult things he'd ever had to do.

"If I don't walk away now, we're going to put on quite a show for Rafferty and his neighbors. Hug Phoebe for me."

Megan's face was flushed, her lips swollen and so kissable. "I will. I'll see you at work tonight."

"And after?" He hadn't planned on pressing her, but he found he couldn't leave without knowing.

"And after. Now go. The sun will be up before too long."

"I'm on my way."

But he jogged backward until she reached Rafferty's front door safely. Then he took off at a full-out run toward the trees. The last time someone was sneaking around back there, it had been Banan. Since he was gone, most likely it was one of Rafferty's employees with a legitimate reason for being there. But all things considered, he'd sleep better knowing that for certain.

Banan wallowed in the human's blood: his fangs, his fingers and his face dripped with the stuff. He licked a few drops off his hands, savoring the rich flavor. It would be a hell of a mess to clean up, but at the moment he didn't give a damn. It was just a shame that he'd had to take his temper out on this human weakling instead of Seamus Fitzhugh or Megan Perez. Even Rafferty O'Day and that bitch wife of his would've provided more entertainment. Humans simply lacked the stamina for this kind of dance.

Eventually his enemies' time would come. Until then, he'd have to make do. At least the human he'd caught had been female, which meant she'd been good for more than her vein. If he hadn't seen Megan Perez walking out of that medic's place, he would have been satisfied with bedding the human and then draining her dry, offering her nothing but pleasure until the instant she realized he wasn't going to stop. That she'd suffered was not his fault. No, that blame belonged to Seamus Fitzhugh for daring to touch what belonged to Banan.

Even from the far side of the field, Megan's body language had been all too easy to read. She had bedded that damn vampire, no doubt about it. The truth was written in the way Seamus stood a little too close to her as well as in the easy touches.

If dawn wasn't so close, he'd wait for Megan to arrive back at her cottage and teach her a painful—and definitely fatal—lesson about betraying him. How sweet it would be to dump her bloody and abused body on Rafferty's front doorstep. Or better yet, the medic's. Let him explain how his lover had ended up dead, her throat ripped out by vampire fangs.

But right now, Banan would dump his substitute date in the creek and then wash up before getting dressed. The water would wash away all trace of his scent. How long would it be before someone found her? He wished he could risk being close enough to watch the security officer's investigation.

The cause of death would be painfully obvious: death by vampire. A chancellor could rip out a throat, but wouldn't have drained the blood. The only real question was which vampire would Conlan suspect first?

It was probably too much to hope that he'd blame Rafferty, although there was no love lost between the two. Conlan seemed to like Seamus a little too much for him to be the leading suspect. Eventually, though, as the attacks continued, Conlan would have to consider them both.

Once they were all spinning in circles and pointing fingers at each other, Banan would find a way to make all the evidence lead straight to one of the two. He was having too much fun envisioning the various possibilities to decide which it would be.

Playing God with lives was a lot of fun and good practice for when he took over the Delaney clan. Things were definitely looking up. He picked up the body and headed for the creek. Then it would be time to get back to the pickup point. He couldn't wait to crawl into his tent and dream of great times to come.

Seamus normally started off his nightly runs at an easy pace, only picking up speed when his muscles were warmed up and stretched out. However, acutely aware that Megan might be watching, he couldn't help but strut his stuff a bit. He might pay for it later, but after all, a vampire had his pride.

He turned off the road to cut across country, preferring the open spaces where he could more easily lose himself in the waning hours of the night. He loved the quiet peace of these last moments of darkness when daybreak hovered just out of sight over the horizon. However, tonight he had little time to dawdle if he wanted to check out the trees for any proof that someone had been lurking there.

A few humans were already stirring in their homes, lights slowly coming on as they started their days. Because of the human affinity for sunlight, they were the ones who did most of the manual labor on an estate like Rafferty's, especially out in the fields. Seamus gave Rafferty credit for treating his workers a lot better than other high-ranking vampires did. He valued them as individuals, not just for their muscles and their blood.

Sure, there were drawbacks to living on the O'Day estate, its distance from any other center of civilization being chief among them. However, his progressive attitudes and an offer of a new start left O'Day with no shortage of applicants.

Seamus's role as the sole health-care provider had already brought him into contact with a fair number of the estate's residents from all three species. As usual, the humans outnumbered the other two combined. Most of Conlan's security people were chancellors, which only made sense. To police any given population, you needed staff who could be out in daylight and were strong enough to handle any problem vampires.

He circled back the way he'd come before heading into the trees. A steady wind had come up, making it doubtful he'd be able to pick up any scents. He slowed to a walk as he entered the copse, quieting his own breathing in order to hear better. Other than the rustling of the leaves, the woods were quiet.

He was alone as far as he could tell. Moving from tree to tree, he studied the ground although it was hard to pick out many details even with his superior night vision. A broken twig here, a crushed leaf there, but nothing that said definitively that someone had been there recently.

Even so, his own predatory nature insisted that someone had been there. What he didn't know was who or why, and he didn't like that, not one damned bit.

It was too late for him to do any more checking, but he could contact Conlan and ask him to take a look around while the sun was up. Maybe he'd pick up on something Seamus had missed. Having done all he could for the night, he walked across the field to the infirmary.

Thanks to the specialized training he'd had in medical school, normally he could function for extended periods of time when the sun was up. But after the night he'd had, he needed to seek out his bed. Once he had some hours of sleep under his belt, he'd contact Conlan before it was time for Megan to arrive. There was no use in worrying her unnecessarily. At least she'd already agreed to spend the hours after work with him. He'd keep her safe—and occupied—until dawn.

Yep, it was shaping up to be another busy day—and night.

Dreams for vampires were rare, especially ones as peaceful as this one was. Seamus smiled at the pastoral scene before him and started down the hillside toward the woman waiting for him at the bottom. Megan waved at him, a bright smile lighting up her pretty face.

Before he'd gone three steps, a rough hand clamped down on his shoulder from behind, preventing Seamus from being able to reach Megan. With a simple touch, his dream went from fine to furious. He struck out, ready to take no prisoners to keep the woman he loved safe. Wait? What had his dream-self said? The woman he loved? Was that right? At least here in his dreams, it was true. But what about when he was awake?

Then the jolt of landing a solid punch jerked him out of his dreamworld and dropped him right in the middle of a painful reality. He came up fighting.

"Seamus, damn it, quit swinging! It's me, Conlan. I'm getting damned tired of being used as a punching bag by you."

Conlan? What the hell was he doing in Seamus's dream? No, wait, he was awake now. So make that, what the hell was Conlan doing in his bedroom? Seamus forced his eyes open and glared at the chancellor, who'd wisely put the width of the room between them.

The clock on the dresser said it was still daylight outside, so for the second time the security officer was waking him up to deal with a crisis. It wouldn't be the last, but they definitely needed to lay down some ground rules before one of them got hurt. He sat up on the edge of the bed and waited for the cobwebs to clear or the chancellor to explain himself, whichever came first.

He glared at the security officer. "I understand that you need my services, but next time, call me. I usually don't punch a phone."

"Thanks for the heads-up. Maybe I'll just poke you with a long stick, but for now, get your ass out of bed. I need you. I'll wait for you out in the clinic." Conlan started out the door, but stopped briefly. "And, Seamus, don't make me wait long."

Seamus quickly pulled on yesterday's shirt and jeans. What had the chancellor's tail in a twist? If it were a medical emergency, wouldn't he have said so? Instead, the chancellor had just looked grimmer than usual. Only one way to find out.

More curious than worried, he left his quarters and headed toward the light pouring out of the closest room. To his surprise, Conlan wasn't alone. Rafferty stood with his back to the door, looming over someone stretched out on the exam table. Seamus's nostrils flared wide as he stuttered to a stop just inside the doorway.

The odor of death easily overpowered the heavy medicinal smell that usually permeated the clinic. That explained why Conlan and

Rafferty were both there as well as the high level of tension in the room.

He moved to the far side of the table and studied the still form outlined by the opaque plastic sheeting that shrouded the body. Feminine for certain, but that was the only thing to be learned at first glance.

"Who is she and what happened to her?"

Rafferty's furious eyes snapped up to meet his, the length of his fangs and the deep lines bracketing his mouth only underscoring the high emotions that thrummed in the room. "Why don't you tell me, Dr. Fitzhugh?"

Okay, so that's how it was going to be.

Before Seamus could pull back the plastic to reveal the body, Conlan blocked him. "Do you have any forensic experience?"

"Only what little they showed all of us in school. I'm a surgeon, not a forensic pathologist."

He tugged harder on the plastic. "However, I'm the closest to it you've got. I'm guessing since you're asking the question at all, this woman was a victim of a crime, not an accident."

Rafferty moved closer to the head of the table and pulled back the sheet himself. "Her name was Maggie Travis."

Seamus hissed when he saw what was left of her throat. "Who did this?"

Conlan ignored the question to ask one of his own. "Vampire or chancellor?"

"I'll need to take a closer look. I'll be right back."

He went next door to the operating suite and picked up a tray of sterile instruments and his surgical telescopic headgear that would allow him to scan the wounds and flash them up on the computer screen. Not that he had any doubts that a vampire had played long and hard with this poor female. Yes, a chancellor's fangs were capable of inflicting that same damage to her throat, but she'd been drained of blood.

However, he'd follow the protocols as he remembered them from school. Preserving the evidence had to take priority, to make sure that a case could be made against the guilty party once Conlan hunted the bastard down.

He slipped on the surgical goggles. After he adjusted the focus, he turned on his voice recorder. Leaning in close, he studied the wounds, starting with her head and working his way down her body. He noted each wound, each bruise, each violation. Then he repeated the journey, this time with a digital camera. He was dimly aware that both Rafferty and Conlan kept their eyes averted from the body, preferring to watch the computer monitor.

He didn't blame them, knowing it would allow them some small emotional distance from the horrific wounds. Whoever had done this had done more than play with his food, resulting in her accidental death. Although Seamus was no expert, it was obvious the vampire in question had deliberately set out to inflict pain, terror and death, but had at some point lost control. This woman had suffered greatly, and she would have embraced death as a blessed release from the horror of her last few hours of life.

Once he'd completed his examination, he quickly summarized his impressions, keeping his voice neutral, professional, his comments succinct. Then he clicked off the recorder, calmly set his surgical goggles aside and left the room. Out in the lobby, he calmly picked up the closest chair high over his head and heaved it against the wall with a resounding crash, putting all of his vampire strength and rage into the effort.

Breathing heavily, he studied the hole in the wall and the heap of broken wood and torn fabric on the ground. It wasn't enough, not nearly enough to vent the fury churning his gut. He started to reach for another chair, but destroying a room full of innocent furniture wouldn't do a damn thing to help that poor woman.

No, what he wanted, needed was to wrap his hands around the guilty party's neck and slowly, slowly choke the life out of the sadistic bastard. And that only after he'd ripped into his arteries to let his blood pulse out onto the ground.

"Remind me not to piss you off anytime soon." Conlan eased up beside him, but Seamus noticed he was careful not to touch him. The chancellor bent down to pick up the broken chair leg. "I didn't see that coming."

"Why? Because I did my job in there?" Seamus growled, his voice thick with anger. "My impressions and descriptions may make the difference in a conviction. I don't want the son of a bitch that did that to get off because we didn't preserve the evidence correctly."

"Thanks. You might not have forensic training, but you did a hell of a job in there." He studied Seamus's expression. "Are you up for answering some questions now?"

"What kind of questions?"

"The same ones we'll be asking all of the vampires on the estate." Rafferty had joined the party. "He needs to know where you were this morning, right before dawn."

Okay, so they needed to do this. That didn't

mean he had to like it. "I was with Megan right up until she dropped me off in front of your place. From there, I took my nightly run."

"Did you come straight back here?"

Not exactly, but how would it sound if he mentioned his suspicion that someone had been out in the woods? However, the truth was still the better route. Lies tended to come back and bite you on the ass.

"When Megan and I were leaving the clinic, I thought I saw someone standing at the edge of the woods across the field out back. I asked Megan to slow down in case it was someone who might be looking for me. But the next time I looked, there was no one there. I decided to swing through the woods on my way back home to check things out. Either way, I was going to call Conlan this morning to have a look around in the daylight."

Conlan was frowning. "Why didn't you call me when it happened?"

"Because it didn't seem like an emergency and I was tired." He still was. "As I was running, I noticed the lights were on in several of the human quarters I passed. I know some of the farm workers head out pretty early, so I figured it was probably a human on his way to work."

Time for a few questions of his own. "Were

you able to narrow down the time of death for Ms. Travis?"

"Near as we can figure, it happened somewhere between three and six this morning. She works the late shift at the dining hall. Her boss said she left a little later than usual to help cover for someone who called in sick. Normally she walks home with a group, but obviously that didn't happen. The last time anyone saw her was when she left work a little after three.

There was real grief in Conlan's voice. "Her family knew she was working late and so didn't get suspicious until close to sunrise. That's when they called me, but some workers had already found the body in the creek before I could get here. At least they had the good sense to back off and wait for me to supervise retrieving the body. My men are out there now combing the area for evidence."

"She was found in the creek? Damn it, I should have guessed that she'd been submerged in water from the lack of blood in the wounds and no scent other than her own." Seamus walked back into the examination room with the other two trailing behind.

"What are you going to do now?"

"I'm going to swab all the wounds to see if we can find any trace evidence. If she wasn't in the water all that long, there's a chance the deeper wounds weren't washed completely clean."

Conlan joined him beside the body. "Those tests take time, and we need answers now. They're also expensive."

Seamus put on a fresh set of gloves. "So what's it to be, Rafferty?"

To give the vampire credit, he didn't hesitate. "Do it. I want my people to know that I'm more concerned about justice than I am the expense. Tell me what I can do to help."

"Use the computer in Megan's office to print out labels with the victim's name, the date and the case number, if there is one. Conlan and I will get the supplies together. Once we're done, we'll all three sign off on when and where the specimens were collected."

"Good thinking. The better job we do in collecting evidence, the better the chance we'll get the death penalty when this case goes to trial."

"So you think we'll catch him?" Seamus asked as he laid out swabs and transport media, along with a scalpel to take scrapings from under her nails.

"If Banan was still here, I'd be hauling his ass in for a long talk. However, I followed up to make sure he really did return to New Eire.

He's still racking up charges at the hotel. Too bad."

Conlan ran his fingers through his hair in frustration. "This whole mess just feels like something he'd do, but since he's out of the picture, we'll have to look closer to home. We pretty much have a captive population, and I'll know if someone tries to leave. It will be a process of elimination after we finish tracking everyone's movements."

A shadow passed over Seamus's soul. What if the vampire in question had managed to hide his movements? Would that leave Seamus the only one with time unaccounted for? Logically, of course, the point could be made that he'd be unlikely to help collect evidence to convict himself. But if he'd refused, they would have already slapped him in chains or worse.

All he could do was hope the evidence pointed out who the real killer was.

Chapter 14

Megan answered the unexpected knock on the door to find her cousin standing there. Joss was clearly agitated, looking both upset and angry.

"Joss, come on in. What's wrong?"

"There's been a death on the estate." Her cousin headed straight for the kitchen.

"Who was it?"

Joss sat down and dropped her head down on her folded arms on top of the table.

"Catch your breath while I put the kettle on to boil."

Considering Joss's background in investigative work, whatever had happened had to have been bad to leave her so upset. Either that, or it was someone who'd been close to her.

A few minutes later, Megan poured each of them a steaming mug of her favorite herbal tea. "Do you want sugar or honey?"

Joss finally lifted her head. "A big dose of honey sounds perfect."

Megan sat down next to Joss with Phoebe in her lap. She'd give Joss all the time she needed to gather her thoughts.

Finally, Joss drew a shaky breath and started talking. "Conlan is investigating a murder that happened near here on the estate. Our first."

Joss's expression was bleak. "One of our human workers, a young female, was brutally tortured and killed this morning right before dawn. Whoever did it brutalized her and then dumped the body in the creek on the far side of the woods that backs up on the field behind the infirmary."

Megan had a bad feeling about where this was going. "Do they know who did it?"

"A vampire, although that's as much as Seamus and Conlan could tell. The creek washed away most of the blood and the scent of her attacker." Joss cradled her mug in both hands, no doubt finding the warmth soothing.

"We have to be careful about assigning blame

until all the evidence is in. But frankly, there aren't that many pureblooded vampires living on the estate."

"And it couldn't have been a chancellor?" Not that there were all that many of them, either.

Joss shook her head. "Not likely. Rafferty said the physical damage could have been done by a chancellor, but the body was drained of blood. That makes it far more probable that a vampire is responsible."

"That poor girl! Can we do anything to help the family?"

"We'll know more when Rafferty sees them after the sun goes down. He was out with Conlan in the early morning, but I made him go home and get some rest."

She took a long sip of her tea before continuing. "After they talk to her folks, he wants to accompany Conlan as he interviews the rest of the resident vampires about where they were this morning."

After setting the cup back down, Joss held out her hands toward Phoebe, who immediately dove straight for her. "Seamus helped with the initial examination of the body. I know Conlan and Rafferty were impressed by how well he did, especially since forensics isn't his specialty."

"At least Seamus is in the clear."

When Joss didn't immediately concur, Megan frowned. "He is, isn't he? In the clear?"

"No one is yet, even though they don't want to suspect him."

Okay, that wasn't a clear-cut yes or no. "He was with me last night, Joss, right up until I arrived at your place to pick up Phoebe."

"But was he with you *all* night? Every minute?"

This was getting way too personal. But she wouldn't let them accuse Seamus of something he didn't do in order to save herself a little embarrassment.

"We were together from the time clinic closed until we got dressed again so I could pick up Phoebe. Is that blunt enough for you?" She knew she sounded defensive, but it shouldn't be anyone's business how she and Seamus had spent their time together.

Joss stared down at Phoebe, letting the baby play with her fingers. "I'll pass that along to Conlan, but that still doesn't account for the time after he left you at our place. The closest they can pin down the time of her death is shortly before dawn."

"Seamus isn't a killer, Joss. He'd never even

consider doing something so awful, much less carry it out."

She hated—*hated*—the sympathetic look Joss gave her, as if her cousin knew something that Megan didn't, something that would change how she thought about Seamus.

"What is it, Joss?" Not that she'd believe it for one instant.

"It's not for me to say. But the next time you see Seamus, ask him why of all the places in the Coalition he could have looked for work, he chose this one." Joss finished her tea.

"Why can't you tell me?"

"It's not my story to tell. Ask him." She kissed Phoebe's chubby cheek. "Look, I've got to go. Rafferty may need my help with any arrangements that have to be made."

Megan let Joss out. As her cousin drove away, she had to wonder what Joss's real purpose in stopping by had been. Maybe she had needed a break or someone to talk to. But if so, why plant the seeds of distrust between Megan and Seamus? What had happened in his past that would lead them to even suspect him in the first place?

Now that she thought about it, though, he'd been pretty closemouthed about his past. All she knew was that he'd had some problem getting his final credentials from medical school, but not really why. Rafferty had intervened to make sure Seamus had a choice of where and how he lived. All of that made sense, but obviously there was far more to the story than she'd been told.

There was only one way to find out. She'd go into work early and see if she could get answers to her questions. If he was too busy, then afterward they'd talk.

Seamus was at his desk when she arrived. Rather than disturb him, she quietly slipped into her own office and settled Phoebe into her crib before booting up the computer. Although she'd rehearsed her opening lines over and over, she still wasn't ready to face Seamus. No matter how she phrased her questions, it came out sounding like an accusation.

But if their relationship was going to last, truth and honesty had to play a major role. After her experience with Banan, she had zero tolerance for lies or secrecy. Finally, she forced herself to confront him.

She froze in his doorway, neither in nor out, waiting for him to notice her. Finally, he looked up, a smile spreading across his face.

"You're early, not that I'm complaining."

He immediately came around the desk to kiss her. Twenty-four hours ago, she would have welcomed the embrace, but she turned her face at the last second so that his kiss landed on her cheek and kept her arms down at her sides. Always perceptive, he frowned.

"Megan? What's wrong?" He studied her expression, his eyebrows drawn down low. "Have I done something to upset you?"

"No, but I heard about what happened this morning, and it's freaked me out a bit. Are you all right?"

He seemed to accept her explanation and stepped back to give her some space. "It certainly wasn't fun examining the body, but it was necessary. I'm furious that someone would do such a thing and worried because there's a killer loose on the estate."

"Joss said a vampire was responsible."

"Yes, that was our conclusion, although I'm sure Conlan would prefer that I not discuss the case in any detail."

Seamus poured himself a cup of coffee, looking even more grim. "However, since Joss has already told you that much, I don't suppose it will hurt. We just don't want to release many details while Conlan investigates and builds a case."

"And it definitely wasn't a chancellor?"

"Not with the way the body was drained. It's doubtful a chancellor could've been quite so thorough."

"Are there any new vampires on the estate?"

Seamus shook his head. "No, not since Conlan escorted Banan off the property. That's what has Rafferty so upset. The few who do live here are all long-term friends of his."

Except Seamus. Before she could point that out, he did.

"With the exception of me, I guess. Rafferty and I have a past, and not one based on either trust or friendship."

"If that's how you feel about him, why did you pick his estate when you needed a job? Especially if you don't trust each other."

For the first time, there was a definite flash of temper in Seamus's eyes. "We've been working on changing that. But out of curiosity, what kind of tales has Joss been telling you about me, Megan?"

Okay, so now she felt guilty for talking about Seamus behind his back. But didn't she have a right to know exactly what kind of man she was sleeping with?

"She didn't tell me anything other than suggest I ask you why you ended up here and not some other place, especially considering how you felt about her husband."

The office was closing in on her as she waited for him to respond. She backed out of the room without waiting to see if Seamus would follow or bother to answer. If he had nothing to hide, it shouldn't matter. But since silence rather than an explanation hung in the air between them, it was obviously a big deal.

She had to get away. "Never mind. It's almost time to open the clinic. Forget I even asked."

After retreating into her office, she slammed the door shut, startling her daughter out of a sound sleep. As Megan comforted her baby, she realized Phoebe wasn't the only one in the room with tears running down her face.

A few seconds later, Seamus walked in without even bothering to knock. His expression was etched in harsh lines. She deliberately turned her back on him, showing how little she feared his temper, as she put Phoebe back to bed.

"Is there something you wanted?" There was no way he'd miss the tear streaks on her face, but she didn't care.

"Hell, yeah. I wanted you to trust me." His words were clipped and cold.

She forced herself to move a couple of steps

closer to him to show she wasn't intimidated by his cold show of temper. "What makes you think I don't?"

"If you did, you wouldn't have let a few veiled comments by a cousin you don't know any better than you do me put this wall between us."

He moved in her direction, leaving her no choice but to either stand her ground or retreat. Well, that wasn't going to happen. She'd run from Banan. She wasn't going to run again.

"At least I trusted you enough to come ask questions instead of assuming the worst. Right now, you're the one making assumptions about me." She clenched her fists, her hands aching to shake him senseless.

Two more steps in his direction put him within touching distance. "So what do you have to say for yourself?"

"You want the truth? Fine. I came here to destroy everything and everyone that Rafferty O'Day cherishes, including your lovely cousin, Joss. I wasn't going to rest until they were both dead and buried."

The shock of his blunt confession hit her like a bucket of ice water. Before she could string together a coherent response, he used his vampire reflexes to capture her. She slammed up against the stone strength of his chest as his mouth engaged hers in a battle for dominance. She wasn't going to surrender without putting up a good fight.

Oh, God, he tasted so good, all temper and heat. When her fangs nicked his lip, she lapped up the small droplet of blood, its flavor rich and powerful. He groaned when she sucked at the small wound.

He lifted her up and set her down on the edge of her desk. Was he going to take her right there amongst the files and office supplies? She hoped so, because as long as he was driving her out of her mind with his touches and kisses, she didn't have to think about what he'd told her.

"Tell me you want this." He rocked against her, showing her without words exactly what he had in mind.

How could she say no when his slightest touch set her aflame?

"Yes, I want this." Right there. Right then.

"Good because I have every intention of finishing this the minute our last patient walks out the front door. Be ready."

Then he was gone, leaving her aching with need and with more questions than answers. Even when her common sense warned her to proceed with caution, her body betrayed her.

She waited for her heart to quit racing and her hands to unclench before standing up. After straightening her clothes, she checked on Phoebe one last time before heading out to the waiting room to greet their first patients.

She hoped it was busy, because otherwise this was going to be a very long evening.

Banan was in a very good mood. Both well fed and well rested, he had a busy night ahead of him. Of course, he couldn't really carry out any of his plans until after midnight when the clinic closed. It wouldn't do to commit murder when the vampire he wanted to cast blame on had lots of witnesses that he was elsewhere at the time.

The only question was how soon after the clinic closed would Megan be heading back to her own home. If she spent the night rolling around in the sheets with that second-class vampire Fitzhugh, it would definitely complicate things. Yet another crime she would pay for when it was her turn to be his playmate for a night.

For now, he'd wait until Riley returned from running up some more charges from Banan's hotel room. If Rafferty's security officer started nosing around, it would appear that Banan was nowhere near the O'Day estate. The ruse wouldn't hold up to close scrutiny, but it should buy him enough time to accomplish his mission.

Once Riley got back, they'd go have themselves a little fun. Both of them had a taste for dark pleasures, but they had to be careful to make it look as if only one vampire was on a rampage. If Conlan detected more than one pair of fangs were involved, he'd have evidence that outsiders were responsible. Then he'd come hunting with sharp stakes and ready to kill.

Even against two vampires the highly trained chancellor would be a formidable enemy, especially since he wouldn't be limited to the daylight hours. If Rafferty joined him, well, it would definitely get ugly.

The only question left to answer about the night's planned entertainment was if the next victim would be male or female, human or chancellor. There were definite drawbacks to each species. The human, although easier to catch and subdue, would be more fragile. A chancellor would put up more of a fight, but once he and Riley had their victim under control, the fun would last longer.

Decisions, decisions. Rather than get his heart set on one or the other, maybe he'd let fate surprise him.

Seamus had spent most of the evening avoiding any contact with Megan while he tried to sort out the confused mess of emotions her simple question had caused. Damn it, one short conversation with Joss had been enough to sow seeds of doubt in her mind about the kind of man she believed him to be. That seriously ticked him off.

Granted, she had trust issues, but he'd thought they'd gotten beyond that.

On the other hand, if he was completely honest with himself, he hadn't told her the full truth about his past for just that reason. He'd told her he had secrets, let her think that he was perhaps embarrassed by them, but not that he'd actually planned to destroy her cousin and Rafferty.

Oh, yeah, this was going to be a pleasant conversation. He walked out into the waiting room, almost hoping that it had filled up again while he was restocking the exam rooms. No such luck. As it stood, the clinic would close precisely on time.

Allowing ten minutes to explain his past to Megan, he could probably be in bed—*alone*—by one, one-thirty at the latest. Even if he could use the sleep, it sure wasn't how he'd been hoping to spend those hours. But despite his assertion that they'd finish what they'd started in her office, he wouldn't push her into something she didn't want. But, damn, that woman burned bright when she was in his arms. Surely that meant something. If only he knew what.

Megan came out of her office carrying a stack of files. "These are the last ones for the night. Once you've signed off on them, I'll update their patient records."

He took the files from her, wishing he dared to do more than brush his fingers against hers in the transfer. "It shouldn't take me long."

"I'll be working on the pharmacy and supply inventories so we can place an order. We're getting low on a few things."

"Thanks, I appreciate it. Rafferty said once we've had enough time to work out an average rate of usage, we can set up standing orders. That should simplify things."

"Yes, it should." She did an about-face to head back to her office. "Holler if you need me for anything."

Now that was tempting, but he suspected she meant the offer to be work-related. The brief snippet of conversation was such a far cry from the easy rapport they'd shared before. Damn Joss, anyway. He fought back the temptation to rip the files to shreds or maybe destroy another chair. Rafferty hadn't complained about having to replace the one from that morning, but he wouldn't appreciate Seamus making a habit of destroying furniture whenever things didn't go his way.

So for now, he'd go finish up his paperwork, lock the door, turn off the lights and try to convince the woman in the next office that he was still one of the good guys.

Megan was waiting for him out in the living room, but not with the same warm welcome she'd had for him last night. What a difference a single day could make. He guzzled a blood pack to replenish the energy he'd burned thanks to the increased stress the past twenty-four hours had brought. He'd need every advantage he could get.

Finally, he could delay no longer. Time to face those doubts and questions in Megan's mind. He wanted to blame Joss for all of this, and she'd certainly played a part. So had Rafferty. But Seamus thought he'd come to terms with their betrayal of his sister, as well as the poor decisions she'd made herself.

Megan looked up when he walked in and sat down. Although he didn't exactly cuddle up close, he refused to put the length of the couch between them. If she didn't like it, she could be the one to move. When she didn't immediately object, some of his tension drained away.

"Okay, I'm going to start at the beginning and tell you how and why I ended up here on Rafferty's estate. When I'm done talking, you can ask me any questions you might have or you can talk to Rafferty and Joss if you'd rather. But hear me out before you interrupt."

"I'm listening."

So he stared down at the floor, as if all the answers he needed were there. Starting at the beginning, he explained that Rafferty's humiliation of Seamus's half sister had resulted in Petra's attempt to destroy Rafferty by setting the vampire up to be convicted of murder. Only Joss's intervention and finding out the truth had prevented him from being executed.

When he drifted to a halt, Megan reached over to entwine her fingers with his, telling him with her touch that she was still there for him. He took a shuddering breath and started talking again, almost choking over the words.

"Petra was tried, convicted and executed. When her assets were confiscated, I lost my only source of income and the medical school canceled my scholarship. Fairness doesn't mean much in vampire politics."

And then he told her the hardest part of all. "I meant what I said earlier. I came here planning on doing a lot more than confronting Rafferty and Joss. I wasn't going to be satisfied with anything less than their total destruction. I was so angry, I wanted them both bleeding and everything they cared about destroyed."

"So what changed?"

He clung to the note of conviction in her voice that made it clear that she knew his intentions toward her cousin and her husband were no longer violent in nature. Slowly, he turned to face her.

"You, mostly. When I came here, I thought I'd lost all chance of ever practicing medicine again. Fighting to save you from the poison reminded me of how it felt to be a doctor, to hold someone's life in my hands. I realized that even as a medic, I could make a real difference.

"And as much as I hated to admit it, I saw that Rafferty was already making changes that are long overdue in our world. It's criminal that anyone would expect you to give up Phoebe just because she's purebred vampire and you're not. No matter how mad I was over what happened to Petra, I'd be a pretty selfish bastard to destroy the one place where you and your daughter could be safe."

Megan immediately let go of his hand and shifted to straddle his lap. She framed his face with her palms. "Now that we've settled that, it seems to me you made a promise to finish our earlier conversation."

"I'm up for it if you are." He flexed his hips to demonstrate that he meant that literally.

Her warm breath tickled his ear. "Want to start out here and end up in your bed?"

"Either is fine with me." He punctuated each word with a kiss. "As long as we get started right now."

What the hell was that noise? Seamus blinked sleepily at the clock as he waited to see if he heard it again. There. Someone was knocking on the clinic door. More than three hours had passed since he'd locked up for the night, meaning it was another emergency.

He eased away from Megan, seeing no reason for her to lose sleep, too. His clothes were scattered on the floor out in the living room. So were hers, for that matter, he thought with a pleased smile. They'd finished up their conversation on the couch and then started a whole new one in his bed. The evening had definitely ended on a high note.

But back to the matter at hand. He was still buttoning his shirt when he turned on the outside light and opened the door. A vampire he didn't recognize was waiting for him. The man was breathing hard, as if he'd run a long distance. He was also dripping wet from the rain that had started sometime during the night.

"Can I help you?"

"Are you the medic?" the vampire wheezed.

"I'm Dr. Fitzhugh, yes. Is there an emergency?" He looked past the vampire to see if he was alone.

"You'll need to come with me. I was working out near the fence when I found an injured female. I was afraid to move her by myself, so I ran all the way here to fetch you. Between the two of us, we can get her back here easily enough."

So why hadn't he called ahead? It didn't make sense, but then not everyone reacted logically when confronted with injuries. Maybe he'd better offer some first-aid classes when he had time to prevent this type of thing from happening.

"I'll get my bag. Once you show me where

she is, we'll call for help if she's too badly injured to carry."

The two of them ran at full speed for what had to be at least three miles before the electric fence came into sight. The vampire at his side slowed to a stop.

"If you keep going straight to the fence and turn right, you'll find her. She's under a pair of trees. I'll go back for help."

Then he took off, leaving Seamus staring as he disappeared into the darkness back the way they'd come. Something wasn't right. He'd said the two of them could get the woman back to the clinic. If that was the case, then why was he leaving?

With a growing sense of foreboding, Seamus continued on toward the fence before turning right. Spotting the trees a short distance ahead did little to ease the knot of tension in his chest. Thoughts of the murdered human female filled his mind. Was he walking into a trap? His instincts were screaming that he was, but he had no choice but to continue on.

A few minutes later, he found her—a human female. The rain did little to hide the scent of fresh blood, triggering his fangs to drop down. He slowed his approach, his night vision still able to pick out all too many details from a short distance away. Death was close if not already stealing the last beat of her heart, the last breath from her lungs.

But he had to try to save her. He knelt in the wet grass, ignoring whether it was blood or rain that was soaking through to his skin. He began cataloging her injuries at the same time he opened his medical bag. When he tried to put pressure on her neck, blood sprayed right in his face. When her eyes fluttered open and saw him hovering over her, fangs out, she panicked and tried to move away, her efforts weak and unfocused.

"I'm Dr. Fitzhugh. I need to treat your injuries."

That only made her more frantic. If she weren't already so weak, perhaps he could have sedated her. However, in her condition, it might only hasten her death. Damn it, why hadn't he called for help before leaving the clinic? Maybe they could have gotten her evacuated to the trauma hospital in time.

But judging by the rattling deep in her throat, that was wishful thinking. One breath, another, and then a quiet exhale that ended her life for good. He rocked back on his heels and cursed. If he couldn't save her, at least he could do as much as he could to bring her killer to justice.

Thanks to the rain, he couldn't readily identify the vampire either by scent or sight. The male had been wearing a heavy sweatshirt with the hood cinched down close to his face. Seamus had assumed he'd worn it that way because of the weather, but now he knew it was to prevent him from being able to describe him.

One didn't make it through medical school without developing some immunity to the sight of horrific injuries. But the degree to which this poor woman had suffered at the hands of her attacker made him sick. Shallow cuts meant to inflict pain, but not death, were scattered over her torso as well as her legs and upper arms. There was no mistaking the similarities between this victim and the one that Conlan had brought to the clinic.

It was definitely time to call for help. But before he could dial the phone, he was hit with a blaze of light that blinded him for several seconds. He'd been concentrating so hard on the woman that he'd missed hearing the approach of a pair of transports. He shaded his eyes against the glare, trying to make out the shadowy forms who were now walking toward him.

Was that a gun?

Rather than wait around to ask, he jumped to his feet and prepared to run like hell. Vampires could survive almost anything other than a head shot, but he wasn't going to wait around to test that theory. He'd head straight for Rafferty's house.

He'd gone no more than a handful of steps when he was tackled from behind. The ground rushed up to meet him, knocking the air out of his lungs. Survival instincts kicked in as he fought to break free. He succeeded in throwing the guy off once, but before he could make it back to his feet a second man joined the party. Together they quickly overpowered him.

His arms were yanked behind him and handcuffs were snapped around his wrists with little care other than to make sure they were painfully tight. So far, his attackers hadn't muttered a single word. The brief scuffle had them all breathing hard.

Seamus muscled his face up out of the mud long enough to identify himself. "Let go of me. I'm Dr. Fitzhugh!"

His captor rolled him over. To his shock it was Rafferty. The older vampire got right down in his face. "I know who you are and what you are, you murdering bastard. When I get done with you, you'll be nothing but dead."

"Are you crazy? I was called out here to treat an injured woman. I didn't kill her."

"She's dead, isn't she? And that's her blood your face is covered with." Rafferty lifted him up to his feet with one hand. Under other circumstances, Seamus might have been impressed.

"Yes, but she wasn't when I got here." Realizing how that sounded, he tried to explain. "I found her lying where you found her. She died right after I got here."

"Sounds like a confession to me. Don't you agree, Conlan?"

"Yeah, boss, it does."

"And you two are idiots if you think I could do something like that."

Rafferty's smile was a horror to behold. "Idiots, are we? You know, I don't much like being insulted."

Then his fist connected with the side of Seamus's head, and the lights went out.

Chapter 15

Consciousness returned slowly, with a jackhammer headache pounding in back of his eyes. Seamus moaned and tried to roll over. Even that much movement made him queasy, confirming Rafferty had most likely given him a concussion when he punched him.

That explained the pain, answering only one of the questions flashing through his head. Where was he? What was going on? He briefly considered those two and came up with nothing other than he was obviously on a bed in a room that was absolutely dark. Even with his superior night vision, he needed at least some ambient light to see. All of which left him in the dark—literally.

He pondered one last question, the only one that really mattered to him: would Rafferty let him live long enough to see if Megan would believe in his innocence? If he was going to die, he didn't want the woman he loved thinking the worst of him.

A wave of bitterness washed over him, knowing that he'd never said the actual words to her. After the night they'd shared, he'd planned on telling her how he felt over breakfast. He wanted her to know that he meant it even in the cold light of day, not just after a bout of hot sex. Depending on her response, he might have even asked if she'd consider moving in with him. The apartment was pretty small for three people, but until Rafferty hired another person to help cover emergencies, Seamus couldn't move.

What a fool for thinking that for once his plans would play out the way he wanted them to! He flexed his fingers, wishing he could have five minutes alone with that rat bastard vampire for playing him like a fool. He'd choke the truth out of him, and then drain him dry, leaving him alive long enough to stand trial for what he'd done to those two poor women.

It was time to do more than lie in the darkness

and brood. He reached out with both hands, feeling for the edge of the bed. His right hand hit a wall, but his left found nothing but air beyond the mattress. Okay, now to see if he could sit up without getting sick. The last thing he wanted to do was to throw up in the darkness.

He made it to semivertical, sitting on the side of the bed as he waited for the pain to ebb to a manageable level again. Before he could stand up, though, he heard someone approaching. Cocking his head to the side, he focused all of his attention into listening.

Sure enough, the muffled sound of footsteps slowed to a halt a few feet away on the other side of the wall. He stayed where he was, waiting to see what happened next. A rattle of keys and a quiet click preceded a door opening directly across from him. He blinked against the light pouring in from the hallway.

"Conlan."

"Right on the first guess. I'm going to turn on the lights, so you might want to shade your eyes."

Even with the warning, the sudden onslaught of high-voltage light sent fresh shards of pain ripping through Seamus's head. He closed his eyes and held his head in his hands while he waited for the moment to pass.

Conlan made a disgusted grunt. "Damn it, I told Rafferty he hit you too hard. When you're able to eat, here's a trio of blood packs and a tray that Megan insisted on bringing by for you."

At the mention of her name, Seamus forced himself to look up at Conlan. "How is she?"

Before answering, Conlan put the tray down on the seat of a straight-backed chair and then dragged it across the room to where Seamus sat. "She's shaken up. It's not every day a woman realizes she's been sleeping with a murderer."

There was nothing Seamus could say to that, at least until he consumed enough blood to kick-start the healing process. Maybe once his head cleared, he could find a way out of this mess. He quickly knocked off the first two packs and then started on the food Megan had prepared for him.

For the first time since Rafferty's fist had connected to his head, things were looking up. If Megan was worried about what he ate, maybe all wasn't lost. Once he'd finished eating, he reached for the last of the blood.

"Thanks."

Conlan stood across the room, leaning against the wall, his eyes on the frigid side of cold. Seamus wasn't fooled by the chancellor's calm demeanor. It wouldn't take much more than Seamus breathing wrong to release Conlan's pent-up rage.

He popped the top of his blood pack. "For the record, I didn't kill either of those women."

"Save the 'I'm innocent' crap for someone who's more gullible than I am, Seamus." Conlan pushed himself off the wall and glared across at him.

"You had opportunity and motive. I may not be part of the Coalition's justice system any longer, but I'd bet those two things are still enough to get you convicted and maybe even executed. That is, if Rafferty had any plans to turn you over to the Coalition in the first place."

Seamus shrugged and consumed the blood. Already his head was feeling better, his thinking clearer. "Did you find any sign of the other vampire? The one who suckered me into taking the fall for this?"

Conlan sneered, his fangs on full display. "There is no other vampire. And before you ask, we checked on all the other resident vampires on the estate. They were all accounted for, including witnesses. The only one out wandering around by himself was you."

Conlan picked up a notebook off a table near the door that he'd obviously left there earlier. "I promised Rafferty I'd take your statement. Personally, I think it's a waste of my time."

It was obvious that both Conlan and Rafferty already had him tried and convicted, but Seamus had to try to make them listen.

"I'm reasonably intelligent, Conlan. Why would I kill two innocent women and set it up so that the most likely suspect is me?" He fought for control. "I was with Megan right up until a vampire I didn't recognize came banging on the clinic door. He told me he'd been working out near the fence and spotted an injured woman. He was afraid of moving her by himself, so he came and got me. We were going to either bring her in together or call for help if I thought she was too badly injured to be carried."

Conlan looked up from his notes. "And where did this mystical vampire disappear to? When we arrived at the site, you were the only one there."

"He turned back to get more help before we actually reached the woman. At the time I thought it was odd that he changed the plans with no warning, but I had no choice but to go on. I was going to call Rafferty as soon as I determined the nature of the victim's injuries."

Seamus frowned. "But how did you know to come at all? To get there as fast as you did, you had to have been on your way before I even found the victim."

"I was meeting with Rafferty when he got a call from someone saying they heard screams out near the fence."

"Did he say who called?"

"No, whoever it was hung up before he got a name." Conlan looked up from his notes. "Rafferty is trying to trace back to find out, but the number wasn't local. That doesn't mean much, because we don't keep track of cell phones and the like."

Maybe the call was a dead end, but at least Rafferty was looking into it. "The woman was still alive when I found her. When I tried to apply pressure to her neck wound, she roused long enough to try to fight me off, which is how I got coated with her blood. Before I could calm her down, she died."

He couldn't sit still any longer, not with that poor woman's eyes, terror-filled and dead, clogging up his thoughts. Conlan must be confident in his ability to stop Seamus from escaping since he made no effort to block the doorway.

"Go on with your story."

"I was just going to call for you and Rafferty when I saw the lights from your transports. I was prepared to run if it turned out to be the killers coming back."

"Killers? Why plural? You only mentioned seeing one vampire."

Seamus paced the length of the room and back several times before he answered. As he walked, he reviewed his mental list of the woman's many injuries. Finally, it hit him.

"She has bruises on her upper shoulders."

"So? Near as I could tell, she had bruises everywhere." But there was a definite glint of interest in Conlan's eyes that wasn't there before.

"I'd have to take a closer look to make sure, but I remember seeing a series of small bruises along the top of her shoulders, like someone was holding her down. And before you ask, the angle was all wrong for it to be the same person who was busy…doing other things."

There was no need to itemize how many ways the woman had been brutalized. Conlan had seen all of it for himself.

The chancellor kept writing for several more paragraphs before he finally set the pen aside. Finally, he stood up. "I'm going to give Rafferty a call."

"Should I borrow that pad to write out my will?" Seamus tried to inject a note of levity in his voice, but suspected he failed miserably.

"Not quite yet. Get some rest. This might take a while." Then he walked out and locked the door behind him.

When had her cottage shrunk to this size? When Megan first moved in, her new home had seemed spacious and yet cozy. Now it was stifling and oppressive. Of course, she was pretty sure the way the four walls were crushing in on her had more to do with her state of mind than any real flaw in the design.

Poor Phoebe had clearly picked up on Megan's foul mood, and it was making her fussy. She wouldn't sleep, and she wouldn't eat. Instead, she demanded to be held constantly. But when Megan tried to cuddle her, her little face turned bright red, her body stiffened and then the crying started.

Megan tried rubbing her daughter's back. "Darn Seamus, anyway. I know he'd calm you right down with those smooth moves of his. Instead, here we both sit, crying and frustrated."

Neither Rafferty nor Joss would tell her where they were holding Seamus. She still couldn't believe that they'd think he was capable of killing not just one, but two women for no reason.

Admittedly, she wasn't the most experienced

woman when it came to the males of any species. But despite that fact, she wanted to believe that she knew Seamus Fitzhugh better than either Rafferty or Conlan did. Maybe her ego didn't want to think she had trusted her heart to a man who would make such sweet love to her and then go right out and kill.

It didn't make sense. She didn't believe it. And she was tired of being kept away from the man she loved. Sure, she'd badly misjudged the kind of man Banan really was. However, looking back, she realized that she'd loved the idea of Banan, not the person he really was. She'd somehow ignored the warning signs that he was all wrong for her.

When it came to Seamus, though, despite his secrets, her instincts insisted that he was a good man, one who could be trusted with her heart. At least Phoebe had finally settled down, although judging by her quivering lip, it wouldn't take much to set her off again.

A new determination settled over Megan. "Phoebe, I'm not going to settle for secondhand information. I want to hear what happened directly from him. He owes me that much."

It was almost dark outside, so Rafferty should be up and about. She'd start with him and Joss. If they wouldn't give her what she wanted, she'd track down Conlan. Surely he'd let her talk to his prisoner. If not, she'd fix Seamus another meal and then sit back and watch for Conlan to deliver it. Yeah, that would work.

"Okay, little one, we're going to find him. And heaven help anyone who gets in my way."

As she spoke, Phoebe relaxed in her arms and contentedly blew some impressive spit bubbles, a clear sign her daughter approved of her plan.

Okay, then. First she'd pack up a meal to go and add extra for Conlan as a bribe. After that, she and Phoebe would start their quest.

"Riley, you did a fine job. I haven't had quite this much fun in a damn long time. Did you see Rafferty clock his pet medic?" He smiled at the memory. "I bet Fitzhugh's head is still ringing like a bell."

Banan's cousin sat cross-legged on the ground. "Yeah, it was almost too easy to be fun. Those noble types make me sick."

"When Rafferty gets done with him, he won't be feeling anything but pain." Banan laughed as he scraped the dried blood out from under his nails with his knife. "Or more likely, he won't be feeling anything at all. He'll be dead."

Riley opened a pack of blood and poured it

into his glass before topping it off with some whiskey. "Of course, once we snatch your woman, they'll know it wasn't Fitzhugh since they've got him under lock and key."

"True, but as much fun as we've had, I'm ready to be done with it. Once the sun goes down completely, we'll check out Megan's place. As soon as it's safe, we'll grab my daughter and call in our ride for the last time."

Riley belched and scratched his head. "Megan's not going to give up her baby without a fight."

Banan's smile showed off his fangs. "I'm counting on it. And when I'm finished with her, you're welcome to what's left."

Considering how helpful Riley had been, he supposed he should offer to let him have the first chance to enjoy Megan's considerable charms. But that wasn't going to happen. First of all, while Riley didn't seem to mind leftovers, Banan was more fastidious about his fun. But more important, he couldn't afford to leave any witnesses behind.

His cousin had become expendable. He'd leave Riley behind, staging his death as if Megan had managed to take him out before dying herself. Then Banan would torch her house with the accelerant Riley had brought along, which was guaranteed to leave nothing but ashes behind. With luck, once the fire was out, Rafferty and his chancellor buddy wouldn't be able to tell whether or not Phoebe had died along with her mother.

By the time they got some forensic expert to tell them any differently, his daughter would be safely stashed away in the Delaney compound where she belonged. His parents and grandparents would be satisfied he'd done his duty by the family and give him free access to the Delaney fortune.

It was time to set the last details in motion. "I'm going to go down to the creek and wash up. Contact your buddy so he'll be ready to swoop in and pick us up. I want to make sure he's in place before we make our move."

"He'll be here. I promised him extra to make sure he'd stay close by."

"That was real smart of you, Riley. You've thought of everything. I appreciate it."

"Anything for you, cuz. After all, blood is thicker than water." Riley held out his glass of the red stuff as if making a toast and laughed at his own joke.

"That's a funny one, Riley. I'll be back in a few."

Banan let himself out of the tent before he gave in to the urge to punch his cousin on general principles. Although it didn't hurt to pay the hired help the odd compliment, he hated to encourage stupidity.

The only comfort came from knowing that by this time tomorrow, he'd be back among his own kind and living in luxury as he so deserved.

"No, Megan. This isn't a social club." Conlan crossed his arms over his chest and planted himself directly in front of the door. "He's a prisoner, not a guest. He isn't allowed visitors."

"I'm not just any visitor, Conlan Shea. I'm delivering another meal." Megan tried to push past the security officer, but she might as well have been pushing against a stone wall.

"Rafferty said no one in, no one out."

"Fine." Megan turned her back to Conlan. "Can you lift Phoebe out of her carrier, please? I need to change her."

He sighed and pulled Phoebe out of the back carrier and then held her out to Megan. Instead of taking her daughter, Megan picked up the basket and slipped past the now furious chancellor.

"Damn it, Megan, come back here."

"Not until I see Seamus, Conlan."

She kept moving, but glanced back to see how he was doing with Phoebe. She would have laughed at the sight of him holding her daughter out at arm's length, but he was already mad. There was no use in making the situation worse. He caught up with her after only a short distance.

"Okay, okay. I'll take you to Seamus."

"Seriously?"

"Seriously," he said, sounding thoroughly disgruntled. "I hope you'll feel real bad when this costs me my job. Rafferty carries a mean grudge."

"He won't fire you for letting me talk to an innocent man."

She injected as much conviction as she could into the statement. It wasn't hard, though, because she believed what she was saying.

A familiar voice spoke up. "You believe I'm innocent?"

She whirled around to find Seamus walking toward her, looking tired but smiling at her. When he held out his arms, she didn't hesitate. It was hard to tell which one of them needed the hug more.

"I've been so worried." She blinked hard, trying not to cry.

"I'm sorry about that," he whispered.

He gently brushed away her tears with his fingertips as he bent his head down and kissed her. She gave herself up to the moment, taking comfort in the strength of his embrace and the promise of Seamus's kiss. Here, wrapped in each other's arms, for a few seconds the world and all of their problems simply ceased to exist. At least until Phoebe let loose with a loud wail. She felt Seamus's mouth turn up in a smile.

"Someone feels left out," he whispered as he eased away.

Conlan immediately handed Phoebe into Seamus's waiting arms. As soon as Seamus cuddled her up to his shoulder, she stopped crying. When he had her settled, he wrapped his free hand around Megan's shoulders and pulled her close. She'd never thought she could trust another man, much less a vampire, but it felt so right for Seamus to offer her and Phoebe the shelter of his arms.

Conlan looked a bit jealous. "One of these days you're going to have to explain this gift you have for charming females."

"Not all females, Conlan. Just these two."

"Yeah, I see that." The chancellor's expression turned serious. "I hate to break this up, but we need to get moving."

Megan looked from one man to the other. "You're setting Seamus free?"

Seamus carefully eased Phoebe back into

her carrier. "We're going to examine the body. Conlan wants to verify what I told him about her injuries. We have to hurry because the longer we delay, the greater the chance someone else will get hurt."

"Can I come?" she asked, but wasn't surprised when he said no.

"It's not safe for you to be seen with me. Whoever is out there could be watching. We don't want to put you at risk by letting them know how much you mean to me."

His words and the heat in his eyes melted her heart. She wanted to tell him about her own feelings for him. But now clearly wasn't the time, and not just because Conlan was still hovering right behind her. She knew Seamus well enough to know he'd want to finish clearing his name before taking that next step with her.

"Okay, I'll go home and wait for you there." She raised up high enough to kiss him again, but kept it simple and sweet. Even so, she flashed her fangs at him. "Don't make me wait too long."

He did a little flashing of his own. "I'll try to hurry. Lock yourself in and stay there unless it's me, Conlan or Rafferty at the door."

His words sent a chill through her. "Do you think I'm in danger? You really think it could be Banan, don't you?"

Conlan nodded as he led the way down the hall. "We thought of him first off, but computer records show he's been in New Eire since he left the estate. I've sent one of my operatives to verify that in person. We should know for sure soon."

They'd reached the door, but Seamus stopped her from leaving.

"All we know for sure is the killer has been going after females, but I have a bad feeling about this whole situation. It can't be coincidence that both murders were done when I had no alibi. The only vampire I've had a problem with was Rafferty, but he's not behind this. If the killer is targeting me for some reason, that could put you and Phoebe at risk."

"Can't I stay at the clinic with you?"

"We don't want anyone to know that I'm out and about, so my warden here was going to slip me out a secret way." He was clearly unhappy about having to refuse.

Conlan spoke up. "Why don't I follow her home and stay with her until you get there? Rafferty will meet you at the clinic."

Seamus held his hand out to Conlan, who gave it a firm shake. "Let's get this wrapped up."

"Sounds good."

"One more thing, Conlan. I'm sorry if

Rafferty comes down hard on you for letting me run loose."

The chancellor didn't look overly concerned. "Either he trusts my judgment or he doesn't. Besides, it wouldn't be the first time I lost a job. I was looking for work when I came here. I can look again."

Despite his nonchalant attitude, there was a definite undercurrent of pain in Conlan's voice. Megan sensed he wouldn't appreciate any questions.

"Thank you, Conlan. I'll feel better knowing you're with me."

"It's nothing," he said.

But they all knew that wasn't true.

In the end, Megan made a show of leaving in a fit of anger, in the hopes that it would throw anyone who might be watching off their trail. Then Conlan let Seamus out of the building through an underground tunnel that resurfaced in a thicket of trees about thirty meters away.

Once they climbed out, Seamus closed his eyes to listen to the night. Other than the usual rustles of small critters and the breeze stirring the leaves overhead, it was quiet. When he looked around, he noticed Conlan was doing the same thing.

"Seems clear. I'll take off for the clinic. If all goes right, I should be able to do a quick examination of the body and take pictures. If I don't catch up with you at Megan's in an hour, come charging to the rescue." Then he added, "But make sure you take Megan and Phoebe someplace safe first."

Conlan smiled. "Man, you've got it bad."

"Jealous?"

"Yeah, maybe I am." He clapped his hand down on Seamus's shoulder. "Don't worry, I'll keep her safe or die trying. See you in a few."

Then he took off at a dead run. Seamus waited a few seconds to see if he picked up on anyone else in the area who might follow Conlan. When all remained still, he headed for the clinic. When he reached the trees across the field, it was hard for him to slow down and proceed with caution. He couldn't shake the feeling that the situation was poised to go from bad to much, much worse.

There was only one vampire who had reason to cause problems like this on Rafferty's estate—excluding Seamus himself—and that was Banan Delaney. According to Conlan, no one had entered through the gates nor had there been any breaks in the electric fence. That didn't mean that the vampire hadn't found some way to go over the fence or maybe even under it.

Once the bastard thought Seamus was out of the way, he would go after Megan again. With the horror of that prospect riding him hard, Seamus took off running for the clinic. He let himself in through the front door and quickly locked the door behind him.

Only a few steps into the waiting room, he came to a screeching halt. He wasn't alone. Another vampire had passed through the room recently. After tasting the air, he relaxed, at least marginally, when he recognized the scent as Rafferty's.

"Okay, where are you?"

The older vampire limped into sight. "About time you got here. I hate to be kept waiting. I've already put the victim in the same room we used last time."

He headed for the examination room to study the victim's injuries. Rafferty followed him.

He got his equipment and then uncovered the body. The injuries looked even worse under the stark overhead lighting. The woman had suffered a lot of pain and violation before she'd died. Seamus clicked on the recorder and did his best to choke back his fury as he started at her head and methodically cataloged the cuts, bruises and worse.

It took a long, long time to describe them all. By the time he was finished even Rafferty looked pale. Seamus forced himself to do a brief summary of the cause of death and then formally signed off.

When he was done, he walked away from the table and out toward the lobby. Rafferty followed close on his heels. Seamus stopped and stared at the furniture scattered around the waiting room, his hands itching to pick up the closest table and destroy something with it.

"Go ahead, because if you don't break something I will. Or maybe we both should." Rafferty picked the table up, testing its weight. "I think it would make good kindling or maybe a whole bunch of toothpicks."

Seamus couldn't help it. He laughed, although it wasn't a happy sound. "Yeah, but it does okay as a table, too. It's not the furniture's fault that someone needs to die."

"So listening to you in there, it was definitely two vampires who did that?" Rafferty's eyes were ice cold.

"It took two to do all that damage. The second one might not be a vampire, but my gut feeling is that both of them are. The kind that like to play with their food."

"When I get my hands on them, I'll do more than play with them. They'll die, and it won't be pleasant."

Seamus shot him a questioning look. "So you're not coming after me for this?"

"Not after I saw your face in there. Any doubts are long gone. Your rage over what was done to her was genuine." He set the table down with exaggerated care, obviously still not quite in control of his emotions. Then he sat down in the nearest chair. "Sit down. I'm too tired to look up at you."

Seamus needed to get back to Megan, but they needed to solve this mess even more. "You want to hear my theory?"

"Sure, because I'm drawing a blank here. If it wasn't you, then it was one of my other friends. I don't like the thought of that any better than when the facts pointed in your direction."

"Both murders were done at times when I wouldn't have an alibi, which makes me think it's someone who wants them pinned on me. The only problem with that theory is that I haven't been here long enough to piss anyone off that badly." He risked a small smile. "Well, except maybe for you."

The older vampire's own smile was a whole lot scarier. "For the record, if I was that mad, you'd be the one who was dead, not two innocent women."

"Duly noted, boss. But there was a vampire here who might think he has good reason to want me dead—Banan Delaney. As Phoebe's father and Megan's ex-lover, he wouldn't like me messing with what he'd see as his property. He might not want Megan anymore, but I'm sure his family feels differently about Phoebe. As a pureblood vampire, she represents their future."

"But why kill these other women?"

"To hide his real target? Remember, he's already tried to kill Megan once. If I hadn't had the antidote in my medical case, she'd have died shortly after Conlan found her. She didn't want anyone to know."

Rafferty's eyebrows snapped down as he flashed his fangs at Seamus. "For future reference, Dr. Fitzhugh, patient-doctor confidentiality be damned if one of my people is threatened. I expect to know about it, and sooner rather than later."

"Knowing what I do about you now, I wouldn't hesitate to tell you. Back then, I had no reason to trust you with her safety."

"Point taken."

Seamus drew a deep breath and launched back into his theory. "I think Banan wants his daughter and knows Megan will fight him on that. If he eliminates Megan from the picture, makes me take the fall for the deaths, he's got a chance at taking his daughter home to his clan. I can't imagine he wants Phoebe for any reason other than a power play within his family. We both know the vampire who ensures there's a next generation carries a lot of clout."

He didn't need to explain that any further to Rafferty. Seamus was the last of his clan. If he never produced an heir, his family name would disappear, and Rafferty wouldn't be taking in strays like Seamus if his own clan was thriving.

"But Conlan insists he dragged Banan off my property himself. I have no reason to doubt that he did exactly that."

"Conlan just told me that he sent someone to make sure that Banan made it all the way to New Eire, but he hasn't heard anything yet. I think Banan came back. It's the only thing that makes sense. Not through the gate, of course, but maybe over the fence some way. I know you've got sensors and stuff, but there has to be some flaw in the system he could have exploited if he was willing to spend enough money."

Rafferty was back on his feet. "Maybe there's another way to find out. I'll call his grandmother. She might not approve of me or what I'm trying to do here, but she won't refuse my call. I have too many friends and too much money for her to risk offending me."

"Won't she be suspicious if you accuse Banan of murder?"

"Give me credit for being more tactful than that. I'll tell her how much I enjoyed his visit and ask if she knows where he can be reached. It seems that he left one of his favorite jackets at my house, and I'd like to return it."

"You really are a sneaky bastard, aren't you? Can you make that call now? The night's not getting any longer, and I need to know Megan's safe."

Rafferty punched in the number of the Delaney estate and asked to be connected to the matriarch of the clan. Seamus waited impatiently for the a few minutes for her to be located. The conversation didn't last long.

When Rafferty disconnected the call, he definitely looked worried. "Seems the lady is not pleased with her grandson. He hasn't been home in a while and is supposedly visiting a distant cousin that she doesn't approve of. Seems Banan's cousin Riley had criminal connections and has been disowned by the family as a whole. No one has seen or heard from either of them in days."

Seamus was already starting for the door. "If he lays a hand on either Megan or Phoebe, he won't live long enough for you to kill him. They're mine."

"Let me warn Conlan that you're on your way." Rafferty was already punching in the numbers. After a few seconds he hung up. "No answer."

"Son of bitch, they're already there."

Rafferty pulled a gun out of the top of his boot and tossed it to Seamus. "Go. Run. I'll only slow you down, but I'll be right behind you after I call in the rest of the security force for backup."

Seamus gave Rafferty a long, hard look at his fangs before snarling, "Call in whoever you want to but warn them not to get in my way. You can have what's left of Banan and his cousin when I finish with them."

Then he ran out into the night.

Chapter 16

Seamus ran full out, not caring who heard him coming. In fact, Banan should know that death was on its way. There was no way Seamus would let the bastard live this time. He wanted a future with Megan. For that to happen, he needed to lay her past to rest, preferably in a shallow grave.

If he left enough of Banan to actually bury.

The urge to go charging in, fangs and gun at the ready, was powerful. Even if it were only Conlan in peril, his predator instincts would be aroused. But with a helpless infant and the woman he loved at risk, those same instincts were at full boil and ready to explode.

By sheer strength of will, he brought himself under control. He needed to know what was waiting for him. Only a fool went in blind, especially when it could endanger the very people he wanted to save. He tested for scents on the air. Vampire. Chancellor—Conlan. Blood. Fresh blood.

Shadow to shadow, step by step, he approached Megan's cottage. Voices, angry but with a spicy hint of fear, carried on the night air. He recognized Megan and Banan, but not the third voice. Conlan's absence from the conversation worried him. Was the chancellor dead? He'd better not be. Banan already had enough to answer for.

He stooped lower, not wanting to draw anyone's attention until the last possible minute. He'd made it within twenty meters of the front door when he spotted a still form lying on the ground just ahead. He froze briefly to make sure no one was watching from the doorway before sprinting forward to verify the body's identity. Conlan. It was too much to hope that he'd managed to take out one of the bad guys.

He felt for a pulse and was relieved to find one. Using his sense of touch, he did a quick check for injuries. The chancellor was bleeding from a shallow gash on the side of his head.

Seamus used his own shirt as a bandage to help stanch the bleeding. Conlan was in no immediate danger, so Seamus dragged him farther from the house to remove any potential of him being used as an additional hostage. Hopefully Rafferty and his security forces would find him if Seamus didn't survive his encounter with Banan.

He had a lot to live for now that he had a home and a woman he wanted to share it with, but he would gladly die to save Megan and her daughter. That might be his only advantage against two vampires in bloodlust.

He positioned himself against the house, pressing his ear against the wall to listen. Hearing the filth Banan was spewing out to Megan in a series of threats infuriated him even further. At least the two vampires had yet to lay their hands on her and Phoebe.

From what he could discern, she'd barricaded herself in her bedroom by shoving the furniture in front of the door. The cottage had no windows in the bedrooms, so the only way Banan could get to her was through the barricaded door.

Suddenly Banan stopped shouting threats and started whispering. Seamus could only make out a few words, but one stopped his heart cold.

Fire.

Before he could react, the front door flung open and a vampire charged outside to head straight for a transport parked at the side of the road. Should Seamus go after him or not? Deciding he should to avoid the risk of him returning before he could subdue Banan, Seamus picked up a hefty rock and went on the attack. He reached the vampire just as he stepped off the curb. Leaping high, Seamus hit the bastard on the back of his head, putting all of his strength into swinging the rock. The blow sent the vampire plummeting to the ground, his face hitting the concrete with a satisfying jolt.

Seamus put his knee in the small of the man's back and bent his arm up almost to the point of dislocating his shoulder. The vampire whimpered in pain when Seamus cranked on it even harder as he leaned down near his ear.

"Let me introduce myself. I'm Seamus Fitzhugh, the vampire who is going to kill you. You must be Riley."

"Banan said you were locked up," Riley whimpered.

"Well, he was wrong, wasn't he?" Seamus laughed nastily, "What's more, boyo, Rafferty O'Day is on his way here. You'll hate meeting him."

That set off a full-blown panic attack as the

frantic vampire tried to buck Seamus off his chest. "It was all Banan! He made me help him."

"Don't bother lying to me. I saw what you did to those women. You and your buddy in there deserve everything you're going to get and then some."

If Megan wasn't still at risk, Seamus might have taken the time to teach the stunned vampire a lesson about playing with his food. Instead, he went right for the jugular, ripping into the side of his victim's throat, inflicting as much pain as possible. As tempting as it was to kill him outright, he decided to leave some of the fun for Rafferty. He drained enough blood to weaken the vampire and left him sprawled on the edge of the road.

That left Banan. Wiping the blood off his mouth, Seamus stood up. If he didn't hurry, the other vampire might come looking to see what was keeping his cousin. Seamus yanked Riley's hooded sweatshirt off his body and put it on, hoping he could get close to Banan before he recognized him.

The house had grown ominously quiet. Seamus approached the front door, his heart in his throat. If he'd made the wrong decision in going after Riley first…

But then Banan's voice rang out again. "Go ahead, bitch, and think you're safe. When I get back, we'll see how much you like being toasted. I know you'd rather see Phoebe with her father than dead. Think about that."

Megan's fury burned brightly in every word she uttered. "Phoebe doesn't belong to you, Banan, and never will. Even if you manage to kill me this time, Seamus Fitzhugh will hunt you down and get her back. And think how many interesting ways a doctor knows for killing animals like you!"

"Yeah, well, your lover isn't here, is he? By the time they put out the fire, I'll be on my way home with the brat. My partner out there will be another unfortunate victim, so Rafferty will think he's found the killer. My parents and grandparents will get their precious heir, and I'll get my inheritance. It's a win-win situation for me."

Megan still had plenty of fight left. "No matter what happens, Banan, you'll be a loser. Do you really think your grandmother doesn't know what a worthless piece of garbage you are? Otherwise, why are they more concerned about the next generation instead of you?"

"Shut up, bitch!" Banan backed up and kicked the door again.

Seamus turned the corner to find Banan standing outside Megan's bedroom. There were huge cracks in the wooden door, and it would have likely shattered if Banan and Riley had attacked it with their combined strength. He shut down that thought. There'd be time later to think about how close he'd come to losing both Megan and Phoebe to this madman.

He eased closer, hoping to sneak up on Banan, but something gave his presence away.

"It took you long enough, Riley. We don't have much time before we have to get out to the pickup zone."

Thanks to the sweatshirt, it took Banan a couple of seconds to realize that he wasn't talking to his cousin. When he recognized Seamus, his eyes went huge and he backed up a couple of steps. That was all the invitation Seamus needed to go on the attack.

"Get ready to die, Banan. Personally, I'm looking forward to watching you bleed out."

At the sound of his voice, Megan called out, "Seamus! I knew you'd come."

"Stay in there, honey, while I take out this trash. Rafferty's on his way with help."

Banan lunged at Seamus. The fight turned brutal quickly. Desperation was driving Delaney, but all of Seamus's protective instincts were running at full bore. He would make this night safe for his females or die trying. The two vampires banged from side to side in the narrow hallway until they finally stumbled into the kitchen.

Banan managed to snag a butcher knife off the counter and slashed at Seamus's chest with it. The blade sliced through his shirt and skin, but he didn't even notice the pain or the blood that immediately soaked through the cloth. Instead, he latched onto Banan's wrist with both of his hands.

Despite Banan's best efforts, Seamus slowly bent the knife around until it was aimed back toward the other man. Lunging forward, he forced the blade upward and into Banan's chest. When he yanked it back out, blood came gushing out in pulsing waves. Banan gave up all pretense of fighting as he attempted to stanch the bleeding with his hands.

Seamus wanted to watch his enemy as Banan's life force poured out onto the floor. But now that he was no longer a threat to anyone, Seamus's medical training kicked in. He grabbed the dish towel off the rack and tried to get Banan to let him apply pressure.

"Let me stop the bleeding! You'll be dead in seconds if you don't."

But Banan was too out of his head with pain and fear to listen to reason. He stumbled past Seamus, heading for the front door. By the sounds of things, Rafferty had finally arrived. He could deal with the Delaney heir any way he wanted to. Seamus had more important things to do.

A few seconds later, an agonizing scream rang out, and then there was silence.

Seamus needed to get to Megan and Phoebe, but he was covered in blood, some of his own, some Banan's. He wiped off what he could with the towel and washed some of the rest off at the sink. The gash on his chest was far more serious than he'd realized, so he got out more towels and did his best to close the wound and slow the bleeding.

When he'd done all he could, he ran down the hallway to the bedroom.

"Megan, honey, open the door. It's safe now."

He could only hope he could stay on his feet long enough for her to come out. He had something to say, something important, and he needed to say it now, before it was too late.

Finally, he heard the last piece of furniture slide out of the way and the door opened. Megan peeked out. When she saw him, she started to smile, but then she noticed the blood dripping down onto the floor.

"Seamus! You're hurt."

His vision was going black around the edges, and he couldn't feel his feet. He was surprised to find he could still stand. When Megan reached his side, she wrapped his free arm around her shoulders.

"Come sit down before you fall down."

"No, that's not what I need to do," he told her, standing his ground. "Need to tell you something."

"It can wait until we stop the bleeding."

"No. Waited too long already." He fought the dizziness and the fog.

"Okay, tell me as we walk over to the couch. That'll work, won't it?" She tugged him along a step or two.

"No, listen. Look at me."

"Stubborn man, what could be that important?"

She propped him up against the wall and positioned herself to catch him if he should fall. Bless her.

He smiled or at least he thought he did. Megan only looked more worried, so maybe he wasn't doing it right. No matter. Words were better. Clearer.

"I came here. Life over. Hated Rafferty."

"Yes, I know. We've been over all that."

"Didn't tell you, though."

"Tell me what?"

"Love you. Love Phoebe." He managed to drag his hand up to her face. It left a blood smear on her pretty skin, but she didn't seem to mind. "Want you. With me. Please."

He was pretty sure that it was tears making her eyes sparkle so brightly. On the other hand, she was smiling, so maybe he was wrong about that. None of it mattered, though, because as he slid down the wall to land on the floor, she said the words he'd been hoping to hear.

"I love you, too. Now can we get you some help?"

"Good idea," he managed to whisper.

Then the lights went out.

Megan walked into the clinic and headed straight for the pre-op room. She'd spent a good part of the day there until Rafferty and Joss ran her off with orders to get some sleep. Since her cottage wasn't exactly livable at the moment, she'd commandeered Seamus's bedroom and slept there.

Joss was staying with Phoebe for a while, freeing Megan up to visit the two patients currently housed in the clinic. Rafferty had flown in an outside doctor to care for Seamus and Conlan.

Banan's body and that of his cousin had been returned to the Delaney clan. The family had agreed to accept Rafferty's offer to report the deaths as tragic accidents. They all knew that if the two had survived long enough to stand trial, they'd be facing execution if convicted. No matter how much money the Delaney clan had, they wouldn't be able to buy their way out of this one. The scandal was buried along with their bodies.

Megan wondered if she should be feeling some regret about that, but she wouldn't lie to herself about how she felt. Banan had destroyed any feeling she had for him with his atrocious actions. Someday, Phoebe might have some questions about her father that would be tough to answer. Somehow she and Seamus would find a way to handle them when the time came.

She could already hear the grumbling from inside the makeshift patient ward before she'd gotten halfway across the waiting room. Both males were due to be discharged within the next day, and neither of them took being invalids particularly well. She stopped in the doorway to study their battered faces. Conlan looked the best, but that wasn't saying much. It terrified her to know how close she'd come to losing both of them.

Pasting a bright smile on her face, she knocked on the door frame. "Up for some company?"

Seamus immediately sat up straighter, his handsome face marred with the yellow-green tinge of fading bruises. He held out his hand in welcome.

"Sure thing." He motioned toward Conlan. "He hasn't stopped complaining since he woke up."

"Yeah, well, he slurps when he feeds." The chancellor glared at Seamus. "I'd rather he snored."

She giggled. "He does."

"Hey!" Seamus protested, even as he tugged her down for a kiss. "I have other redeeming qualities."

Her memory of some of those talents had her blushing. But when he winced as she accidentally bumped his cheek, she was reminded that he'd been willing to die to save her and Phoebe. She tried not to cry, she really did, but the fear was still too fresh, too painful.

"That's it! I'm out of here." Conlan threw

back his covers and stalked out of the room, quietly closing the door on his way out.

Seamus scooted to the far side of his bed and tugged her arm, trying to drag her onto the mattress with him. He didn't have to try hard. She so needed the comforting touch of his body next to hers.

He held her close while the tears soaked through his hospital gown. Cuddling next to him, resting her head on his shoulder felt like coming home. She needed to know where they went from here.

"Did you mean it?"

He didn't pretend to not understand. "I might not have been at my most eloquent, but yeah, I meant it. I love you, I love your daughter and I want you both with me."

"Good, because I've already packed our stuff. Rafferty promised to have it all moved into your quarters this evening."

She looked up into his handsome face, so dear to her. What she saw reflected in his eyes chased the last bit of doubt and fear of the future from her soul.

Then he frowned. "I had a long talk with Rafferty about Phoebe and the Delaneys and any potential claim they might have on Phoebe. I've asked him to officially make me part of his clan. He's going to put through the necessary paperwork today, and he'll officiate at our wedding as soon as I'm up and about. Once you two are legally mine, we'll all be part of the O'Day clan."

Bless his heart, always thinking about her and Phoebe even when he was hurt and bleeding. The strength in this man never failed to amaze her. "Are you sure about all of this, Seamus? I don't want to rush you into anything."

His kiss was meant to comfort, but incited at the same time. "Here, and I thought I was the one rushing you. Do we have a deal?"

"If you're sure, then yes, we do, Dr. Fitzhugh."

"Good," he said, his smile looking awfully satisfied. "I hope it's all right that there won't be time to invite your parents or anyone to the ceremony. We need this all laid to rest as soon as possible."

"I have all the family I need right here. I can face anything life throws at me as long as you're there beside me."

His eyes gleamed with satisfaction. "Then, that's where I'll be."

* * * * *

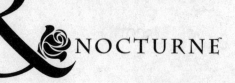